# FUTURE CONTINUOUS

## BENJAMIN PRIVETT WILL HAVE BEEN TRANSFORMING

### SIMON H.G. ROWELL

For Sebastian

# CHAPTER 1

THE *LEGATI* BATTLE cruiser, parked low over Central Park in New York, suddenly announced a call to attention. A deep two-tone warning reverberated around the city. The other nine ships stationed over the other major cities, echoed the same sound.

The population of the world fell immediately silent. Nobody dared make a sound.

The two people standing on the platform that had been lowered below the ship over New York, stepped forward to the edge.

"Hello," said Benjamin. His voice was amplified by the finest sound system ever created and repeated by the other ships across the other cities but translated into the local language. Such was the clarity and lack of distortion that everyone for miles around knew exactly what was being said without effort.

"My name is Benjamin Privett, and I have a very important message for you."

As he spoke, the air on either side the platform, from the height of the spaceship above to a few meters above the heads of the assembled masses, began to sparkle as if it had been visited by multitudes of fireflies. After a moment, the glow transformed into two shapes that took on fine definition. They were projections of Benjamin, two hundred meters high, looking out to each side. The same projections appeared beside the other ships.

There was a momentary pause as the phenomenon that had presented itself became clear, a collective gasp and then the crowds around the world went wild.

Perhaps it was a sense of relief. Everyone knew the name - Benjamin Privett – and now here he was in person, presented as two colossal lightshows through some unearthly technology, for all to see. A household celebrity with a fleet of extraterrestrial spacecraft in tow.

The trance-like and fearful attraction that had drawn many millions to the shadows of the alien behemoths lifted in an instant. It was replaced by huge numbers of people telling one another what everyone already knew.

"That's Benjamin Privett. Remember him? That lottery winner. The one that went to Mars. What the hell's he doing up there?"

The statements of the obvious and unwarranted questions quickly escalated to many people yelling at the Legati ships. Some groups orchestrated chants of "We want to know!" Everyone seemed intent on making noise and not listening. Those people telling other people to shut up and let Benjamin speak, only added to the pandemonium.

Benjamin held his hands in front of him. A signal to attempt to quieten the crowds.

Unfortunately, this gesture simply emphasized the spectacle of the huge three-dimensional images of Benjamin. People instinctively reached out in return, swept up in a sudden carnival atmosphere. The global screaming, chanting and hysteria continued. After a while of this nonsense (as Benjamin perceived it), the ten ships intervened by repeating their two-tone calls for order. The crowds calmed down as the deep bass penetrated their very cores.

"Please," said Benjamin, his arms still raised. "I need you all to listen carefully. And please let me finish." He had a slightly irritated tone to his voice.

There were some mutterings and excited calls but finally there was the attention that Benjamin required.

"Do not be afraid." He paused. "I have been brought back to Earth by a friendly civilization that lives a long way from our planet."

The sound of millions of people muttering to the people by them, erupted again. They were all asking the same questions.

"Does that mean there *was* life on Mars?"

"What were these aliens doing on Mars?"

"I wonder how long our government has known about this?"

"Who's that standing with him?"

"What's that drone thing hovering above Privett?"

Benjamin continued; the sound systems of the spaceships overcoming all the mumblings.

"My hosts are not the only civilization out there. We are not alone. In fact, there is an alliance of these worlds. Hopefully mankind will join this alliance one day. We all have so much to learn about the realities of our galaxy. We are entering a thrilling new chapter in the evolution of our own species and our planet."

To Benjamin, the continued murmurings of the massive crowds sounded like waves gently breaking on the shore. He ploughed on though, despite a mild annoyance at having his historic speech interrupted by peoples' irresistible urge to have something to say.

"Our visitors are known as the Legati. They are not here to occupy our planet. They are simply delivering me home and will be leaving shortly. But what they *will* be doing is helping mankind to prepare to take our place in the galactic community I mentioned. They will be helping us to know ourselves better. We will all learn about the form of this guidance in due course."

Benjamin did not pause.

"I will tell you up front that our visitors will *not* be handing over their technological knowledge. They believe this would be an unwarranted intrusion in our own development and distort our natural progress."

At this, the noise from the masses rose in volume. Benjamin could not hear what they were saying exactly but he was right in his suspicion that this was received as disappointing news. He proceeded in his attempt to finish on a high note.

"I have been asked by the Legati to be their ambassador on our planet. And in that capacity, I will speak to the World Council and the broader World Government without delay.

"I hope we will all learn to appreciate the importance of the arrival today. I hope we will all learn to understand the great value and insight that the Legati want to provide. I hope we will all learn to appreciate the approach that the Legati are taking with our civilization, out of a deep respect for our kind.

"Finally, expect more communications very soon. We are all partners in this new era!"

The platform started to rise back into the belly of the battle cruiser. The demands from the crowd increased in volume once more.

"We will be back very soon," said Benjamin as he rose. His mighty projections dissolved into points of light and then disappeared.

The crowds erupted into further hysteria, demanding answers, calling out Benjamin's name, telling him to come back, asking him where he was going.

When the platform was inside the ship and the outer doors closed, the colossal spaceship ascended effortlessly to an altitude of five hundred meters above Central Park and fell silent. The others did the same over their respective cities.

It was some time before the crowds realized that there was nothing else going to happen, and that they should disperse and make their various ways home.

They had hoped for so much more. They had hoped for a more detailed explanation of who these visitors were. How had Benjamin Privett hitched a lift with them? What sort of guidance did the owners of these spacecraft have in mind? What's the point of aliens turning up, if they don't share their technology with us? Don't they trust humanity?

There was frustration.

But Benjamin had adhered to his script. There was no way to hold a town hall meeting with the entire population of the planet. The true motivation for this brief introduction, Benjamin knew, was to set the expectation that primary communications would be with the people of the planet, and not the politicians of the world.

Baby steps.

And here was Benjamin decades later, watching the recorded video stream of the event for the hundredth time. He let out a sigh.

He tapped the screen of his tablet to pause the stream.

It never got easier watching that first speech. He had said what the Legati had told him to say, but that didn't stop him from wondering every time whether he should have said something more. Had the challenges of the previous years stemmed from those early words?

More uneasily, he could not help but notice how he much younger and younger he looked each time he viewed the footage.

That perception had not been lost on the Legati.

"Good morning, Benjamin," Flight had said a few days earlier. "We must talk about an inevitable subject today."

"Okay…," replied Benjamin. He had a sense of what was coming.

"Your faculties are still strong, and physically you are in average condition." Benjamin flinched at Flight's attempt at diplomacy. "But it has been assessed that it is time for you to retire."

There was a pause while Flight allowed this notion to soak around Benjamin's brain. Necessarily, it was a short pause.

"Thirty-three years is a long time for humans," continued Flight, "and they tend to deteriorate in their final decades." Flight was still trying to be uplifting.

"I understand Mr. Flight. Time for someone else to be taken out of mothballs."

"As you say Benjamin. It is time for one of the other travelers to be revived and to take over from you."

"Any idea who it will be?"

"Yes, that decision has been made. You will shortly be traveling back to SaQ'il with your female companion to assist in the transition and to meet with the Videnti. They are the elders of our race. They wish to thank you for your service."

"When do I leave?"

"In ten days."

That had been two days earlier. Straight away, Benjamin had gone to Christel to tell her the news.

"Oh, Benjamin, you must be so proud. It is extremely rare for the Videnti to meet anyone in person."

To Benjamin, Christel was as radiant as ever. She had not appeared to age as fast as he had, although she insisted that she was subject to the same ageing process as him. He was sure she would outlive him by many years. That thought always made him feel sad; she had been alone for such a long time before Benjamin had come along and she would probably end up alone again. As usual, he resolved to improve on his 'average condition' for her sake.

Nonetheless, there was no getting around it. He was 75 years old. The year was 2094, and he was beginning to feel tired. He'd started this adventure in his early forties and had tried so hard over the intervening decades to make a difference. The fact that the Legati leaders wanted to thank him for his contributions suggested relieved his usual sense of self-doubt.

But Benjamin knew that he had only seen the beginning of the process. He suspected his tenure would be viewed as the most tumultuous given all the new concepts that mankind had had to absorb. But everyone knew that the overall process would take hundreds of years to complete as old biases and prejudices were leached out of the fabric of society.

But what a time he'd had.

# CHAPTER 2

SCHEDULING A MEETING with the World Council had been as easy as a phone call. The main contact point had been the WC spokesman, Gene Harlander.

"Good morning Mr. Harlander," said Benjamin from his newly recharged phone. "I'm sure you recognize me by now. Benjamin Privett."

"Yes indeed – I believe we need to talk," replied Harlander matter-of-factly.

"Would you and the Council members be available later today?"

"Of course. How about 2pm at the Government headquarters? I believe you are local."

"Very good – we will be arriving by the roof."

"Do we need to make any special arrangements?" asked Harlander.

"No thank you – that won't be necessary. See you in a few hours."

Benjamin was rather amused at the deference he was

receiving from the spokesman of the World Government. That would not have happened a few months ago, trip or no trip to Mars.

He put on his newly combined breathing assistant and translation mouthpiece, inserted his earpieces and exited his climate-controlled room. He had been presented with this upgraded device before leaving SaQ'il. It was truly a masterpiece of engineering. On a whim he had decided to call it his BAT gear, for obvious reasons.

He walked down the corridor outside his quarters and entered the elevator at the end. He pressed the only button he understood, which took him to the bridge. He was impressed that the Legati allowed him to walk around the ship unescorted, although he suspected he was under close observation all the time.

The doors opened and he stepped out onto the immense theater that was the ship's bridge. The captain turned toward him as Benjamin entered. He was even more of an impressive spectacle than the Counsellor that Benjamin had met on SaQ'il. He seemed taller and the crest of his skull curved back even more impressively. Not someone to be messed with, quite clearly.

"Are you ready Ambassador?" asked the Legati.

"Yes, we are Captain. We are to be on the building's roof in four hours."

"Your companion will escort you to the transport, and you must take your Centurion with you."

"Thank you. May I ask if there has been any unusual activity?"

"Not really Ambassador. Their little aircraft are still buzzing about, but we just ignore them. The attempts at communication have stopped. It seems that they are slightly less alarmed."

The captain was the only person on the bridge. Such

was the level of autonomy on his ship that very few were necessary to operate it. That was not to say that the captain was the only of his kind onboard. The reality was that there was a skeleton crew of technicians, flight crew and a military squad. They could keep everything going, but by no means was the ship carrying its normal complement of many thousands of military personnel. The other nine ships were the same. But this was not a military assignment, and it was only expected to be a short one.

At the appointed hour, Christel guided Benjamin to the upper flight deck. They entered an immense hangar where two of the scout ships stood gleaming. They were of the type that Benjamin had flown from Mars to SaQ'il. Other than these two, the hangar was completely empty. There, they were joined by Benjamin's new friend, his Centurion.

To everyone else, the Centurion was just a simple security necessity, but to Benjamin it was one of the coolest gadgets he could possibly imagine. It was a drone, but it just hung in the air without the use of propellors and was usually completely silent. It was coded for Benjamin's protection, which meant that it followed him wherever he went. He had been given demonstrations of its capabilities, but fundamentally it could shield Benjamin from incoming projectiles, including kinetic and photon weaponry, as well as immobilize threats through a variety of means. It was quite deadly, but irretrievably loyal to Benjamin. If necessary, it could drill through steel and rock to find him. It was his friend and could even understand a few phrases in English. Benjamin wanted to give it a more friendly name, but that would have to wait for later.

The trio boarded the transport via the extended entry ramp.

On the bridge, Christel issued a voice command. The gigantic doors above them opened, revealing a blue sky.

Their ship then rose in the air and emerged above the huge battle cruiser. The hangar doors closed silently below them, and they accelerated away from the mothership, making their way briskly to the Government building on the western tip of Long Island by the East River. Along the way, they were followed by a couple of news drones and a military helicopter, but no effort was made to allow these pursuers to keep up with them, and they were soon left behind.

They reached the roof of the Government building after a short while and the ship descended to less than a meter of it. From the bridge windows, they could see several people waiting for them. The side door opened, and the ramp extended to reach the roof surface. Benjamin and Christel emerged, along with the Centurion, dressed in their matching white jumpsuits. Benjamin had had reservations about these garments, but felt it was a battle not worth fighting. He would just live with his self-conscious feeling of resembling a character from a detergent commercial.

The seven members of the World Council and a few security personnel, standing to attention, were there waiting for them.

Benjamin and Christel descended the ship's ramp and walked toward the group. Benjamin led the way and outstretched his arm to the Council members and shook their hands with a quick "Thank you for speaking with me today," to each of them. Benjamin could not help but notice that they all seemed slightly distant and kept looking at the scout ship expectantly. It was Div Ballakur that finally explained the detachment.

"Are you alone? We were expecting your new friends to join you today," he said.

"Yes," replied Benjamin. "My function is to represent my new friends, as you put it."

"Well, that's not going to work," interjected May Lin. "If we're supposedly being visited by aliens and they are requesting meetings with the World Council, the least they could do is turn up themselves."

"I agree," added Sylvia Coulthard. "The World Council should be shown the respect for their position as the leaders of this planet. If we are to establish a relationship with these aliens, we should be interacting with them at a peer level."

"Hang on, hang on," said Elena Lenkov. "Let's hear what Mr. Privett has to say. I get the impression that from many perspectives, this won't be a peer level conversation."

"Quite right Elena," said Gene Harlander. "Let's go down to the conference room and hear what Mr. Privett has to say."

Benjamin was expecting this sort of challenge and was prepared for how it should be handled. First and foremost, he had to listen. He said simply:

"Thank you, Councilor. I think I can respond to your concerns. Please lead the way."

The seven Council members filed down the stairs, with Gene Harlander guiding Benjamin and Christel to the Council's private conference room on the top floor of the building. Benjamin's Centurion followed them.

"Is that thing necessary Mr. Privett?" asked Harlander pointing to Benjamin's flying companion.

"Yes, it is," replied Benjamin bluntly. "It is my communications hub, amongst other things."

"I see – very well then."

The group walked down two flights of metal stairs and then through a fire door into a carpeted corridor. Ahead was a pair of heavy wooden doors that led them into an lobby in front of the Council's private conference room. The lobby was crowded with security personnel and some senior members of the World Government that had been alerted to the special meeting.

The Council members filed through the lobby, as if they were processing in a church ceremony. But nobody was looking at them. All eyes were on Benjamin, Christel and the drone that silently followed them. Nobody said a word.

Once in the Council Room, the Council Members took their usual places. Benjamin, and Christel were seated at the head of the table.

Gene Harlander started the conversation.

"So, Mr. Privett, could you please introduce yourself formally and your companion, and then we will do the same."

"Thank you, Councilor," replied Benjamin. "This is my Chief Advisor, Christel. She is an expert on the culture of the visitors. In time, you will understand how she acquired this expertise and why she is critical to this interaction.

"Secondly, my formal function is to perform the function of Ambassador for the visitors, who are known as the Legati."

"Thank you, er, Ambassador, and welcome Chief Advisor," said Gene, nodding to Christel. "Thank you for that clarification. I am Gene Harlander, Spokesman for the World Council from the North American Territories. Elena?"

"I am Elena Lenkov – Council Member from the Eastern European, Middle Eastern and African Territories."

"And I am Lucas Oliveira – Council Member from the South American Territories."

"I am Div Ballakur - Council Member from the West Asian Territories."

"May Lin – Council Member from the East Asian

Territories."

"And I am Sylvia Coulthard – Council Member from the European Territories."

"Gregory Glidell – from the Asia Pacific Territories."

Benjamin nodded to the council members in deference.

"Thank you everyone," said Gene. "All right Ambassador. What do we need to know? Why are the, er Legati, here?"

All eyes were on Benjamin. He took a deep breath and gave the short speech that he had been educated to deliver:

"First of all, I have been instructed to extend respectful greetings from their Excellencies the Videnti, the leaders of the Legati Nation. Their sincere hope and expectation is that Humankind will eventually be able to join the Galactic Alliance.

"Their Excellencies have nominated me as their ambassador to relay their communications to Humankind."

Benjamin paused.

"Will we be meeting any of these leaders?" asked Gene.

"You will have the opportunity to meet their formal Legati representative, the most senior person from the flotilla that is positioned around the planet. He is equivalent to a Fleet Admiral."

"I suppose that will be acceptable for the time being," said Gene. Benjamin decided to let this attempt at equality slide. He pressed ahead with his introduction.

"Now that we know humanity is not alone in the universe, we should also know that there are, in fact, many advanced civilizations in the Milky Way alone. A large proportion of these civilizations are already known to one another and have organized into a structure with agreed laws, assigned space sectors and specific responsibilities.

The Legati, who have been my hosts, are responsible for shepherding emerging civilizations into this Galactic Alliance.

"They have the unequivocal support of all other members of that community. When they encounter emerging civilizations, they will provide guidance on how that civilization can be matured to join the ranks of the galactic community eventually. My role as Ambassador is to support the distribution of this guidance." Benjamin paused for the obvious questions.

"What happens if we don't want this 'guidance'?" interrupted Gregory Glidell. "What are they going to tell us to do? Why do we even need it? Why can't we be left to decide when we want to take our place in this community?"

Benjamin took another deep breath and gave the punch line.

"Fundamentally, this is about the survival of the human race." He noted the skeptical expressions on the faces before him.

"Compared to these other civilizations," he continued, "humanity is many tens of thousands of years behind on the evolutionary, technological and societal development measures. If the human race were to venture out beyond its Solar System without proper preparation, it would not be tolerated and be forced to turn back with extreme prejudice, as they say. In time, you will learn more about the realities of the Milky Way and what is at stake. It is not a naturally harmonious place and eons of effort have been invested in bringing it under control.

"And if humans were to encounter one of the *other* advanced civilizations that are not aligned with the Galactic Community, the outcome could be far worse. Their tolerance for any competition or interference in their activities is reportedly zero. They would happily crush mankind or more probably enslave us in the most diabolical conditions imaginable and then plunder this planet's resources."

"That's a lot to take in," said Glidell. "How do we know this is true and why should we trust your Legati? What's in it for them?"

"With all deference, Councilor," replied Benjamin, "it is these suspicions and an expectation that someone has something to gain, that differentiate the members of the Galactic Alliance from nascent civilizations like ours. The point is that they want us to survive. If humanity decides to ignore the guidance on offer, the Legati will withdraw and leave us to our own fate. But left on our own, humanity's chance of survival will be minimal at best. The Legati have found Earth. If they can do it, they know that other, less friendly, powers will also be aware."

"We have the Legati to blame for this situation?" demanded May Lin.

"No," replied Benjamin. "The Legati have known about mankind for hundreds of years. It is our recent unguarded RF transmissions that have given us away to everyone else."

"Okay," interrupted Gene. "If I understand correctly, the Legati are offering to protect us from these 'unfriendly powers' while humanity pursues policies based on their guidance, so that we can join this galactic community."

"That's it," said Benjamin.

"Good. What are these policies?"

"They are called the Universal Principles. Compassion, community, dialog, equality, respect and peace." Benjamin had been practicing that for hours and was relieved that he had recited it properly at the important moment.

"Is that it?" asked Div. "We could probably legislate to

achieve all of those in an afternoon. They seem obvious moral values that we all aspire to anyway."

"Simple legislation won't cut it." Benjamin looked at Div, who was smirking. "It is going to take fundamental changes in human nature. Corruption, violence, greed, materialism and the unending quest for status over other people are incompatible with the Universal Principles and must end. They must be considered unacceptable universally." At the word 'corruption' Div's smirk was wiped from his face.

"You mean change human nature," said Elena. It was not a question; it was a realization.

"Completely correct. And the Legati expects to see concerted effort and progress. Punting the problem down the line and sticking to the old ways, won't work."

"And that's where this 'guidance' comes in," said Lucas. "Through you, the Legati will be telling us what to do."

There was silence in the room, as the reality set in.

"And where does this guidance come from?" ventured Sylvia.

"The Legati will be issuing this guidance directly. I will be in continuous contact with them and should be able to provide clarifications," replied Benjamin.

"If you can communicate with the Legati, I think it would be preferable that we have direct contact with them, rather than going through an intermediary." It was Lucas Oliveira who presented this challenge. It was an expected challenge. Benjamin had the answer.

"The Legati have a defined process for how they assist civilizations. Negotiating that process is not a possibility. If humanity decides to reject their support, the World Government will continue as it does today. The Legati would simply be onlookers and be indemnified against the fate of our species.

"However, if the Legati's offer of protection and ongoing guidance is accepted, they will expect to see positive engagement and a massive change in the communication structure. That is because their guidance will be far reaching and fine-grained. They will expect to be communicating directly to local authorities around the planet."

"What?" Gene nearly exploded. "You mean they want to circumvent the World Government? How do they expect to do that?"

"The intention is not to circumvent the World Government but rather to streamline the communication flow for effectiveness. How the World Council involves itself in the furthering of the Universal Principles is up to you. Retaining control for the sake of keeping control is not going to work. But attempting to circulate all communications through the World Council isn't going to work either."

"That's outrageous!" Gene was getting red in the face and the other Council members were clearly in a state of disbelief. "You are suggesting we hand over governance of the planet to a bunch of aliens, led by a car mechanic. Just like that."

"Not at all," said Benjamin, glossing over the explicit insult. "The guidance that the Legati will provide will be to highlight where the Universal Principles are being transgressed and leave the resolution to the responsible authorities. If the guidance is ignored, that will be a decision for the World Government, the territorial authorities and the people to make."

"And how are they going to communicate this so-called guidance to all and sundry? Do you have any idea of the level of resources that would be needed to do that?"

"I assume you are aware of the Sperantibus Corporation?" asked Benjamin simply.

You could have cut the atmosphere of the room with a knife. The Councilors looked at one another with questioning expressions on their faces.

"What about it?" asked Gene cautiously.

"They are a creation of the Legati. They were established in preparation for the events that start today. They will help oversee the guidance coming from the Legati in concert with the various authorities."

There was another long pause. Gene finally spoke.

"I think I speak for the Council, when I say that I think that we have heard enough for today. We need to discuss the situation and take advice from other stakeholders. I assume we can reach you on your mobile phone, er, Ambassador." Gene's tone was full of contempt.

"Very well Councilor," replied Benjamin. He rose from the table and Christel did the same. Obviously with reluctance, the Council Members followed suit. Unescorted, Benjamin and Christel left the room, with the Centurion behind them, and returned to the roof to their waiting ship, passing by worried looking Government officials along the way.

Once aboard, as the craft lifted away from the building *en route* to the battle cruiser, Benjamin flopped into his pilot's seat.

"Well, that went better than expected," he said to Christel, "except that I'm a PTRT."

# CHAPTER 3

DELIBERATELY, NO DOUBT, the World Council did not contact Benjamin for several days, which was perfectly fine with him. It gave him a chance to catch up with his friends. He was determined not to let his new responsibilities go to his head.

"Hello Jake – remember me?" he said with a smile on his face.

"*Humm* me, Benjamin. I was wondering if I was still on your quick dial. Welcome back," said Jake with genuine enthusiasm.

"It is good to be back, mate. I have so much to tell you."

"Yes, I think you do. But now you're the most famous person on the entire planet, I expect your social diary is going to be full for some time."

"Jake, irrespective of my change in circumstances, do you think I'd leave you hanging? Just give me a few days and I'll find a way of arranging a meetup. The Bourse might not be practical right now, but I'll think of something."

They chatted for a while and caught up on the essentials. Jake was still between girlfriends and shamelessly asked Benjamin if he could use his new celebrity status to help set him up with someone suitably shallow. Of course, Benjamin told him that he would prioritize that request, without having a clue how he could. They both ended the call happily. Benjamin needed his friendship with Jake, he realized, to remain grounded. Or sane for that matter.

He called up Fabian Price.

"Aha, there you are Benjamin. I was wondering when you'd get round to calling me."

"It's only been a couple of days, Mr. Price. I'm sorry. Fabian. I was just going through the steps that I had been instructed to follow. I assume you saw the feed?"

"I sure did Benjamin. You put the wind up the Council. They've gone into lockdown, with no electronic external communications. They know we have eyes and ears everywhere."

"They can take their time," replied Benjamin. "I'm sure they're busily trying to find a way to maintain their relevance, which is fine. I was told that the preference is to keep them in place for now, for the sake of appearances and minimizing disruption."

"That makes sense. Have you spoken with Flight yet?" asked Fabian.

"No, not yet. I was told to wait for him to reach out to me. I think Christel reached out to him to check the communications through the Centurion."

"Okay. How's it going with Christel?"

"She's great. Utterly curious about everything and that curiosity has gone into overdrive now that she's finally here. Watching too much TV. She even asked if she could go exploring the city with some of my friends, but they're in London, which would be a challenge."

"It's certainly something we could arrange. Maybe fly someone over to New York and they could explore together. Christel is much less of a known face than you."

"I'm sure she would appreciate that," said Benjamin, before moving the subject on. "Do you have any idea how long the Legati are going to be staying here? They can't keep their ships on station forever."

"Well, it's early days yet and they want to stay long enough that their departure is as impressive as their arrival. Frankly other than allowing the Legati Captain of the New York ship to meet the World Council, their primary functions of inspiring awe and conferring authenticity on you, has been completed. In a while they'll want to leave, and you and Christel will be relocated to your permanent accommodations here in Switzerland."

"Somewhere nice?"

"I think you will be very comfortable there, but it is out of the way. Don't expect an apartment in a city."

"Understood. Thank you for your efforts."

"Not at all. We're off to a good start and can't go back now. This is what we've all been working toward. Send me a message when you have your next meeting with the WC."

"Will do."

Benjamin had spent the intervening waiting time with Christel, trying to help her understand her new human hosts. As Benjamin had indicated to Fabian, she was addicted to television, online communities and movies. Benjamin hoped that this addiction would wear off, because at the time, she was behaving like a typical teenager. She was fascinated by silly reality TV stars and commercials for meaningless junk. He decided to ask her about her experiences.

"Christel, could I ask you why you find all this so interesting?"

"I don't know, Benjamin, perhaps it's because it's all so new to me."

"Do you think that you are the audience that the producers of this content are aiming at?"

"I'm not sure. I notice that, fundamentally, someone is always trying to make you purchase something. I recognize that even the non-commercial content is designed to keep you watching a channel, so that you will see the advertisements inserted every 10 minutes. But I don't pay the advertisements any attention. I'm just enjoying these programs – they're very exciting!"

"I see," said Benjamin and paused. "Oh, Christel, would you like something from the fridge?"

"Thank you. Very thoughtful. Could I have a Coke?"

Benjamin grabbed a soda and then left Christel to watch her soap operas in peace.

# CHAPTER 4

GENE COULD NOT just sit there at the table. He was pacing around the room irritably.

"I do wish you'd sit down, Gene," said Elena. "You're giving me a neck ache."

"We've got to do something," he said. "If we agree to let these Legati circumvent us and let them communicate their so-called 'guidance' directly to whoever they wish, they'll have decentralized everything away from us and completely taken control."

"Are we sure about that?" said Gregory. "From what I heard, they were only going to inform local authorities about issues that contravened their Universal Principles."

"But aren't these Principles the basis of a legal system?" asked Div. "I agree with Gene – if they are policing human activity and directing local authorities to take action, they are becoming the law."

"But the Ambassador said clearly that the decision to take action on this information was up to us and the local authorities," added Sylvia.

"Sure, but we don't know what the ramifications of ignoring the information will be," said Div. "If a local authority is informed of a murder, I'm sure they wouldn't ignore it. But if there was some failing in the operations of that authority that was highlighted, they might want to let that slide to avoid looking bad. Would the Legati then announce such an omission?"

"Well, I would suggest that we ask the Ambassador, rather than imagining all sorts of things that might not happen," said Sylvia. "It could be a very good thing for someone to be keeping an eye on what people are doing."

"As long as they're not keeping an eye on us," added Gene.

"Get real Gene," said Lucas. "They already know about our special deal with Sperantibus. That's old news. I agree with Sylvia. Given that we seemingly have little choice, we should view this oversight as simply being additional help."

"I'm with you Lucas," said May. "I would like to know how the Legati are going to monitor societies to see what is going on and what criteria they will apply for reporting transgressions, but I can't see it being too intrusive or fine grained. I think we should, to Sylvia's point, ask the Ambassador how this guidance mechanism will work. No pun intended, but in principle I can't see anything wrong with these Universal Principles. Don't we all want peace and mutual respect?"

"The devil is in the details, May," said Gene. "But let's take a vote."

# CHAPTER 5

DAVID PAGE LOOKED at the calendar on his phone.

"You know, Cyril, they've been here four days now. Other than Benjamin Privett doing his rockstar entrance and the reported sightings of one of their smaller ships landing on the UN building in New York, we've seen and heard nothing. The online community is going mental, and nobody has any answers. There have been no press releases. Nothing."

"That Online Community was never more than a forum for bored hysterics anyway. We should just wait for an announcement. They're not just going to keep those ships hanging over our cities forever, more's the pity. Why don't you give that Benjamin pal of yours a call?"

David laughed. "What, you think he still has his old mobile phone? That's long gone, I'm sure."

"Worth a go," shrugged Cyril.

"Waste of time," said David as he picked up his own phone and dialed Benjamin's old number. "What I should be doing is... hey, it's ringing... Benjamin!"

Benjamin's face was on the screen.

"Good afternoon David. How are you?"

"Wow, Benjamin – I thought I should try your old phone number." Cyril looked at David over his spectacles, "to see if you could still be reached. I am very happy to see you."

"It is good to see you too, David."

"It's obvious why I'm calling you. Can you tell me anything about what's going on?"

"Yes, I can." David resisted doing a fist bump when he heard this. "Given the early state of things, it's pretty straightforward."

Benjamin proceeded to give a high-level description of how he had been extracted from the Martian trip and had met with the Legati. He omitted his visit to *SaQ'il*, his preparation by the Legati leadership and anything about Christel or the other people that travelled with him to Mars. He simplified the scenario by describing himself as the Ambassador representing the Legati. He explained he was in talks with the World Council to show how the Legati could help mankind prepare for a future that could see them living alongside other civilizations. He introduced the Universal Principles and explained why they were table stakes for joining the Galactic Community. Benjamin concluded by saying he was waiting for a response from the World Council to the initial conversation.

David started asking the usual questions.

"Why do we need these Legati? Shouldn't we be allowed to develop on our own?"

"Would you trust a child to grow up on his own to become a useful member of society?"

"Of course not, but that hardly describes the human race."

"Doesn't it?" replied Benjamin with a surprised tone in his voice. "Mankind doesn't create, it discovers. Just like a child. It makes plenty of mistakes along the way. These 'aliens' are the adults in the room, and we should listen to them."

"And if we don't?"

"Then we are going to make some pretty serious mistakes."

"Like what?"

"You tell me, David, and I'm going to leave it like that. If you decide to write anything about this conversation, please just make sure you emphasize that the Legati value mankind and they want to be our friend and ally."

"Okay Benjamin..."

"Thank you, David – someone will be in touch." Benjamin ended the call.

"Plug me," said David as he dropped into his chair.

"From what I overheard of your call, I think that's a reasonable reaction," said Cyril.

"I need to get this out as soon as possible," said David.

"Be careful, though," advised Cyril. "This is not the time to start being 'imaginative'. And make sure you speak with Grant straight away."

David followed Cyril's advice and rushed straight to the office of Grant Everly, the Editor. Apart from a "why didn't you think of that before?" comment, Grant gave David the same advice as Cyril, but as a direct instruction. "Don't enhance!"

The breaking news was on the London Certified News and its global affiliates an hour later. The online forums lit up instantly. It was if the world had been doing absolutely nothing but watching the news for an update, which was quite possibly the case. As per Grant's instructions, no commercials were displayed alongside the article and no

copyright for unaltered re-distribution was enforced.
This information was too important for everyone.

# CHAPTER 6

BENJAMIN THOUGHT BACK on those days with a strong sense of nostalgia. The early days of the arrival had been so simple. They had been hopeful. In retrospect, they were even fun. He recalled a moment that occurred shortly after the LCN bulletin had been released.

He had been in his suite onboard the Legati cruiser, whiling away the time with Christel. She had very quickly progressed from watching mindless reality TV, to documentaries and travelogues, which was good news for Benjamin. They were interrupted by a call from the captain.

"Ambassador, could I trouble you to come to the bridge? We have an interesting situation."

"I am on my way, Captain." He jumped to his feet and headed out of the room. Christel followed.

When they reached the bridge, the captain was watching a video stream on a large screen with a couple of his crew members. Benjamin laughed when he saw what they were looking at.

"What's that doing there?" he said.

"An attempt at humor, I think, Ambassador," said the captain.

Sitting on top of the cruiser was a civilian helicopter and moving around it were several people, clearly excited that they were walking on top of an alien spacecraft. Two of them were holding the ends of a banner that read "We come in peace!"

"I suppose we should admire their courage," laughed Benjamin. "What are you going to do Captain?"

"Obviously, they can't stay there. I could wait for them to get bored and leave, but then that might encourage others to do the same."

"So?"

"I will have to remove them." He turned to one of his crew members. "Put them on the ground with the cranes."

"Yes sir," came the reply.

What followed was probably very alarming for those young people who were celebrating their success at landing on this island in the sky. For everyone else, it was hilarious.

Without warning, plates in the ship opened and two huge crab-like machines rose out of the cavern below. They hovered in the air for a moment and then rapidly approached the revelers, who were less celebratory suddenly. One of the crabs positioned itself above the helicopter. Then, without any visible attachments, the helicopter started rising off the deck. The crab and its cargo then turned and flew down to the park below. It placed the helicopter gently on the grass and without fuss, returned to its hangar in the ship.

That left four people standing on top of the cruiser without a means of departure. They instinctively huddled together. The second crab then flew over the group. They looked up at the monster above them with anxious expressions on their faces. But before they could make any moves, they too were lifted in the air, along with their banner. They looked like sky divers that were frozen in space. The crab rose and then followed the path of the first, flying down to the park below. The visitors were left lying on the grass, staring up at the retreating machine.

"Thank you, Captain," said Benjamin after observing the repelling of the boarders. "I don't think they'll try that again."

The unceremonious expulsion of the uninvited boarders had been recorded by other nearby observers in their own helicopters and ever-present drones. The global broadcast of the footage, while hugely entertaining for all, deterred anyone from trying a similar prank again on any of the Legati cruisers. It was a moment that marked the end of the playful period of the Legati arrival. There were still thousands of people camped out under the spacecraft in all ten cities, hoping to witness something historic firsthand. The atmosphere became less celebratory and more expectant. Almost spiritual.

Shortly after the helicopter incident, Benjamin recalled, he had had his first conversation with Mr. Flight.

Benjamin's phone rang.

"Hello, this is Benjamin," he said. There was no image on the video screen.

"Good afternoon," said a strange androgenous voice with little intonation. "My name is Flight. You have been informed that I will be in touch."

"Ah yes, Mr. Flight. Indeed, I was waiting for you to reach out to me."

"I anticipate, Benjamin, that you have been informed that I will be your guide during your time as Ambassador on this planet."

"That's right. It's a relief to speak to you at long last,

actually."

"Why so?"

"I was wondering what I needed to do next. The World Council is still discussing the first meeting I had with them."

"They are not discussing anything relevant. There is nothing to discuss. We are here to administer impartial assistance to benefit the people of this planet."

"In that case, do you know why the Council has not reached out to me?"

"Yes. They believe that a fast response will make them appear desperate. They are not really concerned about the impact that our arrival will have on mankind, but rather its impact on their positions in your society.

"However," continued the strange voice, "they will be calling you very soon. I can see that several of the Councilors have blocked off the day after tomorrow for the meeting."

"You can see that?" said Benjamin.

"I can see most things Benjamin," said Flight. It was a statement of fact. "I need to prepare you for what they are going to propose."

"I am ready Mr. Flight."

"Good. We shall proceed now."

# CHAPTER 7

"GOOD MORNING AMBASSADOR," said Gene Harlander. "Hopefully this is a good time to call."

"Of course, Councilor," said Benjamin. "What can I do for you?"

"Well, the Council would like to meet with you as soon as possible. How does this afternoon sound? Say 13:00? I propose the Government headquarters again."

"Thank you, Councilor. I will be there." Harlander ended the call without saying anything else.

*And goodbye to you too*, thought Benjamin.

Benjamin was amused that after keeping him waiting for nearly a week, the Council wanted to meet him as soon as possible.

Benjamin called Mr. Flight, who answered immediately.

"Good morning Benjamin."

"Good morning Mr. Flight. Are there any updates before I meet with the Council today?"

"No Benjamin. Nothing has changed. You know what to do."

"Thank you, Mr. Flight."

Benjamin turned to Christel, who was looking at him expectantly.

"Wish me luck, Christel. I think I'm going to need it."

"Not at all, Benjamin" she replied. "Luck is an illogical concept anyway. You are thoroughly prepared and will perform as per plan."

"I hope so."

"I know so, Benjamin."

Benjamin donned his BAT gear and with Christel, headed to the bridge. He passed a few Legati along the way. They stood to attention as he passed by.

The bridge was busier than usual. The tiers of monitoring stations in the amphitheater were all manned with ship's officers.

"Captain?"

"Yes, Ambassador. We are all ready." The answer came without a question, but no question was needed. "Your ship is ready for you."

"Thank you, Captain. I believe I am prepared to perform as per plan." Benjamin was trying to follow Christel's advice on how to speak the way that a Legati would. He found himself just mimicking her.

"We will be following your progress," said the captain.

The prospect of executive oversight didn't make Benjamin feel a lot better. In fact, it heightened his anxiety quite considerably. He didn't want to show how he felt openly but suspected that Christel could sense it.

"You'll be fine," she said kindly, without prompting.

With nothing more to be said, Benjamin and Christel made their way to the flight deck as before and boarded their scout ship. Christel spoke to the ship, which resulted in the overhead doors opening and the ship lifting slowly into the sunlight once more. Clear of the cruiser, the scout ship turned and accelerated toward the Government building, reaching the tall structure after only a minute or so.

As they disembarked with the Centurion in tow, they noticed immediately that there were far more armed security guards lined up on the roof, standing to attention and looking straight ahead. The Council members were not there. A single person in formal civilian clothes was standing at the center of the roof area to greet them.

"Good afternoon, Ambassador. I am Quentin Mategeko, Special Counsel to Councilor Harlander. He has asked me to escort you to the Council Chambers."

"Thank you Mr. Mategeko" said Benjamin. "Please lead on."

The small group headed into the building and down the same stairs as before and retraced their steps to the Council meeting room that Benjamin had visited before. The high number of armed guards was not lost on Benjamin. Quentin knocked on the door to the Council Chambers and then opened it. The Council Members were seated at the table and did not rise when Benjamin and his companions entered the room.

"Ah, good afternoon, Ambassador," said Harlander. "Please do take a seat."

"Thank you, Councilor."

"First of all," said Harlander once they were seated. "I wanted to thank you for your patience while we discussed the implications of the arrival of the Legati and yourself.

"We have asked Councilor Coulthard to lay out the conclusions that we have arrived at during our deliberations. Sylvia, would you?"

Sylvia Coulthard was clearly from the British Territories. Perhaps that was why they chose her to relay their decision to Benjamin as a compatriot. Benjamin could not help but feel the situation was overloaded with subliminal messaging.

"Obviously," she began with a confident tone, "we have only the presence of these large spacecraft over our cities, to believe that we are, in fact being visited by the Legati you speak of. We have observed the incident with the aircraft that landed on the ship in New York and how it was removed along with its passengers in a peaceful manner. It could have all been an optical illusion, but we are inclined to believe that non-earthly technology was used to perform the removal. Therefore, on balance, we agree that we are being visited by representatives from another planet.

"In addition, we see nothing unreasonable about these Universal Principles that you speak of. We are not in agreement, however, that we need some external entity to perform a policing role to force mankind to abide by them. These Principles are nothing remarkable for us and have long been values that we hold dear. We are confident in the developmental trajectory that mankind is making and are proud of the progress that has been made over the centuries.

"We understand that these Legati want to intervene in mankind's development and highlight where they believe there have been digressions from the ideal path. Such so-called guidance would be communicated directly to those authorities that would be expected to handle the claimed transgressions. They seem to believe that mankind will go through cultural, social and behavioral changes by being told what they are doing wrong all the time. They want to stifle mankind's creativity. They want to deprive mankind of the opportunity to experiment, make mistakes and to improve on their own." She paused for effect; perhaps for a little too long.

"May I...?" started Benjamin.

"Allow the Councilor to continue," interrupted Harlander, with no shred of politeness.

"Thank you," continued Coulthard. "These Legati do not offer us anything. We have heard nothing of technology transfers or providing us scientific knowledge. We only hear of this 'guidance' that they want to provide. The arrogance of this notion is extraordinary. It is considered hypocritical that the Universal Principles include respect and yet seemingly no respect for mankind is being shown.

"These Legati arrive on our planet without any warning or prior discussions with the World Government. They secretly build the Sperantibus organization in order to undermine the World Government, the planet's financial system and take control of our off-world mining interests.

"It is for these reasons, that we have arrived at a very simple conclusion.

"We do not want the Legati to remain on this planet. We will also be dissolving the Sperantibus corporation and bringing its assets under the direct control of the World Government.

"The announcement that we will be making to the people of this planet in the coming hour is that the Legati visitors have precisely 24 hours to depart this planet. We no longer have any interest in meeting their delegation or representatives. If they do wish to visit in the future, we require that they find a way to request permission from the World Government beforehand."

Coulthard sat back in her chair. It was clear she had come to the end of her speech. Benjamin did not say anything for a moment. He wanted to be clear that he was not going to be interrupted again. He saw that everyone in the room was looking at him in an expectant manner. He took a deep breath and replied.

"Thank you, Councilor," he began.

"The Legati do not apologize for their unannounced visit. They fully expected the objections that you have raised today. They fully understand the protectionist thinking of this World Council. This protectionist thinking is for the preservation of the status quo on this planet and the authority system that the World Council sits on top of. The one thing that the Council fears most of all is the loss of their authority."

"Now you hang on a minute...," interrupted Gregory Glidell in an angry tone. As he raised his voice, the Centurion moved from behind Benjamin to hovering right beside him. Glidell felt it was looking right at him. He stopped talking.

"Do not worry," said Benjamin calmly. "This device is just very protective of me. Please allow me to continue." All the Councilors were momentarily shocked and so Benjamin continued.

"It is true that the Legati are not about to provide free technology gifts and explain all the mysteries of the universe. Humanity is very creative and there is no intention for that creativity to be strangled.

"It is extraordinarily arrogant of you to attempt to dismiss the visitors without even asking the opinions of the people on this planet.

"As for the guidance that the Legati are offering, it is intended to stamp out corruption, wars, organized violence, engineered poverty, divisive behavior at all levels, hegemony, population suppressions, abuse and collective apathy about the environment. Only when people know what is really going on will they want to stop it.

"I said on my other visit that the Galactic Community is many tens of thousands of years more advanced than mankind, both from a societal and technological standpoint. Their values should be aspired to, rather than rejected.

"The Legati will not be leaving just because seven people feel their self-importance is going to be eroded. Hold a referendum and let me state the Legati case. If mankind wants them gone, they will leave as promised."

Benjamin placed his hands on the table, raised his eyebrows and stood up. There was nothing more to say.

"Thank you for your time today Councilors." He nodded his head and turned to leave the room. There was complete silence as he, Christel and the Centurion left.

# CHAPTER 8

"MY FELLOW CITIZENS," announced Harlander over the global broadcast. "Today, we met with the Ambassador for the Legati visitors, the Honorable Benjamin Privett. We do not know why the visitors could not speak to us themselves, but we learned what we needed to learn from the Ambassador.

"It is with significant sadness that we have to report that the discussions highlighted the arrogance of the Legati and their desire to eliminate our way of life, replacing it with a subservient human race that receives nothing in return. We have told the Ambassador that mankind cannot accept the rule of an invader and occupying force. Humanity should be allowed to plot its own course in history and take its rightful place in whatever galactic societies that already exist, as a peaceful partner.

"It is therefore with a heavy heart that we have issued an ultimatum. The Legati have precisely 24 hours to leave our planet. If they fail to adhere to our wishes, we will consider ourselves to be in a state of formal conflict and will take any measures necessary to evict them.

"Your local authorities will advise how to shelter during this difficult time. Rest assured that this is now our only option to maintain our civilization's freedoms and proud cultures.

"The thoughts of the World Council are with you all."

David Page watched the broadcast with an unusual mixture of amazement, surprise, disbelief and disappointment. He could not understand what had caused the World Council to react so strongly to the overtures of the Legati. He could only assume that they had unearthed some unpleasant motives of the alien visitors. But Benjamin had painted a completely different picture.

David was perplexed.

He picked up the phone and hoped that Benjamin would answer.

"Good afternoon, David," said Benjamin calmly.

"Thank you for answering Benjamin – we really need to talk."

"I agree."

"What the *humm* is going on?"

"That is the question, David. The truth is that the WC is not being forthcoming with the world's population."

"Why would they not be straightforward with the people? What did you tell them that got them so agitated?"

"They understand the enormity of Legati arrival. They understand what it means. For the first time, mankind is going to know what is really going on. Fact-checking systems are all well and good, but they can be worked around. The WC understands that they are faced with a future of open information. How can you retain power when everyone knows what is really going on? Goodbye propaganda and manipulation of public opinion."

David thought about that for a moment.

"Then what happens next?" he said finally.

"That's entirely up to the WC. A referendum was suggested, but that idea seems to have fallen on deaf ears."

"But what if the military attacks the Legati? What are they going to do?"

"I'm afraid I can't discuss that at this time."

"Why not Benjamin? Are the Legati going to wipe out their attackers? It could be a massacre."

"As I say, I am not authorized to divulge that kind of information."

"What do I tell people then?" asked David.

"You can tell them what you like, but I would advise against being divisive. The truth will come out and you don't want to be on the wrong side of that truth. In any case, I think you will find the Fact-Checking System constraining you."

"Okay. Thank you, Benjamin, as always. I'll see if I can calm the nerves a little."

"Thank you, David." Benjamin ended the call.

David got up from his desk. He was unsure about how to proceed and without Cyril being there at that moment, he headed over to the editor's office. David told Grant Everly about the call he had just had.

"I agree with the Ambassador" said Everly. "There's more to this than meets the eye. But the World Council has absolute authority to do whatever they wish, including a military strike. It's a risky strategy. Perhaps they are hoping that a bee sting will be enough to get their message across. I can't imagine that our weapons compare that well to what the Legati would bring to the gunfight."

"So, what do I communicate on the feed?" asked David.

"Time to keep our heads down. Don't take sides right

now."

# CHAPTER 9

TWENTY-THREE HOURS into the notice period, Gene Harlander and the rest of the World Council were seated in the Primary Military Coordination Center with the full contingent of global territorial military commanders. The atmosphere was tense.

"I want to be on record as opposed to a military strike on these ships" said Councilor May Lin. "We would be blindly attacking an enemy with no idea how they will react, or what they are capable of."

"Councilor, we have been over this a dozen times," replied Oliveira. "We don't expect to destroy these ships and we don't want to. Our goal here is to send them a message that we don't intend to be intimidated and can defend ourselves."

"By attacking them?" asked Lin.

"Their refusal to leave this planet is a form of aggression. We are defending ourselves."

"All right. All right" interrupted Harlander. "We have

voted on this and made a decision. We must proceed to plan.

"General Horst, how long before we mobilize for the assault?"

General Horst was a Scandinavian career soldier. He did not like politicians and their general enthusiasm for putting his soldiers in harm's way. His responses to these Councilors were therefore decidedly deadpan.

"Suborbital flights are already in place and local aerial and ground assets are on immediate standby. We are ready to go on the Council's command."

"We cannot proceed until the 24-hour deadline has expired," replied Harlander. "We must wait."

The PMCC was a very large control center that was dominated by a large, curved wall that could project any number of video or data feeds. For the purposes of that day's operation, there were ten video streams, showing the ten Legati ships from overhead, hovering over their respective cities. From the vantage point of the video stream, it was clear that the crowds and nearby traffic had been evacuated. There was no movement.

In front of the massive video screen were rows of workstations, each with communications officers ready to relay the commands of their superiors to the soldiers in the field.

Time ticked slowly by. There was silence.

Then, making everyone jump, one of the communications officers spoke up.

"The Beijing target is moving sir."

"The Delhi target is also moving sir," said another.

The room was suddenly noisy with reports of all ten ships moving away from the position that they had been at for the previous week.

"Do we have vectors for all the ships?"

"They all seem to be heading in different directions," said the Communications Chief.

On the screens, the ships could be seen turning and moving. The drones filming them started moving with them.

"Where the hell are they going?" barked Horst.

"It is difficult to tell sir," replied the Communications Chief. "They are not ascending but are all heading in different directions. They are all accelerating as well, which is making it difficult for the drones to keep up with them. We are tracking by satellite."

The video streams of all ten ships switched to a map view of their respective areas. It soon became clear that they were all heading out to sea. Within five to ten minutes, all the ships were over international waters, all at least 200 kilometers from the nearest land. One by one, they came to a stop. The drones eventually caught up and the video feeds were restored.

"Have they retreated?" asked Harlander.

"I think they have an idea of what's going to happen and have moved away from the cities" said Councilor Glidell.

"Fine" said Harlander. "We can proceed without worrying about collateral damage."

*Collateral damage?* thought Horst. *Now you're thinking about that, you moron.*

"Yes sir – quite right sir," he said out loud.

"It's not too late to stop this," said Councilor Lin.

"Yes, it is May" said Harlander. "General, you have authorization to proceed with the first wave."

"Yes sir" replied Horst. He gave a look over to the other Councilors, who did their best to avoid his gaze.

"Number One," he called out. "Commence initial phase with adjusted coordinates on all ten targets."

"Yes sir" replied the Communications Chief. He made a gesture on his workstation and the other service members in the room went to work confirming the immediate attack command and sending the authorization codes.

High above the Earth several dozen suborbital bombers descended into the atmosphere. On cue, they launched their cruise missiles simultaneously toward their various targets.

"Two minutes to impact," called out the CC.

"This'll wake 'em up" said Harlander with unconcealed relish.

Precisely on time, each Legati cruiser was hit with ten state-of-the-art conventional weapons. Upon impact, the missiles exploded in a crescendo of fire, flame and smoke. The video streams all stuttered as the drones were buffeted by the resulting shock wave.

Everyone peered at the screen as the smoke cleared. They could see debris from the cruise missiles dropping into the sea below each ship, but the ships themselves looked the same as before.

"How much damage did we do?" demanded Harlander.

"Damage report please" asked Horst casually. He knew the answer before it came.

"Well," said the CC, "there is no evidence of any damage whatsoever."

"They must have felt that" said Harlander. "Proceed."

"Commence Phase Two," said Horst.

"Yes sir," replied the CC.

On command, the suborbital bombers released two more laser guided bombs onto each of the cruisers.

"What are these?" asked Harlander. He sounded like he was asking about fireworks.

"They are Bunker Busters sir – they are the most

potent conventional weapons we have."

The huge white missiles spiraled down and hit each of the ships squarely in the back. Again, there was a tremendous ball of fire and rising smoke as they detonated on their targets. The shockwave was clearly visible this time as it raced out from the impact point.

Again, everyone scrutinized the video screens as the smoke cleared.

"Damage report," order Horst.

"I don't understand sir," replied the CC. "There seems to be no trace of damage whatsoever. Not even a scratch."

"What?" demanded Harlander. "What's wrong with these weapons?"

"There's nothing wrong with the weapons, sir," replied Horst. "They must have the most incredible shielding to resist these assaults. I've never seen anything like it."

"What's next then?" said Harlander with a crazed look in his eyes.

"The only other option is thermo-nuclear – the electro-magnetic pulse should have some impact on them."

"Let's do that then," said Harlander.

"Are you sure sir? Those areas of the ocean would be irradiated for decades sir."

"That's not important – do it!"

"STOP!" yelled Councilor Lenkov. "The Council did *not* authorize the use of nuclear weaponry. This attack will stop NOW!"

"But Elena..." stammered Harlander.

"Enough Gene. Come to your senses. This whole thing has been a mistake. I can't believe we went along with you for as long as we did. It is time to listen to the Legati properly, for the good of our people.

"General. Tell your forces to stand down," said

Lenkov.

"Yes, ma'am" he said firmly. He was the most relieved person in the room.

# CHAPTER 10

BENJAMIN THOUGHT BACK to that attack with amazement. During the assault on the New York ship, which had moved itself over 300 kilometers away to the southeast over the Atlantic, he had been on the bridge with the Captain and Christel. There were not many other Legati there. It seemed that they were not needed. They had watched the incoming missiles and seen the massive explosions but had felt absolutely nothing.

"How is this possible Captain? They are throwing everything they have at us."

"So, I see," said the captain. "Humans do not possess any weapons that can damage our ships. They only have kinetic or explosive weapons, which won't get them anywhere against our armor. They were thinking about launching thermo-nuclear devices, but someone stopped them. Those weapons would also have had no effect. We gathered some useful live data during their experiment, so at least something good came out of it."

Benjamin had laughed emptily, although in hindsight the captain probably was not joking.

"And you were able to see that someone stopped that last attack?"

"Yes. Flight will give you the details, but it was Elena Lenkov" he said, looking at the screen in front of his Captain's chair.

"Thank you. Very interesting. But how could the ship handle these impacts like it did?"

"In essence, the more force you apply to the dynamic shielding, the more it pushes back. The net result is that all kinetic or explosive forces are reflected straight back out, which can be deadly to an attacking ship at close quarters. Obviously, there are reactant forces on the ship because of this, but the gravitational drives can maintain complete stability, so you won't feel anything."

"Obviously..." echoed Benjamin. He was in awe. Not for the first time.

# CHAPTER 11

"GOOD MORNING, AMBASSADOR" said Councilor Lenkov in a confidential tone.

"Good morning councilor" replied Benjamin brightly. The Councilor had called him the day after the attacks on the Legati ships.

Benjamin was not surprised at receiving the call. The global reaction to the assault on the Legati ships had been ferocious. Online media had been relentless in demanding formal explanations for the action. But it was the physical demonstrations that had been most poignant. The world had not seen such a spontaneous outpouring of global anger since the start of the Democratic Riots of the 2030s. Thousands of people had assembled where the Legati ships had been stationed, demanding accountability for the bombings and insisting on clarification why the World Council, alone, had the authority to order it without the apparent agreement of the World Government body. What was the point of democracy when executive authorities did not consult with the representatives of the people?

Faced with the extraordinary reaction around the world, the members of the World Government were keen to throw the World Council under the proverbial bus. They demanded investigations in the 'name of the people'. Seemingly, all two thousand Government Representatives were simultaneously appearing on talk shows in their respective territories condemning the unilateral action of the World Council and demanding answers. It was not lost on Benjamin that while these Representatives may not have voted for the attack, they had been informed of it shortly beforehand. Nobody had objected.

"I am calling you in a somewhat unofficial capacity," said Lenkov. "I want you to know that the World Council is in a state of disagreement. I think that's the best way to describe it. There are some of us who were completely against that attack on your ships from the beginning. But obviously a quorum decided to go ahead."

"I see," said Benjamin, simply.

"The expectations of the minority were borne out. That these Legati ships would not be susceptible to our weapons, and they are still here."

"Is that what worries you the most?" asked Benjamin.

"No, of course not. I'm sorry." The Councilor paused. "Our actions were an insult to the Legati and probably proved to them why we need their intervention." She paused for Benjamin to say something supportive.

"Attacks of that nature are standard procedure in situations like this, apparently," said Benjamin. "The way they described it to me, 'these nascent civilizations need to get these tantrums out of their system'."

"They must have a very low opinions of us..." lamented the Councilor.

"I believe they have a very accurate opinion of the

World Council. But what I can say for certain, is that the Legati consider it time for you and your fellow Councilors to start demonstrating leadership. There is no place for impulsive violence in solving societal challenges. The Legati need to keep the Council in place to oversee and develop the planet, which is what the Council is for anyway. You should be able to view the guidance they offer as help in how to make the world a far better place. If the current Council members are unable to do this, they will need to be replaced."

"So, what's next, Ambassador?"

"You need to be honest with the people of our planet."

# CHAPTER 12

"MY FELLOW CITIZENS," said Councilor Lin "I am speaking to you today in the spirit of complete openness.

"The World Council has not acted in a manner that befits the trust that you have all put in us.

"As of this morning, the three World Councilors that voted against the unprovoked attack on our Legati visitors have accepted the resignations of those that voted for it. Specifically, Councilors Ballakur, Glidell, Harlander and Coulthard are no longer members of the World Council. Elections will be held shortly to replace them, as well as the three remaining Councilors. That includes me, of course.

"It is important that everyone is clear that at no point have the Legati, or their representatives, threatened or coerced anybody. Even during the unwarranted assault on their ships, there was not the slightest retaliation or aggression. Even though it has been a hard-learned lesson, we see the Legati as an inspiration and not a threat. We look forward to hearing what guidance they would care to impart.

"One other aspect that I feel compelled to emphasize is that this realization is not the result of our inability to overcome the Legati militarily, although that was a catalyst for our understanding of our visitors. More importantly, it was the assessment of our own behavior and the failures that it resulted in, that brought us to this point.

"We will be resuming our discussions with the Legati and their representatives as soon as possible and will keep you all fully informed of the steps along the way. We will not be operating in a vacuum."

Benjamin recalled being overwhelmed by a high degree of skepticism about the capitulation of the World Council.

Would there have been all this handwringing if the attacks had succeeded in sending the Legati fleet home? Were they so desperate to maintain their dominion over the World Government that they would resort so quickly to a show of military force? Was violence still the default response from people in power when challenged?

Mankind had been given a key lesson, however. Their military was utterly irrelevant against the Legati and, by extension, humanity would be defenseless against any belligerent they might encounter beyond their own Solar System.

There would now be those that were pondering how they could get their hands on Legati technology.

With some urgency.

If humanity was unable to assert itself against the prevailing technology of these visitors, wouldn't that mean that they were destined to be a subservient race?

Since the beginnings of mankind's existence, its societies had been defined by their ability to overcome aggressions of other societies, as well as dominate other societies by imposing their superior technology on them. It didn't matter whether it was flint arrow heads, gunpowder or nuclear weapons. Human desire for status and hegemony was irretrievably dependent on superior flavors of violence.

This was the central consideration and double-edged sword of the Legati announcing themselves to any nascent civilization. They became a blueprint of what was possible technologically and militarily. Everyone craved immediate access to knowledge that seemed magical to them or could give them advantage. Little thought would be given to how that knowledge would ultimately be used or misused.

The Legati knew, all too well, they had to be very careful.

# CHAPTER 13

THE DAY AFTER Councilor Lin had addressed the world with her apology and commitment to be open with everyone, Christel and Benjamin were sitting in their quarters onboard the Legati ship which had returned to its New York location. Christel was very clear in her view of what would happen next.

"Any minute now," she said, "you're going to get a call from that Councilor. She'll want to establish herself as someone in authority. She'll want to demonstrate how close she is to you and the Legati. I wouldn't be surprised if she asks to have one of them appear alongside her at some event, as evidence of the new trusting alliance."

"Well, that needs to happen sooner or later," agreed Benjamin. "At least she'll be meeting them on her home turf. She won't feel so terrified as I was. Remember when you introduced me to my Legati hosts for the first time?" They both laughed.

"But I don't expect she'll want this meeting to be with

just her and the remnants of the World Council," continued Christel. "I expect she'll want to make a... what's the expression?"

"A grand gesture?" answered Benjamin. "I expect you're right. She did promise not to work in a vacuum."

"Has Mr. Flight spoken to you about this?"

"No, he hasn't. Perhaps when we get that call you mentioned, he'll have some advice to provide."

Christel was right, as she so often was. Later that day, Benjamin's phone rang. It was Councilor Lin.

"Good morning, Ambassador. Thank you for taking my call."

"Of course, Councilor."

"The remaining Councilors have been discussing with the territorial councils how best to accommodate a formal meeting between the Government and yourselves... I mean the Legati.

"We are hoping that you will be amenable to a meeting in the General Assembly here in New York tomorrow. We are hoping that representatives of the Legati themselves would also honor us with their presence."

"Thank you, Councilor," said Benjamin. "We would be very happy to attend such a meeting tomorrow. And certainly, senior Legati would want to attend as the primary attendees. They can communicate directly in English, so my advisor and I would only be there in a supporting capacity."

"I understand Ambassador. Hearing from our new friends directly would make this an even more historic event, if that's possible. I am hoping that we can formalize the meeting by having prepared speeches from both sides. Would that be acceptable?"

"Indeed Councilor," replied Benjamin.

"Thank you, we would like to propose 2pm, if that works for you."

"Yes, Councilor. That will be fine. There is one thing, though."

"Oh, yes?"

"I have been informed that the Legati have a strong preference for this first meeting to be held outside and open to the public."

"I see."

"Yes, so we would like the event to take place in Yankee Stadium."

"Oh." The Councilor seemed taken aback for a moment, and then she said, "of course, Ambassador. We will make that happen. We will see you tomorrow at 2pm."

"Thank you, Councilor. We will see you tomorrow." The call ended.

Benjamin leaned back in his chair with a slightly smug grin on his face.

"I thought you hadn't spoken with Mr. Flight?" said Christel.

"I haven't."

"So, what's all this about meeting outdoors at some stadium?"

"Yankee Stadium? Oh, I've just never been there."

# CHAPTER 14

AS SOON AS David Page had heard about the upcoming meeting, he had booked himself onto the next Delited flight to New York. As one of the accredited journalists that could attend such governmental events, he had not waited for permission. He packed a small bag and headed for the airport. The Fact Checking System had effectively curtailed public press events, so under normal circumstances this travel would be unusual. But he, and all the people around him, knew that this occasion was going to be a truly once-in-a-lifetime event.

*A once in a civilization event,* thought David.

He had arrived at the stadium early to make sure he found a good seat in the Press Area. A wide platform had been installed over the baseball diamond. Seating could be seen on it for the remnants of the World Council and other senior members of the Government. The platform was angled to run along the third base and home plate line, so that the banked seating behind the visitors' dugout could accommodate the two thousand Government officials. The Press Area was in the stands behind home plate, affording views of the platform and the outfield.

David was surprised to see that the rest of the stadium had been made largely available to the general public. Even though he had arrived two hours early, these seats were already almost all occupied. There was a celebratory atmosphere, and the continuous sound of a multitude of conversations filled the air. Over fifty thousand people had turned up for the occasion and so security was very tight, but the crowd seemed to be very relaxed and focused on what was going on. The spillover of many thousands more were content to watch the theater outside on massive monitors that had been hastily erected.

The Governmental body arrived a little over half an hour before the start of the meeting. They filed into the stands mostly in silence. Each one was as curious as the rest of the crowd as to what was going to happen that day. The remaining members of the World Council were among this contingent. They made their way, along with some other selected officials, to their seats on the platform.

David did not know any of the people sitting near him, and nobody seemed to be particularly interested in small talk. So, he just sat there and waited.

A line of syndicated news drones flew overhead, training their cameras on the stage as well as the assembly around them, streaming the event to the world. Fixed cameras were deployed all over the stadium. No details of this day were going to be missed.

The clock on the scoreboard clicked to 13:55.

The crowd became noticeably quieter as the anticipation of the start of the meeting became keener.

Just at this moment, a deep shadow was cast over the field as one of the Legati scout ships slid slowly and silently over the roof top of the stadium. As it reached centerfield beyond the platform, it slowed and descended to the grass.

For most, this was the first time seeing an alien spacecraft in their midst. The size and menacing design of the spaceship was so extraordinary that the stare of a hundred thousand eyes could not be pulled from it. There was a broad gasp and murmuring from the crowd as the reality of the situation sunk in.

A platform extended from underneath the ship's nose and Benjamin and Christel emerged into the sunlight and went down the ramp to the grass. The crowd cheered loudly as they recognized who had arrived. The couple strolled to the platform and walked up the ramp that had been installed at the rear. As they reached the top of the platform, David could see that Benjamin had some sort of drone hovering a meter behind him. The noise of the crowd did not subside.

Benjamin waved to the crowd and then approached the Council members. He shook their hands and spoke with them for a few moments. David could not tell what he was saying. Benjamin and Christel took their places in the seats on the stage.

The crowd in the stadium slowly calmed down and eventually became silent. It was a silence of expectation. It was time for the alien visitors to appear. The people were transfixed. You could have heard a pin drop.

David stared intently at the alien ship behind the platform. He held his breath.

The sound of multiple synchronized heavy footsteps on a metallic floor broke the silence. Four Legati emerged from the ship and marched to the base of the ramp. There was an audible gasp from the crowd as these colossal guards set foot on the grass. Even from such a distance, their sheer size was clear for all to see. Eight feet tall, at least, they exuded a singular purpose. Authority.

Every guard was clothed in tight-fitting black battle dress, and each had another drone floating above their shoulder. These machines were altogether more significant than the one that followed Benjamin around. David could only wonder what they might be capable of. The Legati guard formation turned to face the ramp and waited. The crowd continued to hum.

The sound of heavy footsteps on the ramp started again, and the Fleet Admiral, the Captain of the battle fleet descended toward his guard. He was an impressive sight in his heavy coat, seemingly even taller than his guard members. As he reached the grass and his soldiers, the guard saluted him by crossing their arms in front of their chests. The Admiral walked forward and led the way toward the platform, with his guard fanned out behind him. They stopped at the base of the platform and the Admiral continued up to the top on his own.

The crowd was quiet once more. Everyone on the stage stood up slowly. At this signal, all two thousand Government members also got onto their feet. Seeing this, everyone else in the stadium felt compelled to follow suit. Fifty thousand and more people standing, watching in silence, respect and amazement. They could not believe what they were seeing for themselves.

Benjamin walked over to the Admiral as he arrived on the platform and stood beside him. He then guided him toward the Council members and their colleagues.

"Councilors and Honorable Members," said Benjamin, his voice carried by the stadium sound system, "please allow me to introduce you to His Excellency, Fleet Admiral Spear." The Legati tipped his massive head forward. It was clear that the people on the stage were simply awe-struck. They did not move. They stared at Spear in complete bewilderment. This was not lost on Spear, so he spoke first, using the translation device that he was wearing. His voice reverberated around the stadium.

"Thank you for the reception," he said slowly with little intonation. "I am here as the formal representative of the Seniors of the Legati people, the Videnti. They have asked me to extend their greetings on this day of encounter."

Councilor Lin composed herself and stepped forward toward Spear. She bowed her head in respect.

"Welcome Your Excellency – on behalf of the people of this planet," she said with a slight tremble in her voice, "I welcome you and look forward to our ongoing close association."

There was a loud cheer from the assembled crowd. David was impressed at the level of composure that Councilor Lin was able to maintain. The other people on the stage still had a look of great apprehension on their faces.

Eventually the cheers and applause subsided.

"Councilor, may I be permitted to address your people for a moment?" asked Spear.

"Of course, Your Excellency – we are here to understand more," replied the Councilor. Everyone took their seats as Spear moved into the center of the platform. David was able to get his first close-up view of this incredible visitor. It was clear to him that they were quite unlike humans, in almost every respect. The strange mixture of reptile, mammal and insect that Benjamin had described to him, resulting in a formidable and aggressive presence.

He admonished himself for his surprise at how well the Legati spoke, especially given the translation that was being performed. He felt his world being turned upside down as his deeply entrenched notions of human preeminence dissolved as he listened to the visitor.

"Fellow citizens of our galaxy, I thank you for your enthusiastic welcome.

"We understand that it will take some time for you to understand fully why we, the Legati, have decided on this moment to introduce ourselves to you. And we understand that it will be a cultural challenge to adjust to the realization that you are not alone in the universe.

"It is not our intention or place to dictate to your species how you should structure your societies or manage your planet. However, you are not yet aware that you have neighbors. You may view them as very distant, but for some of your neighbors, you are close by. The challenge is that the curiosity that these neighbors could have in your species, may not be welcome or beneficial to you.

"The Legati is part of an aligned community that undertakes to keep such unwelcome intrusions at bay. We wish that developing civilizations such as yours can reach their full potential in peace. But to reach your full potential and join our community, your society needs to advance. That is something you must do on your own. We believe you all know what needs to be done – nothing that the community asks is unreasonable. All we offer, other than a protective shield, is insight into the true behavior of your species. We leave it to you to decide what is right to do with this information.

"Finally, we will soon be leaving your planet. But we will be leaving the Honorable Benjamin Privett as our Ambassador for the coming years. We will remain in contact with him. We will never be too far away, but you must view our ambassador as our direct representative."

Spear turned to the assembled group on the platform.

"I am sure you have many questions," he continued. "But I would ask that you wait to see how we are able to help you in practice, rather than me telling you right now. Remember, it is the people of this planet that must decide what to do, not us."

"There is one question, Your Excellency, that would be helpful to have an answer to," said Councilor Lenkov, "and that is, when will all this start?"

"Thank you Councilor Lenkov," replied Spear, surprising her by knowing her name. "My ships will be departing two days from now. By the time we leave, the system, called Concordia, will be operational."

There was silence on the platform. There was silence in the Government ranks. There was silence in the public masses.

David found himself agreeing with the Legati. If a system, this '*Concordia*', was going to be imposed on them, what choice did they have but to see what happened? It did not seem worthwhile asking more questions.

Councilor Lenkov did not seem to agree.

"Would it be possible, Your Excellency, to explain a little about this Concordia system? The whole world is watching and, like me, they are certain to want to know how their lives are to be affected. Especially if we are to live with this system for years."

Spear shifted on his feet, still commanding the stage. His immense head lifted as he looked around the stadium. His pause spoke volumes to David. He was not planning to discuss details in such a setting.

"I understand," he said finally. "This planet has become accustomed to active monitoring of communications for factual accuracy.

"You are referring to the Fact-Checking System," said Lenkov.

"Yes. This was a very important and impressive development for your planet.

---

72

"Your system is syntactical in nature, and binary. Concordia is different. It is semantic. It highlights the fundamental reasons for problems."

"But...," stammered Lenkov, realizing that was the only explanation she was going to get.

"Councilors. Government officials. People," called out Spear, in an assertive tone. "Concordia will be operational in two days. You will start learning more at that time.

"I thank you for your time today," he continued. "This is an important day for your species, our species and the Galactic Community. But it is just the beginning."

Spear stood to attention and punched his left shoulder in a salute. He then turned and headed down the platform toward his guard. The group headed back to the waiting scout ship. The quickness of the departure caught the Council and Government by surprise.

It seemed to David that Benjamin had also been caught unawares by this sudden end to the meeting, as he and his female companion hurriedly stood up, said the briefest of goodbyes to the Council Members and walked quickly off the platform, down the ramp and across the grass to the waiting ship following the Admiral and his honor guard that had gone ahead of them. Almost as soon as they were inside, the door closed, and the ship lifted silently into the sky and disappeared over the stadium roof.

Councilor Lin just stood there, open-mouthed. She had not even had the chance to deliver her speech.

# CHAPTER 15

OVER THE NEXT 48 hours, the ten Legati cruisers started moving around their regions of the planet. From time to time, they would stop and open their massive cargo doors. The ships' flying cranes would then retrieve components from the hold and transfer them to the ground. Once there, Legati engineers used the cranes remotely to assemble the components into tall masts that towered into the sky, two hundred meters high. Other than being tubular metallic structures, they were featureless except for a slowly flashing red navigation light on their tip.

Hundreds of these masts were deployed all over the planet's land mass. Locals, who found one of these masts in their neighborhood, rushed to the location to view the construction efforts of the robots. But nobody dared interfere with the progress of these monstrous machines. It was an act of simple fascination.

Less conspicuously, the ships then traversed the oceans, periodically dropping objects into the depths.

When these activities were seemingly complete, the ships returned to their original locations over the various major cities of the world.

Benjamin had no idea what the Legati were doing. When he asked Christel, she shrugged and said it was all part of the Concordia network, but even she didn't know the details.

"Mr. Flight will tell you if they want you to know," she said.

But even with the increasingly frequent conversations with Flight, Benjamin was none the wiser for a long time.

"They are an integral part of the *Concordia* information-gathering system, Benjamin," Flight had said. "It is an important upgrade to my existing systems that allow me to perform my tasks."

That was all that Flight would say early on. To tease more details out, Benjamin tried a more personal approach.

"Are we ever going to meet in person Mr. Flight?"

"That would be a challenge, Benjamin. I am not where you might think I am."

"Somewhere here on Earth?" asked Benjamin.

"No. My consciousness was preserved on SaQ'il when the time was right. That consciousness has been assigned to an artificial environment that has been deployed on this planet," said Flight, and then he added, "at a location that will not be disclosed."

"That is extraordinary," said Benjamin. "You're living in a virtual environment?"

"'Living' is, of course, a euphemism, but yes."

"Can you tell me what it is like?"

"From my perspective, it is a real world. Thoughtfully I was assigned as a younger version of my old self.

"I occupy a reproduction of a world that is legendary

to my people. It is beautifully rendered. As my consciousness is fully active here, I continue to develop and learn as if I was in a living world, in a living body."

Benjamin did not immediately say anything.

"In order to suppress psychological stresses," continued Flight, "I feel like I am in a familiar place with familiar people around me. But I know I am in a synthetic world. It is not a labor for everyone, but I was prepared for my future."

"That is incredible," said Benjamin. "Do you go to work every day?"

"Yes, Benjamin. That is how it appears to me."

"Very impressive. Does anyone else know about your status?"

"Fabian Price and the other leaders of Sperantibus are aware. Your companion, Christel, has probably arrived at the correct conclusion. She is a very intelligent person."

"For a human," joked Benjamin.

"Indeed," replied Flight without a suggestion of humor in his voice.

"And it is impossible for someone like me to enter your virtual world?" asked Benjamin.

"It is not impossible but would require facilities that are not readily available."

"That's a pity, Mr. Flight. It would be so much easier to have these conversations in person."

Later that day, Benjamin had told Christel what he had learned about Flight.

"That does make sense Benjamin. As I told you on SaQ'il, revered members of the Legati society sometimes do have the option of having their consciousness and knowledge recorded. Once hosted in an artificial environment, they can continue to serve their community."

"But he said that he was in some sort of virtual world,"

replied Benjamin.

"Well at least he knows it is artificial. Who is to say that we are not living in such a world?" said Christel with a smile.

Shortly after that exchange with Flight, the Concordia system had been activated. There was no fanfare, no announcements. It was just operational. Benjamin only knew, because Flight had told him casually.

With that final task complete, it was time for the Legati ships to depart. Benjamin was summoned to the captain's quarters, along with Christel.

"Today, Ambassador," said the captain, "I must bid you farewell. You will be transferred to your new residence now."

"Thank you," replied Benjamin. "Am I likely to see you again on Earth?"

"Probably not Ambassador. I am scheduled to return here in fifty of this planet's years, by which time you will be elsewhere."

"Yes, I probably will be," replied Benjamin wistfully. "In that case, thank you for everything that you have done for our planet. Please wish us luck."

"Ambassador, I understand this concept of luck, but would prefer to state my confidence that you will execute your role admirably." The captain made a snort, which Benjamin had learned was equivalent to a chuckle.

Christel and Benjamin had departed the battle cruiser soon after on one of the scout ships and were flown to the Sperantibus headquarters in Geneva. They landed on the roof of the building and were greeted by Fabian Price.

Benjamin was glad to be back in his familiar world.

Around the time that he was landing in Geneva, the ten Legati ships departed unceremoniously. They ascended into the clouds silently.

Then they were gone.

# CHAPTER 16

DAVID PAGE WAS not alone in wondering what form the Legati guidance would take. In fact, most of the planet was asking the same question.

David sincerely hoped that the Concordia system would be communicating publicly. What would the point be of allowing the authorities to cover up what the visitors had to say? He tried to busy himself with other news stories but found it impossible to concentrate. He decided to try calling Benjamin, for the fifth time.

"Oh, hello David," said Benjamin. David was surprised that his call had been finally answered.

"Thank you for taking my call Benjamin, you must be very busy."

"When I can answer your calls, I will, David. What's on your mind?" It was a stupid question. David knew it. Benjamin knew it. David got straight to the point.

"Can we have some idea when this Concordia system is going to start telling us whatever it's going to tell us?"

"You know it's been less than 24 hours since the Legati ships departed," said Benjamin.

"I understand," replied David, "but pretty much the whole world is impatient to hear what the guidance is going to be."

"David, let me ask you some questions."

"Okay."

"Do you doubt that you will hear from Concordia?" asked Benajmin.

"Er, no."

"Do you have any idea what the guidance is going to be composed of?"

"Well, no."

"If I were to tell you when you're going to hear from Concordia, what would you do?"

"I'd let all my readers know."

"And what would they do with that information?"

"Wait for the appointed hour?"

"And?"

"Er, they would probably talk to one another about it."

"And then what?" persisted Benjamin.

David was slowly beginning to think Benjamin had a point to make.

"Maybe they'd have more questions?" he suggested.

"So, the value of me satisfying your impatience is what?"

"I give up," said David, realizing he wasn't going to win this game.

"More questions and more pointless public discussion about a topic that nobody has any control over or any knowledge of. You understand how conspiracy theories start, don't you?"

"I guess not."

"They are the result of witless people craving attention

through the selective use of available information."

"I see."

"Good," said Benjamin. "So, no information whatsoever will be released about Concordia, including timings, other than by the system itself. That way, there can be no conspiracy theories, gossip or people claiming to know something they most assuredly don't.

"I will tell you, though, that I spoke with the Legati about this," continued Benjamin. He was on a roll. "They asked me why humans are often so impatient and tend to jump to conclusions without all the necessary information.

"I suggested to them that it might be because we are mortal and so time is precious to us, but they didn't accept that."

"What did they think it was, then?" asked David.

"They told me that it was a primitive psychological disorder, stemming from a belief that one's time is more valuable than others."

"Which it isn't," submitted David. "But this is different, we're all waiting for this information."

"So, you wouldn't describe it as impatience?" replied Benjamin. "Perhaps you might call it keen curiosity. The Legati did not sugar-coat it. They described this keen curiosity as, and I quote, 'unearned entitlement'."

"Wow, that's a bit hard."

"I thought so at first too," said Benjamin a little less testily. "But then I realized that we have become accustomed to acquiring information, useful or not, so easily that we now resent having to wait or make any effort to do the mental weightlifting ourselves. We have become lazy and demand instant gratification."

"Okay, so we're going to have to wait. Right?" said David, trying to keep things simple.

"Yes. I have no control over this, thankfully. But the

Concordia system will be in touch with everyone when it sees fit. It is not going to be bound by some human schedule."

"But," said David, "surely you, or they, are going to let everyone know that."

"Goodbye David." Benjamin had ended the call.

David was annoyed by the rejection to his questions, especially as a journalist. He wanted to know things. But as he sat in his chair, he thought about what Benjamin had said. In the end, he had to agree that most people live their lives frantically absorbing information that they had absolutely no use for. Who cared if a celebrity had had a child? Who cared if a politician was meeting with the World Council that day? Who cared if someone fell off a cliff taking a photo of a friend? People had been trained to absorb useless information right away, either to convince them of some polarized viewpoint or simply to expose them to nearby advertisements.

It made David feel slightly less valuable professionally, but he understood the point. As individuals, nobody is more important than anyone else. Anyone's frustration at not knowing something in their desired timeframe was their psychotic problem alone.

He decided three things at that point. First, he would remember this piece of wisdom next time Cyril was shouting at him, demanding a story to be delivered. Secondly, he needed to take up meditation. Third, no more stupid questions to Benjamin.

Nonetheless, David could not keep this nugget to himself and wrote a short piece, extolling the virtues of patience and reaffirming the notion that mankind had no place demanding timelines and schedules from the Legati.

As David was reporting on his conversation with Benjamin, Benjamin was sitting in his home in a remote but beautiful part of Switzerland, talking to Christel.

"Well, that was two of mankind's deadly sins raised," he said.

"How many are there?" asked Christel.

"According to Flight, there are three. There is the tendency for people to demand information that they don't need to know or couldn't use if they did. That's nosiness. Then there's the irresistible urge to tell other people tidbits of information, usually creating a false narrative that benefits the narrator. That's gossiping. And third, there's the expectation of receiving a reward or praise for doing their job. Call that narcissism or being self-centered, but it's worse than those. I'm waiting for that characteristic to show itself sooner rather than later."

"Why are they 'deadly' sins?" asked Christel.

"I'm not sure whether Flight was being ironic, or what," replied Benjamin. "I always thought there were seven deadly sins, like gluttony and lust, which would damn your soul for eternity. Frankly, I'm glad those two seem to have been dropped from the list.

"But for Flight, he seemed to focus on mankind's overt sense of self-importance and how that could be terminal for our species."

"Okay, but why did he make a point of telling you this?" asked Christel, "Nosiness, gossiping and narcissism seem more subtle than the Universal Principles."

"True. But he indicated that when mankind has stopped exhibiting these characteristics, they will be on their way to having achieved what the Legati is hoping for."

# CHAPTER 17

IT WAS A week before Concordia made its presence felt.

Mail messages started appearing in the inboxes of all network users around the world. These messages were localized to various regions, being presented in a suitable language. The content of the message was simple.

"Dear Citizen – you are receiving this message from the Concordia reporting system. Moving forward, you and your fellow citizens will receive periodic messages. The dynamic nature of the planet's population and their activities precludes a fixed timeframe for these messages.

"The presentation by Ambassador Privett is delivered by his Virtual Assistant in order to support the multilingual requirements.

"As citizens of this planet, the responsibility for deciding how the information provided is to be acted upon, is yours."

Below this, was a link to a video message.

David Page, being on tenterhooks, reacted to the arrival of the message almost immediately. He noted that it had arrived at noon Greenwich Mean Time exactly. Lucky for him, being in London.

He selected the link to the video message and held his breath.

"My fellow citizens," said the virtual Benjamin Privett, "this is the first broadcast from the Concordia reporting system.

"Concordia has the function of highlighting challenges in the structure of human society. These are challenges that are hindering the attainment of the Universal Principles. Specifically, you may recall, these principles are compassion, community, dialog, equality, respect and peace.

"Do not expect that all issues highlighted for resolution will be in a single presentation. Resolving any critical issue is going to have repercussions that may also require resolution. You, the citizens of this planet, are responsible for holding your community leaders to account in their response to the provided guidance. The manner of the response is for you to decide as a community. Concordia will tell you if issues have been resolved or provide updated guidance.

"Your duty is to understand why issues are being highlighted. Only demand that they be acted upon, if you understand.

"The incremental steps that will be proposed by Concordia are going to be small. This is a process that will take many decades. This is a journey.

"As guidance is provided, the status will be maintained at this network site, along with an archive of all guidance that will be provided over time."

The camera angle on the Virtual Assistant changed.

"Concordia     Societal     Guidance     System. Communication Number 1.

"Humanity must understand empathy. Only when you care about other people, will you be able to exhibit compassion. Without compassion, humanity will fail.

"At present, humans demonstrate an almost complete disregard for one another. Unless you have some obligation to care for someone, like an immediate family member, you will more than likely leave them to suffer beside the roadway. You will think that their suffering is not your concern and turn away.

"As of today, you are all being monitored. If you abandon or ignore someone in need of your help, you will be reported to your authorities for potential legislative action. You all know the difference between an opportunist asking for help and someone in real need, so act on it.

"Next, 10% of your time should be spent helping others. We note that many of you are still willing to devote many hours to the worship of gods, so finding the time to help your fellow human should be something you will have no trouble with. We recommend that governments institute a point system for those that complete their allotted time for community service. These points should augment the pension received when you retire.

"It is also noted that community service is often imposed by your judicial system as a punishment. This should stop immediately. Serving your community must be viewed as a privilege.

"Based on historical evidence, many people will try to exclude themselves from adhering to this new directive. Arrogance, exceptionalism, self-absorption, vanity and laziness are the usual reasons. None of these are to be tolerated. Only those that work in community-related professions shall be exempt. Examples are hospital workers, firefighters, full-time police officers, public service providers and social services workers. Of course, those that are unfit for work, through age, illness or disability are also exempt. Your first inclination should not be to find ways to avoid contributing to your society.

"You have the choice how you want to help your community. But this will start in the immediate timeframe. Please expect your local authorities to be in touch.

"Thank you for your attention."

David sat back in his chair. He imagined the reaction of everyone around the world being told that they had to devote the equivalent of a half a day a week to community service. He wondered how the London News Network would react to losing their staff for so many hours. He wondered how *he* would react to donating his time to 'worthy causes'.

*There goes Sunday mornings, then*, he thought.

As he sat and thought about this revelation, this edict, he wondered if it was in fact striking at the heart of the human condition. Everyone he knew was self-absorbed, so they would not want to comply with the edict. But that was the point. At least a carrot was being offered at the end of the tunnel for those that gave their time to the community. Maybe in the future, if this system prevailed, people would take it for granted that contributing to the community was the right thing to do. It would be a shock at first, but it had to start somewhere.

He liked the point in Benjamin's message about people spending time worshiping gods. As an atheist himself, he delighted in the thought that the pious might have to choose between sitting in a church or doing something tangible for their fellow human beings.

*That's going to ruffle some feathers*, he thought with a chuckle.

Sure enough, feathers were ruffled all around the world. All media outlets, online forums, territorial government chambers and drinking establishments were talking about nothing but the first piece of guidance.

In his home in Switzerland, Benjamin was tracking the reaction very closely. He was already somewhat of a cynic, so assumed that most of the objections were because most people had no interest in helping other people.

"Do you think I am being cynical?" he asked Christel.

"You are cynical, Benjamin," she replied honestly, "but that doesn't mean you are wrong. Looking at the direction of most comments about Guidance 1, almost everyone is looking for a way to avoid spending their time on community causes."

"Thank you, Christel. I knew I could rely on you," said Benjamin, smiling. "I really like that Concordia went straight for one of the Universal Principles, compassion. And what do we find? Nobody wants to do it. To me, that speaks volumes."

Benjamin and Christel steeled themselves for a period of debate about Guidance 1, but were surprised when, the following day, Concordia issued a second message.

"Concordia Societal Guidance System. Communication Number 2," said Benjamin's virtual personality.

"Hunger is a major challenge for humanity.

"Your World Government should be afforded considerable credit for their ongoing efforts to resolve this challenge.

"It is counterproductive that greed and theft be allowed to impede this work.

"One of the leaders in your African Territories has been highlighted as one of the largest offenders. Pierre Ilunga, one of the leaders in the Economic Affairs Office in the African Central Region has been part of a group that has diverted 80 million credits to personal bank accounts.

"These funds were either through direct theft of World Government grants or the illicit sale of food shipments that arrived in the region.

"As Mr. Ilunga and his colleagues will have discovered, their bank accounts have already been emptied and the money returned to the donors. However, much of the funds have already been spent on buildings, modes of transport and an unearned lifestyle.

"Details of the individuals concerned and the physical assets to be seized have been provided to the trusted local authorities. They will also be published on the Concordia online repository. The list is extensive as many were willing to participate in the graft, including low level police officers and other state employees that took money to turn a blind eye.

"The list includes those that simply did nothing, even though they knew of the deception. It also includes many of the spouses and some of the children of the offenders.

"Thank you for your attention."

Benjamin found it hard to see a virtual representation of himself delivering these reports. A part of him wanted to be the one delivering them. But the quality of the presentations was so accurate, that he knew he was not necessary. Nonetheless, he had to be fully aware of the reports, because he was the one that received the phone calls from the members of the World Government and selected media members, like David Page.

He was usually briefed after the announcements by Flight.

"I saw the list, Mr. Flight," said Benjamin. "That's a lot of people."

"Yes, and most of them will be acquitted by the local

judicial bodies," replied Flight. "Despite the evidence they have in their possession, they will want to exercise some control and show that they are independent thinkers. This characteristic has been considered as part of the briefings provided."

"So, the goal is to detain the most senior members of the corruption," said Benjamin flatly.

"Partially, Benjamin. The top tiers will certainly be punished. But it needs to be clear that such activity is unacceptable and even less prominent people are not immune from prosecution."

"Fair enough. And it sends a message to anyone else contemplating doing something similar."

"Humans," continued Flight, "are highly prone to breaking the law. Corruption is everywhere. Most people convince themselves that they are doing something minor. They think that other people are far worse, and so they must be safe. They think that their supposedly minor transgression is not going to hurt anyone. But it usually does."

"Does that mean you're going to go after people who falsify insurance claims and things like that?"

"Eventually we will make the authorities aware of these smaller value issues. They are a simple theft or fraud. But we must tackle the bigger issues with an eye to teaching people a lesson.

"We monitor the effects of the guidance we give. If someone stops stealing as the result of our observations, they will be pushed down the list."

"Okay, Mr. Flight. What can I tell the authorities or the media about this particular report?" asked Benjamin.

"This one is straightforward. Everyone on the list must be detained and prosecuted. All identified assets should be confiscated and sold."

Faced with the incontrovertible evidence presented, which included video feeds and documentary evidence, all 83 people on the Concordia list were duly arrested. Unlike the first Concordia report, promoting community involvement, the corruption report enjoyed universal approval and attention. Mr. Ilunga and many of his cohorts received custodial sentences.

Concordia had gone quiet for a while after that, which many took to be a reminder to attend to the first report.

Most people, begrudgingly, accepted that it was an important idea. Nonetheless, the universal resistance remained. But one group was the most vocal in their objections. Benjamin had been waiting for them to start raising objections from the beginning, and here they were. The religions of the world.

No faith group was louder than another. It was if they had come to some agreement to work together on this issue, and perhaps others in the future. Muslims, Jews, Christians, Hindus; all of them approached Benjamin for 'clarification'. They wanted to know why the report had singled out prayer time as seemingly an indication that religious people had spare time on their hands. They felt it was suggesting that going to church and praying was time that could be better used.

Irrespective of the religion, the conversation usually went as follows:

"Do your Legati friends have something against religion?" a priest would ask bluntly.

"They do not have a position on religion."

"Then why do they suggest that prayer, church and communing with God is time better spent?'

"I don't think they do. As part of religion is the care of your fellow man, the suggestion is that those that devote so much of their week in support of that religion should be the easiest to persuade to formalize the help they give to their community."

"But," would say the priest, "surely our teachings should be sufficient to guide the faithful to perform such works. Many already do."

"Which is a wonderful thing," Benjamin would reply, "but evidence shows that statistically less than five percent of the global population do something on a regular basis to help their fellow man."

"I'm sure that can't be right," the priest would protest. "I know that 65% of the world's population identifies with a religion. You are suggesting that most of these people don't do anything with their faith."

"No. No." Benjamin would reply. "Their faith is an important structural component of their lives. They will live by the principles of the religion. They will adhere to the lifestyles and rituals defined by the religion. They will consider themselves good proponents of their faith."

"What is the problem then?" would say the priest.

"The problem is not one of religion. The problem is with humanity. We all know the difference between right and wrong, but usually, people are so self-absorbed that they don't want the overhead of looking after people that could do with their help."

"I think that's a monstrous generalization," would argue the priest.

"Is it? People cross the road to avoid homeless people. They think of tax deductions if they make a charitable contribution. They avoid vacationing in poor parts of the world to avoid confronting poverty, mainly to avoid people that want their money. They consciously take no interest in countries other than their own, as if they were on another planet. They resent migrants coming to their country to escape starvation, in case they'll get some financial handout that they never got themselves. Racism, theocracies and other discriminatory systems still exist, even today. People want to focus on their own lives and families. They don't want to expend time on ungrateful strangers.

"Most people lack empathy."

"I still think you are overstating a problem." the priest would insist.

"Then father, with respect, I suggest you open your eyes to what is going on in the world. Religions are not helping as much as they could."

Benjamin knew that these conversations would not be the end of the matter, and religious people would often retreat to unsubstantiated logic under the heading of 'faith' to support their arguments. But they had to start somewhere.

The one area that he had been told to be very careful about was whether God existed or not. The Legati were, surprisingly, in favor of prayer. They saw it as a societal glue that helped communities align on important topics. They were clear that prayer was not a communication mechanism to a deity but was harmless all the same.

During one conversation with one senior religious leader, he had been confronted with the question, though.

"What do the Legati think about God?" she had said.

"They say that they haven't met a god yet," Benjamin had replied simply. That had seemed to satisfy his interrogator, at least for the time being. Benjamin knew that the religious communities were very sensitive to anything that might challenge their authority in the world, even though more and more people were identifying as atheists, antitheists and agnostics all the time.

Benjamin enjoyed these ongoing interactions with people from around the world. It was important for there to be a dialog about the guidance that was being provided. He knew that his answers were being recorded and used by his many virtual assistants that were answering similar questions in other languages. He hoped his own personal involvement would not be curtailed or rendered unnecessary by technology.

# CHAPTER 18

"WAKE UP! WAKE up!" Christel was shaking Benjamin out of a deep sleep.

"Err, what is it?" responded Benjamin, trying to sit up.

"Benjamin. You have got to see this. It is snowing!" she said, delightedly.

"Oh that. It was on the forecast. This *is* Switzerland." Benjamin slumped back into the bed.

"You have to see it, Benjamin. Come on!"

Benjamin rolled onto his side and then swung his legs over the edge of the bed. He pivoted up into a seating position and then slowly got to his feet, feeling very unsteady. Having blinked a few times to get his eyes used to doing their job, he followed Christel out to the living room and the veranda beyond.

Walking out into the cold air was particularly uncomfortable, given that Benjamin had been nice and warm moments before. But he had to agree that the view of the valley below and the steady fall of large snowflakes around them was very beautiful. The snow was doing its usual trick of muting noise. All was quiet.

Christel had obviously got up some while earlier as she was fully dressed and now happily running around the veranda trying to catch snowflakes in her mouth.

"I never imagined snow would be like this. Everything is so quiet. Everything looks so different. It is wonderful."

"Yes, it's also very slippery, so watch your step," said Benjamin a little late. Christel had not quite fallen but she had discovered the slipperiness of snow just as Benjamin warned her. She laughed that innocent chuckle that Benjamin always found so endearing.

"Any idea what time it is?" he asked rhetorically.

"Yes, it is 5:13 am," replied Christel factually.

"Exactly. You enjoy the snow. I'm going back to bed."


Benjamin had already thought he wanted to take Christel skiing.

He had never been on a pair of skis in his life but living in Switzerland meant it was always on the menu, global warming notwithstanding.

The challenge was how. Everyone on the face of the planet knew what he looked like, and he could not go anywhere without his companion drone. Donning a pair of sunglasses and growing a beard was not going to cut it.

He mentioned this dilemma to Fabian, who came up with a typical Fabian solution. Rent a ski resort for an afternoon.

Initially, Benjamin thought this highly arrogant and an abuse of status. But when Fabian reminded him that it was getting close to Christmas and that Sperantibus could possibly rent a ski run in, say Verbier, for an afternoon as a company celebration, Benjamin changed his mind.

"That's great thinking Fabian – so we could just tag

along to an existing event."

"Indeed," said Fabian. "Let me see if I can get the wheels in motion."

And so it was. A couple of weeks later, Benjamin and Christel found themselves amongst a group of some forty merry Sperantibus employees on a coach, heading for Verbier. For Christel, the occasion was truly momentous. It was the first time she had mingled with a larger gathering of people in a social setting. Even Fabian had agreed to go along, even though his normal idea of a good time was not sliding down a mountain in the dead of winter.

The group made a point of making Christel feel welcome, but the conversations were very careful. There was no mention of her time on SaQ'il or the Legati. There was no mention of the Concordia system and its impact on day-to-day life. People only talked about the afternoon ahead of them and the fun they would have on the snow.

It was not lost on Benjamin that the fellow revelers had been very carefully selected and very well prepared.

Nobody acknowledged Benjamin's Centurion that either hovered nearby or followed them above their coach.

The group arrived at the ski area, disembarked from the bus and headed to the lifts. It was a fine sunny day. The brightness of the snow dominated the vista as they ascended in the open chair lifts. The cold, crisp air filled their lungs. Benjamin was very happy to see Christel so wide-eyed in her excitement to see everything.

When they reached the top of the chair lift, the chairs detached from the fast cables so that getting off was easy. Off to one side was a large open-sided tent, which was filled with skiing equipment.

A tall gentleman approached Benjamin and Christel. He also ignored the Centurion.

"Welcome to Verbier," he said. "My name is Anton.

You are on the Croix de Couer Mountain. There are a few *pistes* that descend to the valley below us. I understand that you are both skiing novices. Yes?"

"I think that would describe us both very accurately." said Benjamin, smiling to Christel.

"Great. In that case, given the time limits we have here, I would suggest you forget skis, snowboards and kites today. How about snow bikes?" asked Anton.

"That would be fun," replied Benjamin. "You'll enjoy these, Christel. All the fun of skiing but not so much to learn."

"Okay," said Christel simply. She had no idea what any of these options were anyway.

Anton led the pair over to some impressive looking machines.

"These are all new models. They all have stability and speed controls on them, so you really just need to point them in the direction you want to go."

Snow bikes were not really bicycles, having no wheels. Instead, they had two short skis at the front, a long seat and below the seat, wide caterpillar tracks. During a downhill run, the caterpillar tracks drove a generator that charged the onboard batteries, as well as the onboard electronics and stabilization system. This system controlled the amount of lean that the snow bike performed in turns and used the caterpillar tracks for braking to keep the machine under the requested speed limit. In addition, snow bikes could reverse the generator to become a motor, allowing them to travel along reasonably level terrain.

Several other people elected to ride on the snow bikes as well, so after donning helmets and choosing someone to lead the way, the group headed off.

There was laughter all round as they all headed down the blue-graded slope. It was wide and groomed, so everyone could quickly become used to how the snow bikes behaved without worrying where they were going. For the next few hours, Benjamin and Christel could forget the framework within which they lived, and simply have fun. At the bottom of the run, they hooked the snow bikes to the lift and headed back up for another go, again and again.

They were tired but happy when they finally arrived in the valley for the last time. They were directed to a lodge that had been prepared for the group. Here, they could all sit together and eat and drink. As light fell, the atmosphere became very cozy, with a fire burning in the fireplace in the corner of the room and lots of merry conversations.

It had been a wonderful day.

When the coach dropped the pair off at their new home a few hours later, Benjamin made a point of thanking Fabian.

"It is not a problem Benjamin. You are right that we need to make sure Christel is looked after. She's a long way from home."

Back in their living room, Benjamin asked Christel what she had thought of the rest of the group.

"Such nice people. They genuinely seemed to want me to have fun today, and they succeeded. I will never forget it. Thank you for coming up with the idea."

"Not exactly a genius move," said Benjamin, "but I am very happy that you had such a good time. That's all that matters."

"And you had fun too?" asked Christel.

"I did. But I must say that having to come up with such an elaborate solution, just to get out of the house, gives me pause for the future. It's unfortunate that we can't just go wherever we want."

"Indeed," said Christel. "But this is the path that we have chosen."

# CHAPTER 19

"CONCORDIA SOCIETAL GUIDANCE System. Communication Number 3," said Benjamin's virtual assistant.

"Many territories are experiencing hunger, poverty and the exodus of their populations. These populations are often attempting to reach other territories that are not experiencing the problems of their homes. While understandable as a short-term reaction, these refugees are often ill-equipped to enter the societies of the lands that they aspire to. Their tendency is to attempt to transfer the culture from their homeland to this new home. The people that built these more stable territories frequently resent the arrival of these foreigners due to their own lack of empathy, the societal changes that the foreigners bring with them, as well as the financial burden that they impose.

"Usually, the more stable societies forget their own culpability for the failures of many of these poverty-stricken nations.

"Ideally, refugees should not be leaving their home countries. If they had the prospect of fulfilling lives in their native lands, they would be less likely to leave and would not need to be accepted as political refugees in other countries.

"Consequently, the so-called Western territories that were previously running these African, Western Asian and Middle Eastern zones shall return as governmental advisors, under the direction of the World Government. The expectation is for secular governmental oversight to be provided such that the economies of these failed territories be resurrected, the rule of law enforced, industry to be established and quality of life for the residents restored.

"Preferential trading agreements between the recovering country and its patron are acceptable but monopolies are not.

"It is expected that some will resist this as an unwanted intrusion. But it is predicted that when the accompanying aid is seen as being managed for the good of the country, viewpoints will be corrected.

"The French Territorial leaders will support the Northwest African nations, with the British, Canadian and Australian Territorial leaders supporting the rest of that continent. The American Territorial leaders shall support the West Asian and Middle Eastern zones.

"Thank you for your attention."

When Benjamin heard this address, he had called Flight immediately.

"How is this expected to work?" asked Benjamin. "Other nations have been trying to get influence in these countries for decades. Forget the native governments, these other powers are not going to be happy with this perceived take-over."

"Benjamin, close management oversight by respected international authorities, backed up by the weight of your World Government, will revive these areas very quickly. The suppression of corruption and the introduction of skilled advisors, will have a significant impact almost immediately."

"But Mr. Flight, how can you know this? How am I to convince the World Government?"

"Those are the right questions," replied Flight. "Concordia is, first and foremost, a modelling engine. Your meteorologists have sophisticated weather forecasting systems. Think of Concordia as something like this, but a system capable of modelling the whole planet. That includes weather, climate, economies and societal behaviors. It models the interactions between these systems. It predicts accurately.

"We will provide these predictions to your people, in a simplified form, so that they can see the expected results of their actions and compare them to what actually happens. They will learn to trust the guidance."

"That would be huge," said Benjamin.

"As you say," said Flight. "Once the response to the latest guidance is underway and professional management is in place, we will start providing guidance based on what they plan to do and what they do in practice. The two are rarely the same."

"I can tell the World Government to start sending these representatives to the hotspots right away?"

"Yes, Benjamin. And they will require military support and protection."

Two days later, Benjamin was sitting in his office reading the news of the day. A great deal of it was the ongoing discussions about the three recent Concordia messages. It was clear that the efforts to encourage community involvement was still encountering the inevitable resistance. On the other hand, there was an equal level of outrage at the reported corruption. As for leveraging the assistance of historic colonialists and partially reformed military interventionists, similar reticence to helping their fellow man was being exhibited at government levels.

*No wonder they said it could take centuries,* he thought.

Shortly thereafter, he received a request for a conference call with the World Council, along with various other senior members of the Government. His heart sank. He did not want to be the only person on these calls. He knew they were likely to become more frequent and more complex. It was time to get Sperantibus involved. It was time for Fabian Price to assign a council of his own.

He was not particularly surprised to learn that the Sperantibus leadership was already thinking along the same lines. Fabian Price had been detached from the corporate leadership team to chair a coordination board that would handle the interactions with the World Government. This board could be expanded as necessary if the Concordia system started generating too much workload.

"The role of this Sperantibus Board," advised Fabian, "is to share the Concordia projections and marshal Sperantibus resources as necessary to assist in the implementation of the guidance."

"All right," said Benjamin, "will they get briefed by Mr. Flight?"

"No Benjamin. You are now the only one with direct contact with Flight. The Sperantibus Board will receive the Concordia missives, like anyone else, and the updated status and forecast reports from the system. If there is the need for more information, they will approach you. It is considered inappropriate for the Board to have access to information that is not publicly available. Fortunately, Concordia is not clandestine, so we don't feel that we're missing out on anything relevant to our task."

"You make it sound like I'm off the hook," said Benjamin, feeling a little superfluous.

"No Benjamin," replied Fabian. "Not unless you want to be."

"Hehe, I think I'm rather too committed for that. Don't you?"

"Indeed." Fabian paused. "No, your role is to interact with Flight and provide any additional guidance that the Board may require. Concordia is a very thorough system, so we are not expecting work overload for you. You'll also need to make the occasional appearances to represent the Legati, of course."

"Okay. Makes sense to me. What's more, it comes as a relief to have some organized engagement here. Thank you."

"And there's better news, Benjamin. We need to have an escalation path available to us. So, you should skip the upcoming Council meeting. I'll reach out to you afterwards."

"Sounds good to me," said Benjamin.

"Yes, and one other thing that you need to do is speak with Flight. You need to meet him properly."

"But he said..."

"Yeah, I know," interrupted Fabian, "but you need to get to know him. Your understanding of the strategy for the application of the Universal Principles and any nuance to the Concordia guidance is going to be particularly important for us. We need you to represent Flight and therefore the goals of the Legati."

"Fabian, you know I'm a team player and will do everything I can to help move all this along," replied Benjamin, "but I have to ask, what do you think I can learn by meeting directly with Flight? You know he's a digital copy of his former self, right?"

"Yes, that was an eye-opener," replied Fabian, raising his eyebrows. "I've had calls with him for years and always assumed he was a glorified voicemail system, not a sentient presence."

"I'm sure he just heard that," said Benjamin with a chuckle.

"No doubt, but he and I have had that conversation.

"The thing is, Benjamin, everyone, and I mean *everyone*, views the Legati presence as a one-way street. Sure, we understand the importance of the Principles. But nobody on this planet, other than Flight, knows *why* they are so important for mankind to adopt. There is a feeling amongst the Sperantibus leadership, at least, that there's more to it than just being good galactic citizens."

"Any theories?" asked Benjamin.

"None whatsoever. We're in the dark. If mankind's shortcomings are such a problem for this 'galactic community', given how much other life there is in the universe apparently, why didn't they just put us out of our misery? They could do it in a moment."

"An ulterior motive..." mused Benjamin.

"Yes. Why do they insist on leading mankind by the nose? What happens when we achieve the levels of advancement that they deem adequate to allow us into this galactic club?

"Talk to Christel, but my understanding is that Flight is an honorable soul, who cares deeply about his burden. He knows what is going on and what is in store for us all. Get to know him."

# CHAPTER 20

"CONCORDIA SOCIETAL GUIDANCE System. Communication Number 4," said Benjamin's virtual assistant.

"Burning fossil fuels needs to be banned globally. If prioritization is desired, eliminate coal burning. Coal mining must stop. But gas and oil burning must also stop.

"Everybody needs air to breathe. Why would you deliberately pump Sulphur and other toxins into your air supply? It will kill you. The carbon dioxide pumped into the atmosphere combines with the water vapor in the air to create carbonic acid. Do you want acid raining from the skies and getting into your drinking water forever? This carbon dioxide also traps heat in the atmosphere, which results in an ever-warmer climate.

"But everyone knows this and has known this for well over fifty years. Why does this practice of burning fossil fuels persist?

"The answer, of course, is shortsighted economics.

There are still people who are employed in these industries, and governments do not know how to wean these people away from them. The solution is as follows:

"First, investment in fossil fuel-burning technology must stop and be transferred to solar, wind, geo-thermal and wave technology. Nuclear power can be safe, and those programs should be maintained and developed.

"Second, the people working in the fossil fuel industries should be allowed to continue until they stop working or retire. No new people should be hired, unless replacing an existing critical safety worker. That means that nobody who is simply maintaining the existing level of production should be hired. As the workforce reduces, so will the scale of the industry. Eventually, the industry will close, and the remaining workers will be retired.

"Third, territories that lack the infrastructure or means to close down their fossil fuel burning power stations, shall be leased small nuclear power stations by the World Government, or receive their power from a neighboring territory. If other technology is desired, the territories concerned must negotiate this. But they must understand that they will have to pay for their electricity and the new power stations. The World Government may consider subsidies.

"Fourth, it should be illegal to import electricity from a neighboring country that was generated through the burning of fossil fuels. Export of fossil fuels should also be banned.

"Pricing of cross-border electricity production shall be monitored and controlled carefully.

"Thank you for your attention."

The scheduled meeting with the World Council and their immediate associates had followed that fourth communication.

"It seems to me that this Concordia system is just issuing blank checks," said Lucas Oliveira in an exasperated tone. "And checks that *we* will have to cash," he added.

Lucas was the only surviving member from the previous World Council and had been elected as the new spokesman. The room was otherwise full of new faces.

"Obviously Sperantibus is in a position to help," said Luther Grand, Fabian's deputy. "Revenues from our off-world mining etc. are going to be offered, but we can't cover everything."

"How much are you going to contribute as a percentage?" asked Lucas.

"We will have to see Lucas, but that is not the right attitude," said Luther. "The work in front of us has to be done and cannot be devolved into a simple discussion of who pays for what."

"Why does it have to be done?" asked Jennifer Xander, a new Council member. "I still don't see what the Legati will do if we ignore their so-called guidance."

"Councilor," said Fabian, a little wearily. "I think we all agree that these early communications are, to a great extent, stating the obvious. These are all things that we know we should be dealing with and have known for decades. Ignoring the guidance would be an insult to our own people, never mind the Legati. In any case, the World Government already has many plans in place to implement similar policies. So why can't we just view the current guidance as bringing some additional focus."

"I get that," replied Jennifer, "but what happens if we don't do what we are told?"

"We will be the ones to suffer through our own negligence," replied Fabian. "It's as simple as that. Do you want me to tell you that the Legati will wipe out our species, or something?"

"Will they?" Jennifer shot back.

"If you view everything transactionally Councilor, you will never be successful." Fabian sat back in his chair. Jennifer glared at him, as she finally understood the point.

"Besides," said Luther, digging the knife in, "everyone here was elected on the understanding that we would support these Legati directives. Are we able to get beyond this continual questioning of purpose, once and for all?"

"The Deputy Chairman is quite correct," said Lucas. "No more second-guessing, everyone. We need to pursue these directives with the help of our friends in Sperantibus."

It was this simple exchange that had finally resolved the ongoing doubts, at least officially. But nobody had the time or desire to spend more time convincing doubters repeatedly. Policy had been set and it was time to execute it.

Benjamin had been a little disappointed that nobody at the meeting had asked where he was. But then again, he realized it gave him more time to investigate Fabian's suggestion.

"Hey Christel," said Benjamin, "can I see you in the bedroom for a moment?"

"Oh Benjamin, it's rather early in the day, isn't it?"

Benjamin smiled. "I have a little suggestion for you to think about."

"Sounds interesting." Christel stood up, took Benjamin's hand and led him to their room.

"Now what is this little surprise?"

"Sit down for a moment," said Benjamin sitting on the edge of the bed.

"Okay..." Christel sat on the bed and looked at Benjamin in an expectant manner.

"I wanted to have a quiet word with you."

"Oh." Christel sounded genuinely disappointed.

"This is the one place we can talk without being overheard."

"I see..."

"I was talking to Fabian the other day. He has proposed that you and I investigate the Legati's motivations behind the Concordia directives. What do you think?"

"But we know what their motivations are, Benjamin. They are establishing the Universal Principles."

Benjamin gazed out of the window. He surveyed the green valley below and the mountain rising on the other side, a prelude to the taller peaks beyond. The valley appeared serene, basking in the afternoon sun. By contrast, the mountain summits were cold, white and unwelcoming. Imperious.

"There are always so many perspectives on the same thing," he said. "Today is a sunny day, but is it warm or cold?"

"That depends on where you are," replied Christel crossing her arms.

"Exactly Christel. Perspective is subjective."

"You want to gain some additional perspective on the *Concordia* communications?"

"Exactly. I know the Legati want us just to do what we are told, but human nature is what it is."

"You mean people are more motivated when they know why they are doing something?"

"Actually, yes," said Benjamin, "but they're more likely to do something when there's something in it for them. That's what I think might be missing."

"Do you have a plan?" asked Christel.

"Fabian suggested that I try to get to know Flight on a more personal level."

"That's interesting." Christel raised her eyebrows in bemusement. "Good luck with that."

Benjamin flopped backwards onto the bed. He stared at the ceiling.

"I need to get into his world," he said.

# CHAPTER 21

"CONCORDIA SOCIETAL GUIDANCE System. Communication Number 5," said Benjamin's virtual assistant the following day.

The real Benjamin was wondering how long Concordia could keep up this daily schedule. There had to be some time to attend to some of the tasks. He leaned back in his chair in his office, folded his arms and absorbed the latest directive.

"The oil drilling rig at Bu Danar in the Persian Gulf equidistant between Doha and Dubai is rapidly approaching a high-pressure zone. The blowout preventers on this rig have been maintained incorrectly and will not activate when the high-pressure zone is reached. Drilling must be stopped immediately.

"Thank you for your attention."

*How do they know that?* thought Benjamin. *But at least*

*this is one where the benefit is blatant. That'll help.*

He was sitting on the veranda, even though it was October and there was a chill in the air. Christel was in the living room streaming old classic movies. Benjamin felt the need to get her out of the house and show her something of the world. She may be used to living in golden cages but that needed to change.

He picked up his tablet.

"Call Flight," he said. Immediately, his call was connected.

"Hello Benjamin," said Flight.

"Mr. Flight. I hope you are well."

"Yes, thank you Benjamin."

"I was impressed by the message from Concordia today."

"Yes, that was an interesting one," said Flight. "Our guidance is usually behavioral in nature, but it was calculated that the damage would be too extreme. Damage that was the result of human error."

"Do you think the oil company will admit the maintenance issues?"

"They will not," replied Flight bluntly.

"Oh well, at least it'll protect the marine life, nonetheless," said Benjamin.

"There is something on your mind, Benjamin." As usual, it was a statement, not a question.

"Yes, Mr. Flight. Does it make sense to you for us to meet?" Benjamin did not waste time repeating his earlier conversations. He knew Flight was fully aware of them.

"The original mandate was for our interaction to be through this medium, Benjamin."

"I am hoping that if we can meet in person, it might

help me, at least. I need to understand the meaning of the ongoing communications."

"They are not obvious already?" asked Flight.

"Superficially they are. But to understand how you choose these issues when you do, would be so helpful for us. Why are they the priority? What are the thought processes?"

"And you don't think you and your World Government can work this out on their own?"

"No, I don't," said Benjamin. "I think there is a danger of misunderstanding."

"And you think meeting me in my virtual world will help somehow?"

"Maybe it's a small point but, as I say, it would help me understand you. It would help me understand how I can help your process. Phone calls for the next 30 years are going to be very abstract for me."

There was an uncharacteristic pause.

"Very good Benjamin. Please await further instructions," said Flight.

# CHAPTER 22

"CONCORDIA SOCIETAL GUIDANCE System. Communication Number 6," said Benjamin's virtual assistant.

"It is understandable that some people are curious about the information gathering towers that have been deployed around the planet. Their function is to collect climatic, tectonic, atmospheric, magnetic and seismic information, and not necessarily in that order.

"It is interesting and educational that this curiosity is resulting in some people planning violent acts against the towers. The Concordia system knows exactly who is planning this vandalism but will not report anyone to the authorities unless they act on their plans. Please note that all towers possess defensive capabilities. These capabilities will be surprising to anyone attempting to damage the towers, at least for that moment before they are vaporized. Remote attacks will be addressed in a similar fashion. The attacking devices will be destroyed, and the controllers of the devices will be reported to the authorities for judicial remedy.

"Thank you for your attention."

Benjamin liked that one. There was a tinge of humor mixed into the deadly warning. He chuckled to himself.

Benjamin was not chuckling a few hours later when he received a call from Fabian.

"Concordia must have known something," he said. "Barely an hour after that warning, a group of, and I quote, 'good old boys', in the US Territory state of Wyoming decided to go on a 'hunting' expedition. They got in their work vehicles and headed into the back country to have some fun with a Concordia tower."

"Whoops," cringed Benjamin.

"Yes. It seems they arrived with some mining explosives. It also seems they tried to detonate these explosives at the base of the tower."

"How much?"

"No idea," said Fabian, "but they thought it was enough, no doubt."

"What happened?"

"Well, from the police report, it seems they laid their explosives and then retired to a hundred meters away. At the moment that they triggered the detonator, it seems that the tower's security system activated and atomized the explosives before they could go off."

"That's impressive" said Benjamin, relieved. "I would have liked to have seen that."

"The perpetrators were not impressed. They were still bumbling around when the police turned up and arrested them all." replied Fabian.

"Who called them?"

"Concordia - it even stipulated the charges that should be applied."

"No damage done then?" asked Benjamin.

"No - but there have been other attempts at interfering with these towers. There are some conspiracy theories doing the rounds that the towers are controlling the way people think. There have been several attempts to damage them in various parts of the world. That may be why that directive was released."

"Has anyone been killed?"

"Not that I am aware of – we just get diagnostic reports from Concordia. Anything else is on the Concordia site. Maybe Flight will be able to tell you more. Any luck with that?"

"I spoke to him, and he agreed to get back to me with a solution," replied Benjamin.

"It is good to hear that he is being flexible on this," said Fabian.

"Do you get the sense that Concordia has a sense of humor?" The directives didn't appear merely informational but had other qualities of embellishment. As if the system enjoyed its work.

"I do Benjamin. You recall the previous directive about that oil field?"

"Sure."

"Well, the oil company denied that there was a maintenance issue with their equipment. They announced that they had found no problems and were aware of the high-pressure zone they were approaching. There was no danger of a blow-out, they said."

"Oh yes...?"

"Concordia published a video clip from one of the corporate leaders. It's on the *Concordia* site."

"Let me see, Fabian." Benjamin windowed his

conversation with Fabian on his tablet and navigated to the Concordia pages. "Oh, yes. I see it." He hit the play button. A subtitled video started. There were two people sitting at a table speaking Arabic.

*"We can't admit this finding. Think what it would do to our share price," said a lady in the video.*

*"But madam," said a man sitting opposite her, "if they knew about the imminent catastrophe, surely they'll know we're lying?"*

*"Ha," scoffed the woman. "Let them prove it. And make sure the maintenance 'economies' are lifted for a while."*

"That is a classic. Nice one," said Benjamin, laughing.

"Of course, it's not a laughing matter," said Fabian, chuckling, "but, neither of these characters are employed by that oil company anymore."

"Do you think people are going to object to the invasion of privacy that seems to be necessary to expose corruption like this?" mused Benjamin.

"That's certainly a risk. I agree. But while such exposures are in the global interest, it's hard to get too idealistic."

# CHAPTER 23

"CONCORDIA SOCIETAL GUIDANCE System. Communication Number 7," said Benjamin's virtual assistant.

"The concept of sovereign nation states has long been replaced with territories, under the governance of local authorities and the central World Government. A carry-over from those nation state days involves the personal ID card or passport. These digital documents are standardized across all territories and their examination is so automated through their association to personal biometrics, that very little thought is given to them anymore.

"The problematic element of these sources of identification, is the requirement for individuals to state the territory of their upbringing, even though they may live in another territory. This record permits individuals to return to that original territory as if they never left.

"Immigration to another territory should be

undertaken with the intention of integrating fully into the society of that new territory and contributing to that society. Those that turn up and expect to recreate their old neighborhoods and ways of life are being disrespectful to their new hosts. This is especially so if they happily accept the social benefits of the new territory. Community engagement is of paramount importance. Isolation, ghettos, enclaves, ethnic quarters only encourage racism and prejudice.

"Consequently, the concept of dual residency shall be abolished. Once someone moves to a new territory, they shall relinquish their right to live in the old territory, unless they reapply for residency without preference.

"Furthermore, ethnic origin and race, should never be used as a mechanism for characterizing an individual in any periodic government census or profile records. No social benefit or penalty should be associated with ethnic origin or race.

"Thank you for your attention."


"Mr. Flight," said Benjamin to his tablet, "thank you for calling me." He was relaxing on his sofa in the living room of his house, enjoying the glow of the artificial fireplace that hung low on the wall. He was not as happy to be disturbed as he made it sound.

"Good morning, Benjamin. I have an update on your request for more direct communication."

"Oh good. How can we make this work?" Benjamin perked up.

"It is probably easiest if you use your standard AVR headset. I will send the number where I can be reached. Would you like to try it?"

"Most certainly," said Benjamin more enthusiastically, "I'll go and get it, and call you back."

Benjamin went to his office, retrieved his AVR headgear and returned to the living room. He slumped back down on the sofa and put the device on his head. He saw the message that Flight had sent him with the number to call.

As the ringtone purred away, he could see the virtual office that was the default view of the AVR system. A small room with a desk and wood-paneled walls all around. Not exactly modern, but Benjamin had never bothered to customize it.

The ringtone stopped as the call was answered, and a prompt appeared in front of him.

"You are being invited to join a third-party chat room," it said.

Benjamin waved his hand over the acceptance target and the office faded away. It was replaced by an extravagant room with many tables. It looked like a restaurant, and Benjamin was seated at a table by a very large window. There was an empty seat opposite him. There was nobody else in the restaurant and the table was bare, except for a white tablecloth.

Benjamin looked out of the window. It was a huge panoramic landscape. Clearly, the restaurant was located at a high altitude, perhaps on a mountain. The ground sloped away into a valley, only to be met by other rolling hills and mountains in the far distance. It was a beautiful sunny day and the view to the horizon was completely clear.

At a whim, Benjamin winked as he looked across this vista to take a photograph. He heard the traditional noise of a shutter to confirm that the image had been stored. It was a truly breathtaking view that he wanted to remember.

He sensed movement to his right and saw a Legati

walking across the room toward his table. Benjamin assumed that this must be Flight. He wished he could stand up as a sign of respect, but his AVR headset only gave him head and hand movements.

"Benjamin," said the Legati, "welcome to a corner of my world."

"Mr. Flight?" asked Benjamin, as the Legati took the seat opposite him. He was another one of these very tall characters, although somewhat slimmer than other Legati he had met.

"Indeed," he said. "These translation systems don't do a good job of differentiating one speaker from another, but it is me."

"Thank you for doing this," said Benjamin, "you honor me by allowing me to enter your world."

"Not at all Benjamin. I was surprised by your suggestion at first, but I can see the benefit. I hope that we can have many fruitful conversations using this medium."

"I hope so too, as long as you don't mind my immobility."

"This interface has been configured so that I see your Virtual Assistant image. So, it feels reasonably lifelike for me. After all, you are seeing a virtual image of me, are you not?"

"Yes, it looks very realistic. Much more realistic than what I'm used to, I must say."

"Good," said Flight. "Other options are being considered, but we should see how this goes for now. Fixing the problem of immobility might be possible." He paused and looked out of the window.

"Where are we?" asked Benjamin.

"It is a sacred mountain for the Legati which features in our ancient history. It is a place of meditation and serenity. It was chosen by the architects of my virtual existence as a reward for my past contributions to the Legati community. I am very thankful for this consideration."

"But it looks like a restaurant. Did they have such things in your ancient history?"

Flight made that rattling noise that Benjamin had learned was a chuckle.

"No, this is an accommodation for you. Much better than sitting on the grass, don't you think?"

"Indeed, I do," replied Benjamin. "But it certainly is a wonderful location." They both admired the view for a few moments.

"Now Benjamin, what is it that you would like to talk about?"

"Everything and nothing, Mr. Flight," replied Benjamin. "I would like to get to know you and how you got to be here. I would like to understand how you work with Concordia. Fundamentally I want to learn how I can be more useful to the process of evolving my planet's culture."

"Maybe we should talk more about Concordia," said Flight. "That seems more immediately relevant. I have already described how it is a modelling system. The model comprises the physical and societal structures of your planet. These models are continually being updated through observations collected from the masts that we have installed, terrestrial networks and other receivers. Perhaps I should show you."

"Can you?"

The restaurant faded and Benjamin found himself seated in a reclined chair, staring up into darkness. Flight was seated in a larger chair beside him, dimly illuminated. He made some gestures in front of him and the heavens above them exploded into color. Benjamin found he was in a hall with a massive hemispherical ceiling like a planetarium. But instead of a view of the stars above him, he was viewing a map of Earth's surface. It was an undistorted view.

Flight made a sideways gesture and the view shifted to Europe. He then made other gestures with his hands moving together and the view zoomed into Switzerland. He made another selection, probably a shortcut, and they could see Benjamin's house. Benjamin could see traffic in the distance. It was a live view.

"If you had been on the veranda, Benjamin," said Flight, "you could wave to us." He gave another of those *Legati* chuckles.

Benjamin had not uttered a word. He was spellbound. He was used to historical views of the planet's surface from satellite imagery, but these live views were altogether new. Even the World Government didn't have global live coverage and with such quality.

"Can you go to my old address in London?" he asked, finally.

"Certainly."

The view zoomed out and scrolled north toward the British Territories. There were clouds covering the city, as usual. Flight zoomed in through the clouds, with details of the city becoming clearer under 500 meters. He descended farther until they were viewing a live view of Benjamin's old house. Very little had changed. The backyard was still untidy. The rusty swing was still there.

"Does anyone live there now?" asked Benjamin sentimentally. There was a slight pause from Flight.

"Yes. Sperantibus bought the house from the previous property owner and have leased it out to a young family."

This was news to Benjamin. He had thought that everything had been left as it was in his absence.

"I know this may sound rather trivial, but do you

know what happened to my possessions? Is my car still in the garage nearby?"

There was another of those Legati chuckles.

"Everything was put in storage. Speak to Fabian about it."

"I will," said Benjamin with relief. "This is all very impressive."

"What I want to show you, Benjamin, is the forecasting capabilities of Concordia. Live views are useful, but the real power of the system is in modelling the future."

"How far can you go?" asked Benjamin.

"That is a very good question. Climate, local weather and tectonics are reasonably deterministic processes. That means they are simpler to predict with accuracy. Human impact on the climate is slowing, which helps here too. For those types of forecasts, we can accurately predict weather, for example, up to a year ahead.

"The societal modelling is nowhere near as simple. As the result, given that our focus is on human society and its betterment, we can only model up to 6 months ahead. After that, we can be sure that human nature will have changed the model fundamentally."

"How long does it take to model this societal future?" asked Benjamin.

"It can be calculated dynamically," said Flight. "For example, let's view your old house over the coming day at sixty times real-time."

Benjamin watched as the day got brighter and then started dimming as evening approached. Cars zipped along the road in front of the house. As the evening settled in, a car stopped fleetingly in from of the house and then drove off. Lights started coming on in the little house.

Flight paused the view and let Benjamin take it in. He felt nostalgic, seeing the light from the kitchen illuminating the shoddy lawn behind the house. He thought briefly about his earlier life spending his evenings in that little room with Fiona, happily catching up on the events of the day. It all seemed like a different world.

Flight did not let the nostalgia last too long.

"Of course, there are more practical uses of these forecasting capabilities. Watching houses is rather dull."

He zoomed the view out and scrolled to Death Valley in California in the American Territories.

"I am advancing the date to next August. I have something to show you that I spotted earlier."

The salt pans glared in the sunlight. The desert areas lay bare and devoid of any life.

"You'll have to take my word for it, but those figures up there," he pointed to some symbols that hovered over the view, "mean that the temperature in your measurements will be 65 degrees Celsius. A record, apparently."

"I'll try to remember that one," said Benjamin.

"Yes. It's acceptable for me to tell you this forecast as it has no impact on humans, but I cannot share other forecasts."

"Because that would interfere in how we run the planet?" ventured Benjamin.

"Exactly. If I were to tell you about the next earthquake that would cause a Tsunami, it could ruin peoples' lives."

"Not save them?"

"But people would not be able to insure against the certain disaster. They would abandon their communities and cause burdens elsewhere. Ultimately, people would become dependent on Concordia to run the planet. It would destroy human society."

"So why," asked Benjamin, "did you warn us about

the imminent oil spill in the Middle East?"

"It was a demonstration of how the Legati are trying to help humanity. I hope I have answered the question about why we will not be warning about everything. Humans will have disasters, but they will learn from it. In the case of the oil spill, it was decided that a timely demonstration of our good intentions would avert a calamity caused by corruption."

"So, there may be other help like this?"

"Yes, but not often. Humans must learn from their experiences. It will be random."

Flight waved his hands once more and the view spun around to the Persian Gulf.

"This is what Abu Dhabi would have been like."

Benjamin could see the oil slick oozing its way eastward toward the city and entering the waterways north and south of the city peninsula. As Flight zoomed farther in and quickened the time-lapse, the sickening pollution of the beaches and islands, the dead and dying wildlife, became gruesomely apparent.

"And you won't share that forecast video with us?"

"Our goal is to have the warnings be adequate. We understand that humans need to understand the implications of not following our guidance. But we do not believe that proving everything to your authorities is worthwhile. We are not interested in debate. If humans decide to ignore our advice, they will learn the consequences later. It may seem very strict, but we know it is the most effective approach."

"I have to say I agree Mr. Flight. Humans have the annoying habit of only learning from their own experiences..."

"Sometimes..." interjected Flight.

"Well, yes," conceded Benjamin. He paused. "But

what about societal guidance? What about forecasting the effects of territorial management of developing areas by ex-colonial powers?"

"As I noted earlier, such modelling can only reliably forecast up to 6 months in the future. We can keep going but the fidelity of the model becomes less certain. That is why generating the model, sometimes daily, is useful. Small changes in the real world can affect the model's view six months out. This is especially true at the beginning. But once an initiative has been executing for a few months and we can discern behavioral trends, the algorithms can become very accurate. The systems are always learning and refining patterns."

"The processing power of your computers must be colossal, that's all I can say."

"They are, Benjamin. But other than that, not so very different in principle to your own."

"Just give us a few thousand years..." mused Benjamin.

"As you say. There is one other thing I would like to mention. It is likely that future Concordia guidance may appear to contradict earlier guidance."

"Because of the system's learning of human behavior?" posited Benjamin.

"As you say."

Benjamin lost track of time as he stayed with Flight in that virtual theater, exploring the world and the forecast impacts of the guidance that had already been provided. The information layer that could be positioned over geographical areas to graph population and economic trends. The weather patterns that would be present in weeks or months to come. The climatic trends over years to come.

It was Benjamin's neck that finally gave out, as well as

some eye strain.

"I'm sorry, Mr. Flight," he said, "but my real-world body is in pain from lying on a sofa too long. I hope that I will be permitted to join you again soon. This has been extremely enlightening. Thank you."

"You are most welcome Benjamin. I will speak to you soon."

Abruptly, the call ended, and Benjamin's view returned to his default tiny office. It seemed so unimaginative compared to what he had just been witnessing. He ripped his headset off.

Christel was standing beside him smiling.

"Been having fun?" she asked.

"I have so much to tell you, Christel."

# CHAPTER 24

"CONCORDIA SOCIETAL GUIDANCE System. Communication Number 8," said Benjamin's virtual assistant.

"Violence between civilian factions attempting to control commerce in urban areas is commonplace. Nowhere is it more pernicious than in some South American cities. Poverty is the primary cause of this activity. As a result, there is no instant solution.

"As a starting point, Concordia has identified the core 964 faction members that dominate the Honduras city of San Pedro Sula. The Honduran authorities have been provided this information.

"Arresting these faction members is not considered effective in dismantling these groups and allowing the local police force to regain control of their city. Instead, the global positioning coordinates of all 964 faction members will be recorded and continually updated.

"When an individual has not been associated with a criminal, violent or abusive activity for an undisclosed period, they will be removed from the tracking system. New and indirect faction members will be added as they become involved in these activities.

"Police will be provided the identities and precise locations of all relevant faction members for criminal acts, that will be reported to them by the Concordia system. Additionally, currency bank accounts of all types, ongoing transactions, public records and travel outside the immediate jurisdiction will be tracked and blocked as appropriate.

"Other cities will be added moving forward.

"Thank you for your attention."


Benjamin was beginning to get used to being impressed. The latest Concordia announcement was something that the police forces around the world had been trying to do for the longest time. But because their solutions usually required facial recognition, there were the usual complaints about invasion of privacy and the over-bearing state. With Concordia not revealing how it knew where all the gang members were at any time, Benjamin thought there would not be any complaints.

He was wrong.

"Good afternoon, Fabian," said Benjamin answering his phone. "What can I do for you on this fine day?"

"Good afternoon, Benjamin," answered Fabian. "We have a slight problem."

"Oh, yes?"

"You remember Gene Harlander, the ex-spokesman of the World Council?"

"Of course, I do. What's he up to?"

"Although he was thrown out of the World Council, he somehow managed to retain his representative status in the World Government. As a member of the WG, he has been agitating against what he calls the WG's prostration before the Legati visitors."

"Prostration? That's a bit strong, isn't it?" Benjamin didn't think he had ever used that word.

"There are those that agree with his attempt at trying to warn the Legati off militarily," continued Fabian. "They think that not hitting the ships with neutron bombs, specifically, was a mistake."

"Really? They think that would have made the Legati go away?"

"What I am hearing is that they believe it would have provoked the Legati into a response. They believe it would have shown the world that the Legati are not the friends they make themselves out to be."

"Who is this 'they', Fabian?"

"They are a group that calls themselves the 'Freedom Alliance'," replied Fabian. "They are led by Harlander but have several high-level government officials in their ranks, and..." Fabian paused.

"And...?" Benjamin did not like the pause.

"The leadership of the American and Chinese Territories."

"Uh oh."

"Exactly. Having the second and third largest economic blocs joining together to oppose the commitments of the World Council is very serious."

"Not to mention the largest military blocs," added Benjamin.

"Indeed."

"Have they made any announcements yet? I have not seen anything on the news," said Benjamin.

"No, this is not public knowledge yet. I'm sure Flight knows about it. But I am getting back-channel information that suggests they are about to make some formal announcements."

"Any idea what they're going to announce?"

"Obviously I have no details, but the expectation is that it will be a big 'thank you, but no thank you' message to the Legati."

"Why do I feel that this was inevitable?" said Benjamin.

"I agree with you. It's nothing to do with freedom. These powers are objecting to their dominance being threatened."

"Their *status* being threatened," added Benjamin.

"And they have the religious institutions on their side too," added Fabian.

"That's not surprising either, is it. Another group trying to maintain their relevance."

"I have set up a meeting with Lucas Oliveira in the morning and would like you to join via video conference please."

"Of course. Have your admin send me the meeting information. I will speak to Flight and see if he has anything to say."

"Okay. Speak to you tomorrow." Fabian ended the call.

Benjamin rested back in his chair. On SaQ'il, the Legati Counsellor, Mentor, had warned him about what was likely to happen sooner or later.

*Sooner,* thought Benjamin exhaling deeply.

# CHAPTER 25

THE TWO DRONES flew low over the landscape. They were not flying fast but hugged the terrain closely. They were silent.

In the distance was the Legati mast. A solitary feature in the prairie landscape. Its single red navigation light glowing brightly in the night.

At a distance of one thousand meters, the drones suddenly rose in altitude and then each fired their four air to ground missiles at the base of the structure. The drones banked away sharply as the missiles bore down on their target, aiming at the structure as well as the ground that it stood upon.

As the weapons reached the tower, it was as if time stood still. As if someone had hit the universal pause button. For the tiniest moment, the missiles hovered motionless in space, their blue engine plumes frozen. With a flick, tall doors in the Legati mast opened and a broad red beam illuminated its foes, reducing them to a charred powder that hung in the air.

When time resumed at that precise moment, the back residue joined the light snow that was meandering its way to the ground.

Benjamin's tablet was ringing. It was a call from Flight.

"Good morning, Mr. Flight," said Benjamin, answering.

"I assume you have not seen the news yet, Benjamin," replied Flight.

"I have just got up. Sorry. What have I missed?"

"The Chinese and American Territories are systematically attacking the Concordia towers in their zones."

"What?"

Flight didn't say anything.

"I was going to call you this morning," said Benjamin, "in preparation for a conference with the spokesman of the World Council. Fabian told me that Harlander was trying to get a coalition together called the Freedom Alliance. I had no idea they were moving so quickly."

"Yes. They have created a network that is not monitored by Concordia."

"How many towers have they targeted, Mr. Flight?"

"Two hundred and six. That is 36% of the total deployed."

"And they did this overnight?"

"Yes Benjamin. You need to speak with Oliveira. The Legati position is that the World Government is clearly rejecting the guidance."

"So that means that the Legati could effectively leave?" said Benjamin with alarm.

"We are prepared for this type of behavior. There will be no retaliation. We are not at war with mankind. The

Concordia guidance system will be paused for the time-being."

"The towers defended themselves, I assume?" asked Benjamin.

"They defended themselves and terminated the attacks, but the scale of the attempt is the important point. Unfortunately, eight towers had to self-destruct due to nearby terrain damage," replied Flight.

Benjamin suddenly felt that now was the time to show some leadership. He felt the time for continuous questions must start coming to an end.

"The World Government was in formal agreement with the Legati. So, this means that the Chinese and the Americans have acted unilaterally."

"Apparently so."

"Which they can do, per law, if their territory is under attack. But it wasn't."

"They will interpret the situation differently, Benjamin."

"Yes, I'm sure," said Benjamin.

"The most senior people within the territorial governments must have authorized these attacks. This means that you must ensure that the World Government still has authority. If it does not, the Legati will withdraw." Flight's deadpan voice, however artificial in its translation, resonated deeply within Benjamin. It was clear what he had to do.

A short while later, Benjamin was dialing into the conference with Fabian and Lucas Oliveira. Christel sat by his side.

"Good of you all to join today," said Oliveira. "I'm sure you are aware of the unfortunate events last night."

"Yes, we...," started Fabian, but he was interrupted by Benjamin.

"I'm sorry Fabian," he said. "Councilor, what exactly did you know of these attacks or the preparation for them?"

"Er well," stuttered Oliveira, "we knew that this Freedom Alliance was gaining traction amongst some members of the government, but we had no idea that they had already planned these acts of aggression."

"Why didn't you know?" pursued Benjamin. "For any territory to use military force, they are required to gain the agreement of the government and the Council."

"The territorial leaders in China and America are stating that they viewed the Legati installations as sovereignty impositions. Therefore, it was an invasion that did not require central governmental authorization."

"Do you agree with that Councilor?" demanded Benjamin.

"Of course not, Ambassador. But we must work with these territories to find a solution."

"Councilor, does the World Council have the final word or not?"

"We do Ambassador, but we are still a democracy and things can be, let's say, fluid." Oliveira was sounding defensive.

"I'm sorry Councilor," continued Benjamin, "but to go from a peaceful understanding, with the Legati providing helpful guidance to mankind, to an unprovoked attack on *two hundred and six* Concordia *towers* in the space of 12 hours is not a mere 'fluidity'. It is a declaration of war."

"I wouldn't go that far, Ambassador," said Oliveira weakly.

"Perhaps, if I may, Ambassador," said Fabian, "Councilor, do you know what demands the Freedom Alliance is making?"

"They are not making public statements," said Oliveira, "but one of the government members that sympathizes with them has said that they want the Legati to leave us alone and take their protection with them."

"Pretty simple, then," said Fabian. "May I ask Christel a question?"

"Of course, Fabian," said Christel.

"Do you really think that the Legati will simply 'go away'," said Fabian, making quotation marks in the air.

"Oh yes," replied Christel, "they are bound by their word. They will leave. And if any other power decides to visit Earth, it is very unlikely that they will come to your aid."

"Unlikely?" prompted Fabian.

"They will not," said Christel emphatically.

It was Benjamin's turn to speak next.

"Who in China and America authorized these attacks? Was it just their leadership or their territorial governments?" he said.

"We heard nothing about this in advance," replied Oliveira, "so it is only feasible that the territorial leaders made these executive decisions alone. I will do some more digging but that is the only possibility I see."

"Got it," continued Benjamin, "so that means that only a dozen or so people plus Harlander are at the middle of all this."

"But that's all they need," said Fabian.

"Only if the people agree with them," said Benjamin. "Councilor, how long would it take to get a referendum vote completed?"

"Using the Data voting system, we could have it set up and responded to before the end of the day, but we are required to give the electorate a week to revisit their electoral profiles," replied Oliveira. "What questions would you suggest asking?"

"Simply, do you support your leadership accepting

the help of the Legati visitors?" replied Benjamin. "Or something like that. I would say that's the question that goes to the root of the issue. Anyone want to ask anything else?"

There were shrugs from everyone else on the call.

"Could you run the referendum through the Data system now, so we can see where we stand? You know, and keep the results to ourselves?" asked Benjamin. "A sort of unofficial run?"

"Technically we are legally bound to report the results of any Data system use to guard against potential manipulation," said Oliveira. "But we could treat this as a system test for now. I admit it's something we've done before."

"Very good Councilor," said Benjamin, after a moment of considering how many elections had only been held once the result was known. "If the electorate disagrees with the actions of their leaders, how do we get them removed from office?"

"The territorial governments would have to hold a vote of no confidence," replied Oliveira, "and if 55% vote for dismissal, they will be gone."

"Well let's see what the referendum tells us before we go to that step," said Benjamin.

"Things could change for the real referendum, though," noted Oliveira.

"By a lot?" asked Fabian.

"Electoral profiles could be updated before the official vote. And yes, there could be significant changes."

"I suppose this referendum would attract more attention than most," said Benjamin.

"Undoubtedly," said Olveira. "You have to know that people do not always vote logically. For us, the Legati support is a very good thing. But there are many who will be convinced that there is some underlying conspiracy working against them. Throw in an off-world involvement and we should prepare ourselves for something off the charts."

"Are people so susceptible to such invented stories?" asked Christel.

"Yes, Christel," replied Fabian. "Sadly, human history is full of examples of leaders convincing their followers of an invented narrative. A narrative that supports their political goals. Sometimes, the more ridiculous the narrative, the more successful they are in getting people to believe it. Humans are highly susceptible to brainwashing."

"This is why I'd like to see the referendum results from the Data voting system before the referendum is announced and held formally," said Benjamin.

"That is extraordinary," said Christel rather too loudly. "You make it sound like humans don't know their own minds."

"They think they do," said Fabian. "It's just that they only believe what they have been trained to believe. Humans are naturally bigots so once a viewpoint has been locked in, they simply look for anything that supports this view and reject the rest. It's a psychological condition called confirmation bias."

"How sad," said Christel.

The sun shone brightly outside Benjamin's house, contradicting the clouds that were gathering in his mind. He sat with Christel in the living room, the monitor on the wall displaying the news. The reports of the missile attacks on the towers were beginning to come in, but nobody from the Freedom Alliance had made a statement.

"How was Mr. Flight this morning?" asked Christel.

"He was his usual self. No obvious sign of emotion.

But that could have just been the translation device."

"The Legati like to maintain their composure, but I am sure he was not happy."

"No," said Benjamin. "They only put those towers in place once we'd agreed to their help. Fortunately, I suppose, only eight towers were damaged. Imagine if the attacks had been successful, the costs would have been astronomical."

"Maybe the costs would feature, but it's more likely that the Legati would simply be incredibly disappointed that humans have let them down."

"I feel let down as well, Christel."

"I can understand that" she said.

"What do you think the Legati will do?"

"As I said on the call, they will do nothing. They will wait to see what happens with this Freedom Alliance and Harlander."

"The only solution is following world opinion and the referendum," said Benjamin. "I suggested to the World Council to do this before, to be honest. But at least we now have something tangible to get the people to vote on."

"Hopefully we'll hear something soon."

# CHAPTER 26

GENE HARLANDER WAS feeling upbeat. From the moment he'd been dismissed from the World Council, he had been obsessed with getting his revenge.

He had just sent the biggest "plug you" to those that had deposed him – and it felt good.

Convincing the American and Chinese leadership councils to resist the Legati had been surprisingly easy. For the longest time, there had been a lingering resentment in both territories that their aspirations for global dominance had been curtailed decades before. They knew they could not overcome the Legati in a straight fight but were counting on guerilla tactics to get rid of the interlopers. If they could make the presence of the Legati so costly to maintain, they would give up and go away. The old gravy train could get underway again.

"Ladies and Gentlemen," said Harlander over the video conference from his home in Montana, "I think you will agree that the first phase of the plan has, well, gone to plan."

There were ten other people on the call, American and Chinese council members. Most of the Chinese wore translation headsets.

"Gene," said one of the Chinese, "it is gratifying to know that our union has been successful, even though our weapons were mostly destroyed, we did have some successes. I note that we have not heard any more nonsense from the Concordia system."

"Indeed Chunhua," said one of the Americans. "I wonder how long that will last. Gene, do you have a meeting set up with Oliveira yet?"

"Not yet. The public announcement needs to go out first. We wouldn't want the World Council to think they are a priority."

There were a few chuckles from some of the participants.

"It is important," Gene continued, "that you all step up your communications to your populations with the message that we must escape the repression of the Legati. Emphasize that they are the enemy of the people. That we continue to show how defenseless we are. That even our combined military is unable to protect us from a future of servitude. Leverage the online communities to drum up support."

There were nods all round. Gene looked at the clock on the wall.

"The public announcement will be going out in twenty minutes, at the top of the hour. I will give Oliveira a call after that."

The call ended.

He settled back in his chair and turned on the main video monitor in the room and selected a news station at random. On schedule, the program was interrupted.

"I am just receiving an update," said the news anchor. "We have a statement from the leader of the Freedom Alliance that attacked the visitors' towers."

"My fellow citizens," began Gene in his pre-recorded message. "By now you will have heard about the action that was reluctantly taken against the alien infrastructure that was left all over the sovereign territories of America and China. You will have heard how these alien installations destroyed most of our weapons that were trying to retake our independence. However, we were successful in terminating nearly ten percent of our targets. They demonstrated their clinical resolve to eliminate anything that would threaten their dominance over our species. We showed that they are not invincible.

"The Freedom Alliance learned a great deal about our enemy, as the result of our action. By no stretch of the imagination is this the end of our fight.

"We understand that some of the messages that the alien propaganda system was delivering may seem benign. But it was clear, even in these early days, that the system is using deeply intrusive technology that is spying on all of us. Our lives are rapidly becoming no longer our own.

"The World Government was sitting idly by, while the surveillance of the public expanded uncontrollably. Fortunately, the leadership of the American and Chinese Territories had the wisdom and courage to stand up to this threat. They acted when nobody else would, sending an unmistakable message of protest that all the alien surveillance towers that had been planted on their zones are now legitimate targets.

"This preliminary military operation took skill and detailed planning by our brave men and women in uniform. We owe them a debt of gratitude for putting their lives in danger.

"We fully expect the aliens to mount some sort of counterattack to cow us into submission, but we will all stay strong and resist any attempts to take away our liberty.

"The Freedom Alliance will communicate soon, once the situation develops.

"In the meantime, God Bless the United Nations and God Bless our troops."

"That was a message from Gene Harlander, spokesman for the Freedom Alliance..." said the news anchor. Gene muted the audio.

One of his better speeches, he thought. He felt it might have been an anachronism to invoke God to bless soldiers, given their role to impose a particular point of view through violence or the threat of violence. But it would be a nod to the leaders of the religious groups that were keenly supporting him.

It was regrettable that they had not been successful in destroying more towers, but the successes they had had showed the way forward. Soon, they would use bigger weapons that would disrupt the ground around the towers – that would certainly have a greater effect. But for now, the coordinated attack by the world's two biggest military powers put them on a war footing, which was the main thing.

Around the same time that he had succeeded in convincing the Americans and Chinese to attack the Legati towers, he had been visited by a delegation of representatives of the planet's six major religions.

"Mr. Harlander," said one a clergyman, "while we appreciate the moral and helpful tone of these Concordia communications, we are concerned that some might interpret them as commandments from the Lord."

"We would not want the Legati to be accused of heresy," added another. "Ideally we would like to be able to review these edicts before they are released. Without review, we feel that our people will become confused. They won't know where to go for spiritual guidance – the churches should be issuing some of these directions, in our view."

"Indeed," said the first. "And our governmental representatives should be issuing the others. Otherwise, we are just doing the bidding of an alien power."

"I understand," said Gene, "we wouldn't want to be simply following the instructions of some all-powerful invisible alien."

The first clergyman looked at Gene sideways. "I hope you are taking us seriously," he said.

"Oh, I am, completely Father," said Gene. "The Legati are not gods. People of faith reserve their beliefs for God."

Gene received another of the sideways glances.

"In any case," said the clergyman, "we also have concerns about the message we are receiving from this Ambassador Privett character regarding God. He has told us that the Legati have no view on religion and have never met a god."

"Well, maybe they haven't," replied Gene.

"We don't want that sort of message getting out," said the second clergyman. "If an advanced society like the Legati don't have a belief system, it could be a terminal challenge to the beliefs of our people."

"Well," said Gene, "it is better than the Legati trying to impose their religion on us."

There was a silence, and then an elder clergyman who had not spoken before said:

"Mr. Harlander, you are clearly not a religious man. That is your burden. But allow me to summarize why we are here.

"We see the arrival of the Legati as an existential threat

to the religious establishments of our respective cultures. Prior to their arrival, the unknown nature of the universe could only be made sense of by the existence of a higher being, our Creator. While science has threatened the world's religions over the centuries, this new arrival has taken away any religious authority we had left. We are left posing the question, who created the Legati? We see it as the end.

"There are still many who depend on their faith for the direction in their lives and we do not wish them to lose that direction. To put it bluntly, we need to lose the Legati."

And that had been it. The religions of the world wanted the Legati to leave and never come back. From Gene's perspective, he just saw it as an electoral boost. So, he had confided with the religious leaders of his overall plans to resist the Legati but gave no details. He had asked for their support, which had been readily given.

That meeting had only taken place a few days before the attack on the towers. By now those clergymen and women would know that Harlander was serious and a person of action

"I am a pluggin' genius," he said to himself smugly.

# CHAPTER 27

"GOOD MORNING LUCAS. How are you today?" said Harlander cheerily.

"What the hell are you up to Gene?" replied Oliveira.

"I see... Lucas, it should be obvious by now, don't you think?"

"What I think is that you are still pissed that you were kicked off the Council and are looking for revenge." Lucas Oliveira was usually a man of mild words. Today was not usual.

"I'm over that unpleasantness Lucas. I was simply selected by the leadership of China and America based on my many years of valued experience as Council Spokesman." The gibe was not lost on Lucas, but he decided to skip over it.

"The use of military force is only authorized when you are under armed attack."

"Well, that is how the Alliance felt. We have had a visitation from aliens in mighty battleships and they have attacked mankind's very foundation by imposing this Concordia system with a gun pointed to our heads."

"No aggression whatsoever has been displayed. You are living in a parallel universe Gene."

"It is you, Lucas, and the World Government that has been duped. If you go much farther down this road, mankind will be at the beck and call of these aliens forever."

"You have no evidence to support your so-called Alliance's actions."

"No Lucas. *You* have no evidence that the aliens are being honest with us. They won't even share technology with us."

"I would say that the Concordia guidance was beginning to become very useful. Now you have screwed it all up."

"Really? Oh, they throw a little bit of advice about an oil well blowing up and they're saints suddenly?"

"They averted a disaster. That was impressive." Despite his best efforts, Lucas felt like he was on the defensive.

"Maybe there was a problem. We don't know. There was no blow-out, so how do we know?"

"Okay Gene, so that's going to be your game, is it? Invent your own warped sense of reality and then spread fear, uncertainty and doubt. FUD. The oldest technique in the book."

"Not at all Lucas. We're just facing the real world." Gene was enjoying this. He felt he had Lucas on the hook.

"Well, whatever your warped sense of justification may be, you will not beat the will of the people."

"What does that mean?" asked Gene. Lucas was busily kicking himself under the table. He had not wanted to divulge the referendum that was underway.

"I mean that World Government represents the

world's total population and we have agreed to the Legati involvement." It was the best Lucas could come up with in the moment.

"You did it without asking the people. Your arrogance is beyond compare." Gene had hit on the key issue, helped along by Lucas's slip.

"In my capacity as the World Council spokesman, Gene, you and your so-called Freedom Alliance are hereby ordered to cease all military operations against Legati infrastructure. A vote of reprimand is to be tabled today against the leaders of the Chinese and American Territories. We will not have any further escalation of this."

"Or what?" asked Gene. "You'll go to war against the Alliance? Don't make me laugh."

"There will be legal consequences Harlander – we will get to them in due course."

"Oh, 'Harlander' is it? Let me tell you... Oliveira... the Alliance has no intention of ceasing any of its legal defensive actions in its territories."

There was a pause. Lucas then said:

"You have your orders. That will be all." He hung up on Harlander.

Gene looked at the blank screen. He had enjoyed that call. He enjoyed provoking Oliveira, even though Oliveira had been quite correct about his motives of revenge. His dismissal from the World Council had been the most demeaning thing that had ever happened to him. From that very moment he had started lobbying his contacts in the government and the territories to find the best way to push back on the Legati and the members of the World Government that was supporting them. He was consumed with the prospect of regaining the authority and respect that he had lost.

His mind went over what Oliveira had said. He had

the impression that the spokesman had nearly given something away. Something related to the people not standing for what the Alliance was doing.

He tapped his stylus on his desk. The World Council had failed to ask the global population what they thought of taking Legati advice and protection. What did they have to say now?

It suddenly hit him. "Oh plug. They're not taking the judicial route. They're going to the ballot," he said out loud.

At that precise moment in Brasilia, Lucas Oliveira was still kicking himself under the table. He realized that he had given the referendum away. He knew that he had to act fast.

He dialed a number on his workstation and almost immediately a face appeared.

"Where are we with the system test, Carlos?" he asked.

"I have been trying to reach you. The results have been in for a little while. Based on the existing electoral profiles, there would be a clear mandate. They would be 76% in favor and 17% against. The remainder are indecisive."

"In favor of what, the Alliance bombing the crap out of those towers?"

"No sir, in favor of maintaining the relationship with the Legati, keeping the Concordia system and censuring the Freedom Alliance and the leaders of the Chinese and American Territories for the unprovoked attack on the visitors."

"So, we would win."

"Yes, sir," said Carlos.

"Thank you. Please be ready to inform the population that a referendum on this topic is coming."

"You mean this wasn't a system test, sir? You know that's..."

"Yes, yes. Don't lecture me." Lucas hung up and

dialed another number.

"Yes, Councilor?" asked a young man.

"Please could you get Fabian Price and Ambassador Privett on the phone as soon as possible.

Lucas was feeling very agitated. He stood up and started pacing around his large ornate office.

After a few minutes, the phone in his workstation starting purring. He rushed back to his desk, composed himself for a moment and then accepted the conference call. Benjamin and Fabian were looking at him.

"How did it go?" asked Benjamin without the formality of greetings.

"Gene is a tricky character. He was blunt. He told me that his alliance had no intention of changing their position on Legati infrastructure on their territories."

"Not surprising. Did he indicate any other actions being taken?"

"No," said Lucas, "but I do think he suspects that we are going to have a referendum."

"How would he know that?" asked Fabian.

"It was something he said about the World Council not having asked the people what they thought a while back."

"All right," said Benjamin, "what would the referendum tell us if we had it today?"

"That is the good news, Ambassador. The resolution to keep working with the Legati and censure the leaders of the two territories for their behavior would pass 76% to 17%. That would allow the vote of no confidence to be submitted straight away."

"Okay, those are good margins. Can we trigger this referendum officially now?" asked Fabian.

"Yes. We must give the electorate one full week so they can update their profiles, if they wish. So, we will have the results one week from today."

"Got it," said Benjamin. "It is important that the Government encourages people to make sure their profiles are up to date. For the sake of appearances, we don't want to appear underhand. At the same time, we need to step up the online activity to discredit the Freedom Alliance."

"I will get the referendum process rolling immediately, gentlemen."

# CHAPTER 28

THE NIGHT WAS crisp and cold. Two figures clad entirely in black slipped through the darkest shadows in the gardens behind Benjamin's house. There was no moon but streetlights in the distance cast a faint eerie glow over the grounds.

Silently, the pair approached the wall of the house. They paused by a corner, checking to make sure they had not been detected, and then descended the stairs that led down to the basement. They crouched back-to-back. One guarded their escape, while the other used an electronic device to open the lock.

*Click.*

The door opened and the two people slipped inside, closing the door silently behind them.

The house was silent. All the lights were off. The two visitors crept along the passageway that led to the stairs up to the house. Using night vision goggles, they had no use of lights to guide their way into the living room.

With utmost stealth they started making their way toward the main bedroom that was down a passageway to their right. The door was shut.

One of the figures reached for the door handle. As soon as his hand touched it, a sharp chirp noise made them turn around quickly. It was the last thing that they would ever do.

A brief but loud percussive thump and a bright green flash hit the two uninvited guests. Darkness fell again.

A commotion in the bedroom followed. Lights went on and the door flew open. Benjamin was faced with the scene of two motionless bodies lying in front of his door and his Centurion hovering over them.

Benjamin did not call the police. He called Fabian. Within half an hour, vehicles pulled up in front of the house and Benjamin allowed a dozen men dressed in overalls into the house. They said very little. Their job was to retrieve the remains of the two would-be assassins and secure the premises.

"I will be staying in the living room tonight, Ambassador," said one of the nameless cleaners. "We will have a car parked outside for the duration. These are the strict orders from Mr. Price."

"Okay. Well, thank you for your help. Good night." Benjamin started turning to return to his bedroom.

"We will not be sleeping, sir."

"I'm not sure I will be either," said Benjamin.

The following morning, Benjamin and Christel did wake up from sleep, albeit a restless one.

When they finally emerged from their bedroom, the same man in the overalls was sitting in the living room, reading his tablet and drinking a cup of coffee. The

Centurion was hovering nearby.

"I hope you don't mind me helping myself to a coffee," he said.

"Not at all. What shall I call you?"

"Just call me Fred," he said.

"Well Fred, I hope the Centurion didn't worry you."

"Actually no, Ambassador, it is a very interesting thing. It must be very good at judging risk. A couple of times I went down the passageway to your room as part of my rounds and it didn't even follow me. It must know that I'm not a threat somehow, even though I am armed."

"Usually it just follows me around," said Benjamin. "I leave it to do its own thing."

"Judging by last night, that sounds like a good thing."

Fred walked over to the kitchen and placed his cup in the sink.

"Mr. Price will be here soon, and then I will take my leave."

"I appreciate you coming along at such a late hour. I assume you work for Sperantibus?"

"Yes, sir."

The doorbell rang.

"That will be Mr. Price. I will see myself out and let him in."

"Thank you again... Fred."

Fabian came up the steps from the foyer to the living room a few moments later.

"Had a fun night?" he said with a grin. "Are you all right Christel?"

"Yes, thank you Fabian," she replied simply. Benjamin felt that he was the only one who realized that someone had tried to kill them both.

"Any idea who those two were?" he asked.

"They were contract assassins," said Fabian, "at least

according to the police databases."

"You informed the police?"

"No."

"Can we guess who hired them?"

"Another question I cannot answer with certainty. Can we call Flight please?"

"Of course," said Benjamin. He walked to the low table in front of the sofa and picked up his tablet. He dialed the code for Flight. The tablet chimed merrily.

Benjamin stood there while the tablet rang and rang. He ended the call and tried dialing again. Again, the device rang, and nobody answered.

"Well, that's a first. He always answers within a ring or two," said Benjamin. "Let me try my AVR headset. That's a different number."

Benjamin put the headset on and found himself in the virtual non-descript office. He looked for the number that Flight had called him from when they met in his world. There was no answer.

"That's not good," said Benjamin.

"Maybe he will call later, Benjamin," said Christel.

"Let's hope so," said Fabian. "In the meantime, we are moving you both to my house in Geneva for the time-being. It's not so discrete as this house, but there's more safety in numbers."

"Now that they know where we live," added Christel.

"Yes," replied Fabian.

After grabbing a few essentials, the trio and Benjamin's Centurion headed out of the house. Waiting for them was a single non-descript car.

"This isn't your usual style, Fabian," remarked Benjamin.

"Ha, people who drive around in limousines with police escorts and flashing lights don't understand the first thing about security. They just crave the attention. We don't."

"Or your style, Christel," added Benjamin with a grin, referring to her exquisite car back on SaQ'il. Christel simply raised her eyebrows, effectively telling him to shut up.

They got into Fabian's car and headed off. As Fabian had indicated, their journey was entirely uneventful; nobody paid them the slightest attention. Christel said nothing for the entire journey, fully enjoying the sights of the towns that they passed through.

Later, when they were sitting in Fabian's living room in his highly ostentatious house, Benjamin tried calling Flight again. Again, there was no response.

"We need Flight to tell us what to do," said Fabian. "It is the Legati that is under attack. The referendum results will be coming soon, and we may lose control of events, if we haven't already. I just hope he hasn't called in the cavalry."

"The cavalry?" asked Christel.

"Sorry Christel. Legati reinforcements," said Fabian.

"That will not happen, Fabian," she said.

"I'm not that worried about Flight," said Benjamin. "I spoke to him immediately after the attacks. He told me the towers simply defended themselves and demonstrated no aggression. I think everything's completely under control."

"That doesn't explain why we can't reach him though," said Fabian.

"My impression of Flight," said Benjamin, "is that even in silence, he is trying to tell us something. Maybe he wants us to find him."

Benjamin stood up and walked toward the window. Fabian's house was not far from the Sperantibus headquarters and shared similar spectacular views of Lake Geneva and the main city beyond. It was a moving painting.

He could watch it for hours. He was sure that Fabian did.

"So where might he be?" he said. "I think we agree it must be on this planet somewhere."

"Or in orbit," suggested Fabian.

"Probably not," said Christel. "There are going to be substantial processing systems with significant power requirements."

"What do we have to go on?" asked Fabian. "Benjamin, you are the only one to have met him, virtually at least."

"We met in a restaurant on top of a mountain and then transferred to his control room."

"Where was this mountain?" asked Christel.

"No idea. It was not too high because it was grassy outside. The view led down to a valley beyond."

"Did Flight say anything about the location?" asked Fabian.

"He said it was a sacred place," said Benjamin.

"What, a restaurant?"

"No, Fabian. Although I asked him the same question." Benjamin chuckled.

"And you didn't go outside and have a look around?" asked Fabian.

"No, I was using my AVR headset, so was... rooted... to the spot... Hang on a minute. I took a photo!" Benjamin lunged for his backpack and grabbed his tablet. He brought up his photos and found the image that had been saved from his AVR headset.

"Wow, Benjamin. Lucky you're a tourist," said Fabian. "Project it onto that main monitor on the wall. It's called 'Living Room'"

Benjamin found the device in his tablet's list of nearby devices and pushed the image to it.

Everyone got up and went over to the monitor to

examine it closely.

"I took the photo because of that view," said Benjamin. "Flight said the restaurant was just for my benefit. Better than sitting on the grass, he said."

There was silence as they all scanned the picture.

"The only thing that isn't generic about this picture is that mountain range on the horizon?" asked Benjamin, peering at the closely. "Anything look familiar?"

"I don't know. They could be anywhere. Who's to say this is even somewhere on Earth. You said Flight referred to it as a sacred place."

"Yes, but that pointy one. It looks like Everest to me," said Benjamin, peering even closer.

Benjamin grabbed his tablet and looked up images of Everest.

"It looks very similar Fabian."

"Really...? Yes, I think you're right. What about this mountain to its left? It's a similar height."

"The second highest is K2," replied Benjamin. "Let me check." He brought up images on his tablet.

"Yes, it could be," he said. "What does this tell us?"

"Is it triangulation?" asked Christel.

"But in the view, they are right beside one another," said Benjamin. "According to this, in reality they're over 1300 kilometers apart."

"But Benjamin," she continued, "what about their orientation?"

"What do you mean?" asked Fabian.

"I was just thinking that perhaps the images of the mountains are taken from a particular side."

"Good thinking, Christel," said Benjamin. "Let me see what I can dig up. This'll probably take a while."

"In that case," said Fabian, "I have an idea, Christel. You should meet my wife. I think she would be delighted to show you the sights."

Christel's eyes lit up.

"That would be wonderful, Fabian! Benjamin can handle the map reading."

"Come with me Christel. Anne will be so happy that you are finally here."

He extended his arm and gestured Christel to follow him. Christel gave Benjamin a sheepish grin and followed Fabian out of the room.

"Yes, don't worry about me doing all the hard work while you gallivant around town," Benjamin called out after them. "Really, it's okay. I'll just save the world on my own. Yeah?" But Fabian and Christel were gone.

*Typical*, thought Benjamin.

He tutted to himself and started working. It took a while to find a three-dimensional model of the mountains, but when he did, he rotated them, so they appeared the same as in the image he had taken. From what he could see, the Everest image was taken from a heading of 21 degrees, just east of the North Face. The K2 image appeared to be from a heading of 114 degrees, just south of the only-recently climbed East Face.

Benjamin drew a line from K2 along the noted heading and likewise from Everest on his mapping application. The two lines converged in the middle of nowhere in Tibet, specifically, just north of a high-altitude lake called *Serbug Tso*.

Benjamin did not feel good about his conclusion. He checked his calculations and his use of the mapping tool. He confirmed the location.

"A long shot, if I ever saw one," he thought.

He put his tablet down and walked to the bar in the corner of the room and checked out the fridge. Happily, he saw that Fabian had stocked it with a few beers. Even more happily, Benjamin found some bottles of Hefeweizen. He snagged one, opened it and poured the contents into a tall glass that was sitting on the shelf. He admired the beer for a few moments, as the occasional bubble made its way to the two-centimeter head at the top. He breathed in and then took a long drink from the glass.

Absolute heaven.

Suddenly, he wished his old friend Jake was with him. He needed to do something about that.

Benjamin walked over to the main window, took a seat and enjoyed the moving picture of the lake laid out before him.

# CHAPTER 29

DAVID PAGE HAD not spoken to Benjamin in long time. After their last conversation, he felt that the best thing to do was spend his time analyzing the Concordia communications and leave his access to Benjamin for special circumstances.

Since word had surfaced about the Freedom Alliance and their campaign of attacking the Legati towers, circumstances had become distinctly special. He had been calling Benjamin for days and none of his calls had been answered.

David spoke to his tablet to dial Benjamin's number again and returned to reading his mail. He did not expect Benjamin to reply.

"Hello David. Good to hear from you," said Benjamin, being uncharacteristically friendly.

"I've been trying to call you," said David.

"Yes, I know – you can imagine there has been a lot going on."

"Are you going to tell me what *is* going on?"

"I think it's fairly straightforward," said Benjamin. "We have a disgruntled ex-Council spokesman firing up the leaders of territories that miss their old arms race."

"But now those territories are on the same side, aren't they?" said David.

"Since when were arms races about fighting the other side? They are merely an excuse to build up one's military, enrich your arms industry and acquire power."

"That's rather cynical."

"Not really. There will always be an adversary to motivate public opinion in your favor. It's an age-old technique. The Legati are now just an excuse to get all high and mighty."

"The Freedom Alliance," ventured David, "seem to be reflecting a common view that we don't need, or want, this so-called guidance from the Legati."

"Well, David, that's why we need to have this referendum. Yes, we should have had it before, but the World Council thought they had the mandate. Clearly, that was not the case and the leaders of two large territories think *they* have the mandate to oppose the Council's agreement."

"Which way do you think the referendum will go?"

"I do not know," replied Benjamin. "But I do know that we are displaying a characteristic of mankind that shows we are not ready to be part of any galactic community."

"Which particular characteristic are we highlighting? I can think of several."

"Yes David – perhaps it is more than one. This Alliance has stomped all over the Universal Principles. So much for dialog, community, respect and peace, for starters. No, let's just start blowing stuff up."

"Yes, that was extreme. I bet the Legati were livid."

"I think," said Benjamin somberly, "that they were deeply disappointed."

"Do you think they will give up on us?"

"It's a distinct possibility. We probably won't get a second chance, which does not bode well for humanity's future."

"I can't speak to our future," said David, "I just don't know what's at stake. But pissing off an alien civilization that makes us look like, I don't know..., rocks, can't be a good thing."

"They know what will happen to mankind, if we are left to our own tendencies."

"You mean, like someone less benevolent coming along?"

"Definitely. We're on the map now. It will only be a matter of time."

"Do you have any idea what could happen?" asked David.

"There you go again. One minute, you are likening us to rocks compared to the Legati, and the next, you want to know how bad it will be if we reject them."

"I'm sorry, I'm just asking the obvious question," said David.

"Yes, and I'm sorry too," said Benjamin. "I find it frustrating that we can't simply trust our friends. We always want to know the other side of the transaction. It is an arrogant side of human nature, especially in this case. We think we have the right to know, as if we have any influence on the outcome.

"I think sometimes that humanity should find out the hard way. Maybe we'll survive, but I have no idea what's coming."

"Plug. That sounds dire," said David.

"It is."

"What can I do, Benjamin?"

"In my opinion, the safest path is for us to reject the violence of the Freedom Alliance and embrace the guidance of the Legati."

"What about the consequences of rejecting them?"

"That's the thing, isn't it?" said Benjamin. "You can't tell them of the fears. That would be putting them under duress, holding a gun to their heads."

"So, what then?"

"Well, best case, people leave their electoral profiles alone. But if they were to update them, they should make sure that their profiles reject military action, nationalism and embrace the care of community."

"All right Benjamin, I will spread the word. Are you going to be speaking? It could be powerful."

"Yes, I will. I was thinking I might be viewed as biased. But I am, so to hell with it."

They ended the call and David started spreading the word over the networks. He had to be careful because the Fact Checking System would block anything about alien retribution or the end of mankind. It would be viewed as mere conjecture and be flagged as such. David appealed to peoples' moral compasses. He emphasized the importance of the Universal Principles. He highlighted the folly of rejecting the relationship with the sole extraterrestrial contact mankind had ever made.

Sometime later, Fabian returned to Benjamin in the living room. Benjamin told him about his conversation with David Page.

"Well, that will help. And I will get a speech drafted for you to review and then deliver."

"Thank you, Fabian. I'm not one for writing stirring

speeches."

"Oh, I'm sure you'd do a fine job, but time is pressing. How did you get on with your research?"

"I think I found the spot, but I'm not sure it's right."

Benjamin showed Fabian the triangulated location he had found in Tibet, *Serbug Tso*. They both stared at the map. It was a barren area, apart from some lakes and some distant small towns. There were no interesting features.

"Maybe the Chinese blew something up in the area?" suggested Benjamin.

"Let's see what's there." Fabian switched on his own tablet and logged into the Sperantibus corporate network. He opened his mapping application, navigated to *Serbug Tso* and added a layer that showed the Concordia towers.

"Oh, my giddy aunt..." he said.

"What?" said Benjamin. Fabian showed him the map on his tablet.

"It's 80 kilometers away to the northwest, but there's a tower located on a mountain called *Muggargoibo*. Or should I say, there *was* a tower. This was one of the towers that the Chinese managed to destroy."

"That could be it. Getting those headings from the mountains wasn't going to be entirely accurate."

"The tower is at 6300 meters. Getting to it is not going to be easy," said Fabian.

"Yes, especially without the Chinese spotting us."

Just as they were saying this, Christel entered the room. She was looking bright and happy.

"Have fun seeing the sights?" asked Benjamin.

"Yes, thank you. It is a very interesting city. Anne was very kind to show me. There were so many people!"

"Happy to hear it," said Fabian.

"We think, Christel, that we've found something interesting." Benjamin showed her the map and the location of the destroyed Concordia tower on *Muggargoibo*. "We were just wondering how to get there."

"Why don't we take the scout ship?" said Christel simply.

There was a pause.

"I thought we could only control that through Flight," said Benjamin.

"Oh no, your Centurion can summon it," replied Christel.

"What? Why didn't anyone tell me that?" Benjamin felt stupid.

"Maybe we didn't ask," said Fabian, avoiding Benjamin's eye and with a chuckle.

"Fabian is right," said Christel.

"All right then," said Benjamin, trying to change the subject, "when shall we go?"

"It'll have to be just you and Christel," said Fabian. "I need to oversee the referendum preparation after getting your speech out."

"Maybe I could record it later today?"

"Okay Benjamin, it won't take too long to prepare."

Benjamin and Christel spent a while discussing what they needed to take with them for their trip. Not knowing what awaited them, other than a wrecked tower, the best they could come up with was sturdy shoes, warm clothes and powerful flashlights.

"We can always go back, if the situation demands it," said Christel. "Let's just check it out."

"Okay," said Benjamin, loosening up a bit.

# CHAPTER 30

"HELLO. THIS IS Benjamin Privett," said Benjamin in his recorded message. "In a few days, your votes will be tallied for the most important referendum in the history of our species.

"That is not an exaggeration. Depending on the views you express in your electoral profiles, the Legati will either continue to provide us with help and guidance, or they will discontinue their involvement with our planet.

"Mankind has been given a special opportunity. An opportunity to align with a civilization that is motivated to build a peaceful and progressive galactic community. An opportunity to choose between a future guided by benevolence or a future with no guidance but replete with peril.

"No updates have been made to the profile gathering system, so for most of us, no action is necessary. But if it has been a long time since you updated your electoral profile, it might be good to make sure it reflects your current views on the world around us. We all know they can change over time.

"The precise query for the Data voting system will not be disclosed prior to the referendum as usual, but clearly I am hoping that collectively we agree that the Legati will be able to remain as our supportive friends for the future.

Best wishes to you all."

Benjamin was very critical of himself when he saw the message streamed, but it was too late. He reminded himself not to look down so much in the future.

As for the content, he knew he was getting as close as allowed to guiding people in how they updated their electoral profiles. But the Fact Checking System had not blocked him or flagged him, so that was a relief. But he reminded himself not to agree to use pompous expressions like "replete with peril" again.

It had been a restless night for him, although he noted that Christel had slept very soundly. He was highly anxious about what they would find during the day ahead. He hoped that they found more than just a chunk of twisted metal.

Consequently, Benjamin was up and about by 6am. He was not being particularly quiet, so it was not long before Christel reluctantly got up. Within the hour, they were both ready.

"Centurion, please summon our ship," said Benjamin.

Centurion sounded two tones of the same pitch, meaning, 'no response'.

"Centurion. Ship. Here," he tried again. Happily, Centurion made the two tones, one low, one higher, confirming the command.

"Hopefully, that means what I think it means," said Benjamin to Christel.

"I think that will do it," she said with a smile. "Your

Centurion is a simple thing."

Behind their backs the Centurion turned toward them, but they did not notice.

"How long will it take for the ship to get here, do you think?" asked Benjamin.

"The ship is highly stealthy, so it could be anywhere. It could have been following you around like your Centurion...," said Christel.

As she said this, the room darkened as if something had blocked out the early morning sun.

"Plug me," said Benjamin, "is that it already?"

"Fabian's wife, Anne, told me that 'plug' was not a very nice word, Benjamin."

"Quite right Christel. Sorry," he said. *Shit*, he thought. "Shall we go?"

They both headed out of the back door of the house. The ship was parked over the house, only two meters above the roof. Towards the side of the house, the lawn sloped up. It was there that the nose of the ship was closest to the ground and where the small crew entry ramp was deployed. They hurried up the slope and then after a momentary pause, walked up the ramp into the ship. The Centurion followed them in.

Once on the bridge, Benjamin's sense of leadership wavered.

"Er, Christel, can you do the talking thing with the ship?"

"I thought you'd never ask," she said, rolling her eyes. Christel then spoke something in the Legati tongue, to which the ship's command system responded. She added another instruction, to which the ship's voice responded again.

Through the front windows, they could see the ship rising slowly and Lake Geneva passing smoothly below them.

"I hope we are in stealth mode again, Christel."

"Yes, Benjamin."

"Good, otherwise we'd be putting people off their Muesli."

The ship continued to climb, accelerating rapidly. From the bridge, they could see that they were flying briskly upward toward the clouds. Momentarily the view was obscured by a blanket of white and then replaced with bright sunshine as they emerged into the clear skies above. They continued to climb, seemingly effortlessly, until the sky darkened. The curvature of the Earth was clearly apparent.

The pair did not have much time to admire the vista below them before it became clear that they were descending. The ship announced the descent in the Legati tongue. The skies regained their blue tone, and the ship re-entered the thin clouds below.

As they emerged from below the clouds, they could see ahead an expanse of desert. Barren plains bordered by high mountains. As they flew closer to the ground, it was clear that there was little vegetation. No forests or prairies. The mountains were capped with snow.

They continued their descent, clearly flying toward a group of particularly high peaks. Their destination, *Muggargoibo,* was soon directly ahead. The remains of the Concordia tower came into view, as the ship slowed. It had been deployed on a relatively flat area near the peak, which afforded an adequate landing zone for the scout ship.

As they came to rest beside the remains of the tower, Benjamin was relieved to see that there was no evidence of a Chinese military presence.

*No doubt the result of the remoteness of this site*, he thought.

Christel and Benjamin put on their jackets and picked up their other gear and exited by the ramp that had extended down into the snow. The Centurion followed them.

Benjamin looked back at the ship. Other than the ramp, their transport was a shimmering ghost, barely visible. Then the ramp withdrew and even the ghost was gone.

"Hey, Christel, I don't know how your breathing was adapted, but I'm going to have issues at this altitude. So, I can't stay out here for too long."

"Good point Benjamin," said Christel. "I'm probably going to be the same as you."

"All right, well let's just keep going until we feel ill effects and then return to the ship."

They trudged through the snow over the fifty meters to the tower, or what was left of it. The missiles that had attacked it had been lucky. Quite clearly, they had not reached the tower but had instead hit a rocky outcrop nearby that had dislodged some huge boulders. These boulders had obviously hit the tower hard on its side, some five meters above ground level. The result had been to bend the tower over some twenty degrees until it was leaning against a ledge above it.

The red navigation light was off. There were signs of intense fire up and down the column. Sections of the mast were clearly melted.

"I suspect all that scorching is the result of the tower's systems self-destructing," said Benjamin.

They walked up to the base of the tower. Benjamin hit it with his hand. There was a solid thump, as if he were hitting rock.

"I'm surprised the Chinese were able to bend this," said Benjamin.

"Maybe the tower isn't so robust farther up," suggested Christel.

"Possibly, but why would this base be so solid, then?"

They walked around the base, examining it carefully.

"Maybe all the intelligence of the tower is here in the base, so it needs to be protected, with the rest being expendable," added Christel.

"So that would suggest an entrance, so someone could maintain it. No?"

"Let's see if your Centurion can open it."

"Really?" said Benjamin.

"Give it a try," said Christel.

"Centurion. Door. Open." commanded Benjamin.

The drone made its confirmation tones and turned toward the tower. They could hear a grinding sound on the other side of the tower and rushed around to see what it was. A portion of the wall of the tower had sunk into the ground revealing an entrance.

"I really need to give this Centurion a better name. He's turning out to be so useful," said Benjamin. "He's much more than a bodyguard."

"He?" said Christel, with bemusement.

"Good point, but 'it' doesn't seem to do her justice."

They walked forward and peered into the darkness in the tower. They couldn't make out anything, except a floor inside. Benjamin stepped inside, with Christel and the Centurion following closely behind them. The Centurion automatically turned on its headlight, which revealed that they were on a landing with a steep metal ramp leading down.

"Ready?" asked Benjamin.

"Yes, of course."

As they started down the ramp, the external door closed behind them. They paused, looked back and then proceeded down the ramp to the floor several meters below. They found themselves in a circular room, considerably larger than the base of the tower above. A doorway was set in the stone wall ahead of them. There was no obvious opening mechanism, so Benjamin tried his new trick again.

"Centurion. Door. Open."

The Centurion gave its confirmation tone and the door slid down into the floor. Ahead was a passageway lined with stone, leading to the right. It was illuminated. The trio entered the passageway. The door closed behind them, and they followed the passageway down in a long spiral. By the time they reached another door, they had lost their sense of direction.

This time, the door opened without prompting, much to their surprise. Beyond was a small featureless anteroom. Once they were inside, the door behind them closed and another ahead of them opened. They stepped through into a large dimly lit hall.

"Now what?" said Benjamin.

"We should look around," said Christel, logically.

They shone their flashlights around the room. They could see the ceiling was approximately five meters high. The room was square, about twenty-five meters on each side. Light was entering the room through narrow horizontal slits in one wall. The only furniture in the room were tall chairs in the center of the room. The walls were paneled with smooth dark gray rectangular slabs. Upon closer inspection, using flashlights and the Centurion's headlights, they could see that some panels had large inscriptions on them.

"This is not the Legati language, Benjamin," said Christel as she peered at the inscriptions.

"That is correct," said a voice behind them. They spun around and both gasped at what they saw. A life-size projection of Flight was standing in the center of the room. It was very detailed. From more than a few feet away, he appeared solid.

"Mr. Flight," exclaimed Benjamin. "It is *so* good to see you!" Christel and Benjamin approached the figure in front of them.

"I am impressed that you were able to find this place," replied Flight. "Please take a seat."

Christel and Benjamin hoisted themselves up onto the tall chairs in front of the projection.

*Are humans the smallest species in the universe?* thought Benjamin.

"Well, thank you for the hints, Mr. Flight," said Benjamin. He looked around and with his palms up, said, "But what is this place?"

"It is part of a settlement from an early civilization. They built this complex before the mountains rose up. It was fascinating how the complex was preserved intact. Are you warm enough?"

"It's warmer in here than up above. Are you okay Christel?"

"Yes, I am Benjamin," she replied. "Mr. Flight, is this facility where Concordia is hosted?"

"Part of it Christel. That is why it is somewhat warmer here," said Flight. "The intelligence systems generate a great deal of heat."

"So, they are still running?" said Benjamin.

"Oh yes. They never stopped." said Flight. He shook his massive head, reminding Benjamin of a splendid horse. "I think you should know that the towers are purely cosmetic."

"So why did the Legati put them there, for goodness' sake?" asked Benjamin with an essence of irritation in his voice. "Were they bait?"

"In a manner of speaking, Benjamin," replied Flight. "Humans often do not differentiate between symbols and reality. Your history is full of examples of militant groups destroying statues, temples and other representations of ideas.

"It is a human urge that only emphasizes how far the species has to go."

"I know," said Benjamin reluctantly. "But they will think they succeeded because Concordia went silent after these attacks."

"It is not important what they think," said Flight. "Their psychosis is focused purely on maintaining their status and their control. They have been hypnotized by Gene Harlander's promises of continued hegemony."

"But" said Christel, "he is only a former spokesman of the World Council. He does not have any authority anymore."

"He is still an elected official," said Benjamin, "meaning he still has access to other Government officials. He is still a player."

"Yes," said Flight, "he is leveraging the innate desire of these former so-called superpowers to resume that role."

"Well, their leaders anyway," added Benjamin.

"We must wait for the results of the referendum to see what the American and Chinese people really think?" asked Christel.

"The referendum was a wise decision," said Flight. "The result will be interesting but will not tell us anything, unless it is a landslide."

"What happens," asked Benjamin, "if the result is not a landslide?"

Flight gave one of his signatory head shakes. "It is not possible to force a population to do something they do not wish to do."

"With respect, Mr. Flight," said Benjamin, "that doesn't answer the question."

"I know. But Benjamin, it is your planet. You must provide the solution."

Benjamin felt like he was being put in a precarious position. Not only did he have no immediate answer, but he did not want to be responsible for such a far-reaching decision. He stood there in silence.

It was Christel that broke the silence.

"May I suggest," she said hesitantly, "even if the result is not clear, that Concordia simply continues?"

Flight stood there impassively.

"You mean just ignore the attacks?" asked Benjamin.

"Why not?" replied Christel. "It will send a message that this violence was not effective. It will send the message that the Legati are above that type of thing."

Benjamin thought about it for a moment. But Christel was right; doing anything else would be viewed as a victory by the belligerents.

"I like it," he said. "But when should Concordia resume?"

"Immediately after the results are declared, irrespective of what they are," replied Christel.

"But the challenge will be if the referendum is strongly against continuing the cooperation with the Legati," said Benjamin. He did not want to be the one to raise all the negative possibilities, but there were some questions that had to be asked.

"But it won't be," said Flight.

"Oh shit, of course. You know the result already," said Benjamin, putting his head in his hands.

"Yes," said Flight calmly, "unless the electoral profiles change greatly between now and Saturday, seventy-four percent of the global population will desire continuation."

"Is that enough?" asked Benjamin.

"Yes," said Flight.

"Can the Concordia communications continue?" asked Benjamin.

"Yes," said Flight.

"Is it a stupid question to ask how?" asked Benjamin.

"Not at all," said Flight. "Humans' knowledge of communications does not extend as far as gravitational technologies. They have no comprehension of how our systems operate."

"Great," said Benjamin. "What would have happened if we hadn't come here, Mr. Flight. Would you have started again anyway?"

"No, Benjamin – I would have called you after the referendum."

"I see, so our trip here was unnecessary," said Benjamin.

"From that perspective, yes," replied Flight. Benjamin remained amazed that Flight could be so blunt. If Flight had been human, he would have sworn he suffered from Asperger's syndrome. Christel was a little like that too, he'd sometimes thought.

"And from another?" asked Benjamin.

"Indeed, Benjamin, it is good to consider all perspectives, Coming here is useful. It allowed you to avoid other assassins – a clumsy attempt to silence our messenger. You learned more about your Centurion. Though I would recommend not being so confident about its lock picking skills – I let you into this complex." The Centurion flinched almost imperceptibly.

"Most importantly, Benjamin, you will have learned of the Q'anua."

'The Q'anua?"

"The builders of this complex and the author of those

inscriptions," said Flight pointing to the engravings on the wall.

"What were they doing here?"

"They had settlements here a very long time ago, but they died out."

"Why?"

"The usual reasons. Earth's history is full of civilizations that went away. The only difference with the Q'anua is that their species was already elsewhere."

"Where did they go?" asked Benjamin.

"The people on this planet didn't go anywhere. They had *already* colonized other planets. Earth was just one. They became one of the preeminent civilizations in the galaxy."

"Really?"

"Yes, in fact they are now what we describe as an advanced civilization. We understand that they have evolved beyond the physical and are now an energy-based lifeform."

"No contact with them anymore?" asked Christel.

"Our leaders, the Videnti, are believed to be in contact. The rest of us only know of their legacy, which includes structures like this one."

"Which I recall you saying was a sacred site," said Benjamin.

"Yes. Legend says that the Q'anua were unable to help their brothers on this planet when a disaster struck. That is why this place is considered sacred by the galactic community. A lesson for everyone."

"What do the inscriptions mean?" asked Christel. She stood up and walked to the wall and traced a finger over the engravings.

"Our scholars believe they are an expression of their justice system and their beliefs. But that is only based on the recurrence of these symbols in other similar formal rooms like this one."

A door at the rear of the hall slid open and revealed daylight. A cold breeze entered the hall.

"Please," said Flight, gesturing to the open door, "move into the room over there. The view is much more interesting."

Christel and Benjamin stood up and walked past the projection of Flight and entered the indicated room. It was a large circular balcony with square openings that looked out over the snowy landscape below.

They couldn't see Flight, but his voice was clear.

"Your craft is above here. But this is the view from the restaurant that we met in recently, Benjamin."

"Except a lot higher," said Benjamin.

"As I said, the mountains in this region have risen up since the Q'anua left."

They admired the view for several minutes, but it was getting cold, so they went back into the hall. The balcony door closed behind them.

"There is one other benefit of you coming here," said Flight.

"I'm glad to hear that," said Benjamin.

"It is something that was delivered along with your arrival," said Flight, "but needed to be configured for my virtual world.

"Please go to the room at the bottom of the ramp to your right."

As Flight said this, a wide door opened in the wall opposite the balcony. It was six meters wide and clearly a main thoroughfare. Christel and Benjamin walked to the doorway and then down a long ramp to a broad corridor that ran perpendicular to the ramp. Looking left and right, the corridor extended into the distance. Directly ahead of them was a regular doorway, leading into a room with rows of tables and some high reclining chairs. They entered the room.

Sitting on the table closest to the door were three c-shaped headbands. Flight's voice came over speakers in the room.

"Take one of the headsets, but do not place them on your heads until you are seated on one of those chairs. They are special virtual reality headsets."

Christel and Benjamin went over to the chairs and laid back on them. Benjamin placed his headset on his head like a hairband. For a moment, nothing happened. Then, disconcertingly, his vision went dark, as though someone had completely turned out the room's lights.

A few moments later, Benjamin was amazed to find himself back in the same room as before, lying on the chair, but with Flight standing in front of him. This was no projection. Benjamin looked to his right and could see Christel, also looking around.

He felt Flight pat him on his right foot. *How is this possible?* he thought.

"You can stand up," said Flight. Benjamin swung his legs over to the left and slid down onto his feet. He was standing, with Flight standing right there, towering over him. Christel also stood up.

"How are you solid, Mr. Flight?" asked Benjamin, bewildered.

"I am not Benjamin. You are in my virtual world - follow me and I will explain." Flight turned and walked out of the room and headed up the wide ramp opposite. Benjamin and Christel followed. Nothing appeared different from before. They entered the large hall and headed over to the balcony door. As they entered the balcony, they found that it was no longer the stone balcony from before but rather the plush restaurant that Benjamin had visited on the previous occasion. But this time, he was walking about. He could see his hands and caught his reflection in glass cabinets. He was not wearing a headset either.

"This is a very faithful emulation," said Christel, with less amazement than Benjamin was feeling. He reminded himself that she had grown up with this type of technology, but still felt more praise was needed.

"This is real, Mr. Flight. I am really here," he said. "What is that headset doing?"

"It is coupled with your cerebral cortex. Your brain is receiving all its external cues, vision, hearing, smell, equilibrium, taste and touch, from the simulated world that I inhabit.

"This is why you must be reclined before placing the headset on. Your body in the real world is paralyzed. You should always be in a locked room or have your Centurion nearby when using this headset as you are at your most vulnerable."

Benjamin was simply staggered by the realism of the simulation. He could even feel the air breeze against his hand as he waved it about. They had thought of everything. Nothing detracted from the experience.

He walked over to the window and looked out over the green meadow that spread out before him and descended into the valley below. It was a beautiful Spring day.

"How far can you wander in this world?" he asked.

"A few kilometers in all directions, so I have a sense of freedom."

A thought struck Benjamin.

"Why have you gone to such lengths for us to be able to visit you here?"

"That is the right question. This is not the main purpose of this tool, though it will make our discussions in the future much more pleasant. You can even use the third headset to take another person on your travels."

"Aha, travels..." added Benjamin.

"Yes, you see Concordia is a monitoring system, as well as a modelling system. It receives information from a myriad of sources. It is therefore possible for us to enter these models."

"You mean, see what Concordia sees?"

"Yes, exactly. You can visit anywhere that Concordia is monitoring. That means any point on the planet's surface. The monitoring is live, so you can see what is going on anywhere at any time. The only difference between this simulation and the observer mode, is that you cannot interact with people or artifacts. You will be a ghost. You will be able to walk through walls." Flight chuckled.

"You will only be able to see, hear and move around. You will only be able to communicate with others wearing a headset or over a Concordia external communication channel."

"Aha, so I will be able to find out what Harlander is up to," said Benjamin brightly.

"Yes, if you so wish. You should respect peoples' privacy though."

"Can you show us how it works?" asked Christel.

"Of course," replied Flight, "It is voice commanded. You simply tell Concordia to go somewhere. Both of you must go to the same place. Your starting point is 'home', by the way. Saying 'End Connection' will turn the simulation off."

"Go ahead Benjamin," said Christel. "You know this planet so well. Take us somewhere interesting."

"Okay... Concordia, go to Bourse Pub, Chiswick,

185

British Territories." Their vision went dark for a moment, and then came back, Benjamin was delighted to find himself standing right in the middle of his favorite pub. He looked around. There was nobody there, except for him, Christel and Flight, looking very much out of place.

"I was hoping that the simulation would include people," said Benjamin with a disappointed tone.

"Well, it would Benjamin. But it's 6AM. Look out of the window," said Flight.

Benjamin went to the window and, sure enough, the early commuters were heading to work. He walked a few steps forward and passed through the wall onto the street outside. He looked back at the pub, just as someone walked straight through him. He jumped.

*That's going to take some getting used to,* he thought.

Christel walked up behind him. "When I said 'somewhere interesting', I didn't mean your old drinking establishment," she said.

"Right. Sorry. I couldn't resist. Um," he said semi-apologetically, "Concordia, go to Shibuya Crosswalk, Tokyo, Japan."

Their vision went dark again for a moment. When it came back, they were assaulted by people rushing past, seemingly in all directions at once. Looking around they were surrounded by extremely tall buildings, their sides pulsing with digital advertisements in the late afternoon sun.

"Better?" shouted Benjamin over the noise of the traffic and pedestrians.

"Not really," replied Christel. "I guess I will have to explore on my own later."

"Mr. Flight," continued Benjamin, "how will I know where people I want to view are currently located?"

"Just try asking Concordia," replied Flight.

"Okay, Concordia go to Gene Harlander, ex-spokesman for the World Council."

After the usual momentary darkness, they found themselves in a white room with writing on the wall."

"It says that access is restricted," said Christel.

"I suppose that makes sense," said Benjamin, "he's probably asleep at 1AM."

"One thing I should mention," said Flight, "is that you should restrict your time connected to these simulations. We have not done long-term testing on human brains. We do not want to cause damage through overload.

"Concordia, End Connection."

After a few moments, Christel and Benjamin found themselves back in the laboratory, reclining in their chairs. Flight had gone. They removed their headsets.

"That was a wild experience, wasn't it?"

"Apart from the pub, yes," she replied with a stare.

Benjamin laughed. He picked up the third headset and then they headed back into the main hall. Flight's projection was waiting for them.

"One other piece of information you may find useful," he said, "is that you can view a simulation from a period up to 24 hours earlier. You cannot view future models, for technical reasons.

"And finally, only you and Christel can command the headsets to navigate to a location. That is for security, especially to avoid loss or misuse of Legati technology.

"And speaking of security," added Flight, "keep your Centurion close. Those against the alliance with the Legati are probably not finished."

With that, they agreed that it was time to leave. They could travel with Flight through the Concordia-generated world whenever they wished. There was nothing else to see in the Q'anua complex, that they could understand at least, so it was time to return to warmer climes.

The scout ship lifted silently away from the mountain top, with Christel, Benjamin and the Centurion on board. Being in stealth mode, it was invisible to all detection, not that anyone was looking.

At Benjamin's request, Christel turned the spacecraft to look back at the peak. There was no evidence of the Q'anua dwelling. Just a bleak, beautiful, rocky edifice streaked with snow, marred only by the wreckage left by the futile Chinese assault on the Legati tower.

They turned east and ascended into the sky and made their way, effortlessly, back to Geneva.

# CHAPTER 31

GENE HARLANDER WAS on a private connection to the leaders of the American and Chinese territories. He had been told of the failed attempt to assassinate Benjamin Privett.

"Whose people were these?" he demanded.

"They were freelance contractors," replied Scott Lindgard, from the American team. "They were untraceable to any of us."

"That is not what I asked," replied Harlander. "Who authorized this attack?"

"It was suggested on our side, and we gave it the go-ahead," said Lindgard.

"What were you thinking?" continued Harlander. "Precisely, what were you trying to achieve? We never agreed to this."

"First of all, Gene," replied Lindgard, "we don't need authorization from anyone. Secondly, it was calculated..."

"Calculated..." sneered Harlander.

"Yes, *calculated*, that demonstrating our lack of tolerance for a mere nobody, like Privett, lauding about like some sort of Messiah, would cut off the head of the snake."

"Mei? Do you agree with this?" asked Harlander.

"Gene, the Chinese Territories do not recognize any authority from Privett," replied Tsao Mei from the Chinese leadership. "We also find the patronizing edicts from Concordia to be entirely unnecessary and offensive to the will of the Chinese people. We are not against the attempt to silence this so-called Ambassador."

"At least our actions against those alien towers on our territories seem to have silenced Concordia," commented Lindgard.

"All I can say is that I'm glad our fellow alliance members from the churches are not on this call," said Harlander.

"They were aware of the operation, and were in support," said Lindgard.

"What?"

"Yes, Gene. They don't want a Messiah running around, especially not *their* Messiah."

"Well," ventured Harlander in one of his more lucid moments, "that just adds to the lack of wisdom in trying to kill off Privett. We all know what happens when Messiahs are killed."

Lindgard shook his head dismissively. "In any case, the operation failed. We will be denying any knowledge of the attempt."

"Look," said Harlander, "can we at least agree on these initiatives beforehand in the future?"

"Gene, you were the one who decided to try align our common interests under this 'Freedom Alliance' banner of yours," said Tsao, "But we are not bound to this alliance. Our agreements allow us to act in coordination, but our territorial interests come first."

"So, you're saying that someone could do something like this again," said Harlander. It was not a question.

"Let me put it another way, if I may," said Lindgard. "We should keep in close communication with one another but agree that independent action is a right of us all."

"I don't think I like the sound of that Scott," said Harlander calmly. "We are faced with an existential threat. We should be handling this in a coordinated fashion."

"All right Gene," replied Lindgard, "the American Territories are not answerable to anyone, except the World Government, but as leaders of our respective territories, I could agree that we won't execute any operations without ratification with this group, unless time is of the essence."

"That's all I'm asking Scott," said Harlander, "is that okay with you Mei?"

"Yes, we can agree to that as well," she said.

"Excellent. I am glad we're aligned on that."

Gene was getting tired of the old-world attitudes of his American and Chinese counterparts. Despite the end of formal animosities that were brought about by desires on both sides to dominate the planet, the residue of that conflict was still clear. The claims of cultural and societal superiority were still all too common on both sides. Grudges borne of many decades of petty disputes and mindless nationalism were alive and well.

It was at moments like this, that Gene could reluctantly agree that the Legati were completely correct. Mankind needed an adult in the room to help them grow up. But these moments always passed quickly. He reminded himself of his personal humiliation at being ejected from the World Council. He reminded himself of the lack of respect shown by the Legati, turning up unannounced and then issuing edicts to the World

Government. Most importantly, he reminded himself of his reduced stature, and wealth, at the hands of Sperantibus. Gene Harlander was an individual consumed with a desire for revenge at any cost.

"What are we going to do about the referendum?" asked Tsao. "Our projections are that a significant majority are going to support it."

"Yes, we see the same thing," said Lindgard. "We are duty-bound to respect the results. To go against it could damage the World Government terminally, and they are not our target."

"Aren't they?" said Harlander. "Maybe that is something we should reconsider. They are the ones that got us into this so-called partnership with these aliens."

"No Gene," said Tsao bluntly. "The will of our people is paramount. We would not be aligned with any action that did not comply with their wishes."

"Of course, Mei," said Harlander soothingly, "but referendums are not like regular elections. The precise wording of the proposition is critical. We won't know what that wording is until tomorrow, when the results are announced. This gives us an opportunity to appeal the question and replace it with something more favorable for us."

"So, we wait, and see?" said Lindgard.

"We wait and then we appeal."

# CHAPTER 32

DAVID PAGE LOOKED out of his apartment window. It was a foggy day, almost living up to the old stereotypical view of London as a city shrouded in eternal so-called 'pea-soupers'. It was ironic, he thought, that smog had returned to the city over a hundred years after the original event that had resulted in the Clean Air Act. That law had curtailed the unfiltered coal burning and had ultimately relieved the city of its biggest health burden.

Now the smog was a problem of the whole northern hemisphere of the planet. Polluted air from countries came mostly from the so-called 'Lion' economies of the African continent that still insisted on burning abundant and cheap fossil fuels. These combined with the warmer climate caused by the earlier century of broad inaction from the wealthier countries.

Sometimes, the British Territories would have glorious days when the prevailing winds over the island would sweep the smog away. But insidiously, cold fronts would cross the land and trap the planet's pollution again at low altitudes. All of Europe was affected, as we were all northern hemisphere territories. It was nasty. It was unhealthy.

David was used to the view from his window and the grime that accumulated on the other side of the glass. HIs apartment was high up and almost completely shrouded in the fog. He could make out other tall buildings nearby, but not with normal clarity. It was depressing.

It was Saturday morning, and the referendum results were due to be announced imminently. He grabbed a synthetic coffee from his Gastro and turned back to the desk in his room. He tapped the touchpad on his browser and the large screen sprang to life. He navigated to the government online site where the officials would be reporting the outcome and saw that they were gathering in a press room. After the usual unexplained delays that politicians and administrators enjoy inflicting on mere mortals, a gray-haired gentleman stood up and read from his handheld device.

"One and all, thank you for your patience. My name is Anthony Hobbs, Returning Officer for the Data Electoral System.

"Today, we have the results of the extraordinary referendum called to vote on the following proposals:

"ONE: Does the global population agree to accept, consider actively and implement appropriately the guidance provided by the Off-World Visitors, known as the Legati?

"This resolution has been passed with 74% of votes. The remainder were either unclear or against the proposition.

"TWO: Does the global population agree that they understand and accept the Universal Principles as defined by the Off-World Visitors?

"This resolution has been passed with 69% of votes. The remainder were either unclear or against the proposition.

"The following caveats have been determined from the electoral profiles.

"First, that this referendum should be repeated every five years. This periodic referendum shall coincide with regular elections, so it is as much a referendum on the politicians that are entrusted to implement the Legati guidance as it is a referendum on the guidance itself.

"Second, tangible metrics that pass an audit by the Fact Checking System, shall be published every five years to report on progress against all guidance received.

"Third, no individual territories should be allowed to exempt themselves from any globally-relevant messages from the Legati.

"Fourth, even though the Legati have nominated Ambassador Privett to be their representative on this planet, it is considered vital that the Legati visit our planet periodically to reinforce their direct commitment to this undertaking.

"Fifth, and finally, there is a general desire for a formal process to be established whereby Legati technology could be made available to assist in our development.

"The resolution affirming the World Government's commitment to the cooperating with the Legati is therefore passed.

"Thank you for your service."

David watched the broadcast carefully. The FCS monitor had stayed green throughout, meaning that everything said was factual. On the face of it, therefore, it looked like the Legati were back in business. Like everyone, though, he wondered if the Americans and Chinese would accept the result. He knew their leadership would not be happy, but it looked like their populations were in favor of working with their new-found alien friends.

Online discussions exhibited their usual repetitive debates. People wanted to express an opinion based on little knowledge or hearsay. They knew how to circumvent the FCS which would flag lies and valueless conspiracy theories promoted by attention seekers. Instead, they posed supposedly innocent questions. What were the real motivations of the Legati? Why should they be trusted? What would happen if the World Government failed to implement the guidance? The usual questions that had already been asked and answered a thousand times, continued to circulate as if someone thought they were original.

For David, it was becoming tedious. It felt as if humanity had no desire to improve itself but would rather spend forever vacillating over irrelevancies. What was it about human nature, he thought, that people preferred the act of pontification, over actually saying something intelligent? He found it to be a huge relief, as well as surprising, that the referendum had been as clear-cut as it was. Still, a significant portion of the population simply did not grasp that humanity had entered a brand-new chapter. The old transactional way of thinking, where some reward was expected for doing something, was now in the past. The adults were now in the room and telling mankind what to do. He could not fathom why some people still could not grasp this new reality.

He wondered what it would take, finally, for people to accept that they were being offered an incredible opportunity by a benign superior intelligence. Who, with any synapses in their head could reject such an opportunity, he thought? Added to that, even if the Legati proved to be a malevolent force, what choice did mankind really have? The world's militaries had already shown themselves to be impotent against the visitors. Crucially, they had not retaliated. So, what was in the heads of the Chinese and Americans, thinking they could impact the status quo by attacking Legati infrastructure? What message did it send?

David knew the answer, of course, Perhaps everyone did, but some were in denial. To the Legati, it told them that mankind really was a primitive species. To those humans more intellectually curious, it sent the message that the Chinese and Americans were petrified of losing the vestiges of their primary influence on the planet.

This was why the referendum votes had fallen as they did. It was the final repudiation of the old way of living. Humanity was finally waking up to the realization that their future was not bound to an internal power system on their planet. Humanity's future was tied inextricably to the other members of this galactic community that they had not yet met. It was a future that most humans wanted to grasp with both hands. There was an inevitability about it.

David started writing on his home workstation. He laid into the naysayers and hinderers, exposing them for the mindless drones that he considered them to be. He celebrated the outcome of the referendum. He celebrated the rejection of the status quo and the problems that the status quo refused to resolve.

A few hours later he submitted his article for publication and syndication. He knew the anti-progressives had yet to make their case, but he was happy to get the first salvo in the battle launched.

# CHAPTER 33

BENJAMIN WAS A little reluctant to start spying on people, but he knew that with the referendum results having just been announced, now was the time to start using his new Concordia headset.

"You are going to join me Fabian, aren't you?" he asked.

"Sure. Are we going to check out Harlander?"

"We have to. We need to know what he is contemplating. It's too important."

"I agree," said Fabian. "Let's go."

"Christel, are you joining us?" asked Benjamin.

"Sure," she replied simply.

The three of them reclined on sofas and comfortable chairs. The Centurion watched over them.

"Fabian don't be alarmed when your eyesight blanks out for a moment. It's quite normal," said Benjamin. "Freaked me out the first time, to be honest."

"Okay, I'll just lie here."

They put the headsets on and waited for Benjamin to command the system.

"Okay, Concordia go to Gene Harlander, ex-spokesman for the World Council."

Their vision went blank for a moment and then they found themselves in a living room. Gene Harlander was seated on the edge of his seat watching a large television monitor in front of him. There was no sound.

"I'm not hearing anything," said Christel.

Fabian was still at the stage of waving his arms around and realizing that he could control his ghost that was standing in Gene Harlander's house, completely unseen. Fabian said nothing.

"I expect that's because Concordia doesn't have access to any microphones in this room," replied Benjamin.

"And the video feed?" asked Christel.

"That's probably derived from that home security camera up there," said Benjamin pointing above a doorway.

"Could be," replied Christel. As she spoke, Harlander's wife entered the room. With her arrival, the audio from the room immediately came on. She sat down next to Harlander.

"She must be carrying her mobile phone with her," said Benjamin with a smile.

"Not good news then, honey," said Mrs. Harlander.

"As expected, people don't know what's good for them," replied Gene churlishly.

"What now then?" asked his wife.

"We'll appeal the wording of the proposition."

"Will that help?"

"Yes, if we can force a wording that works in our favor. You have to ask the right question."

"How will you know if you've got the new question right, dear?"

"We've already done it. We used a development system that most people had forgotten about. The electoral profile data was a little out of date, but we found the wording we need."

"You are so clever, dear."

"Yes, I am, aren't I?'

Benjamin groaned. "What a plonker," he said.

"Anyway, dear, I have to head out – lunch with Sheila today," said Mrs. Harlander.

"Have fun," said Harlander, not taking his eyes off the television monitor.

His wife stood up and walked out of the room, without saying anything else. As she did, the audio from the room stopped.

"Looks like that's all we'll get for now," said Benjamin.

"May I just look around for a moment?" asked Fabian. He started walking around the living room and then walked into the kitchen. A minute or so later, he rejoined Benjamin and Christel in the living room.

"This is phenomenal. Some things are clearly approximations, but the simulation is stitched together incredibly well," he said.

"We'll need to learn its limitations," said Benjamin, "but as long as there are sources for Concordia to tap into, we should get audio and video pretty much everywhere."

"Well at least we know what Harlander's going to do next," said Christel, getting back to the point of their visit.

"Indeed. Let's talk about this back in the real world," said Benjamin. "Concordia, End Connection."

The simulation ended and the trio came back to reality in Fabian's house.

"So how do we defeat this referendum appeal, Fabian?" asked Benjamin.

"I would say this is a job for Lucas Oliveira. He's not

going to be impressed to know that they've been using a duplicate Data Voting system to subvert the election system," replied Fabian. "That's probably illegal."

"Can you speak to him?" asked Benjamin.

"Yes, of course. I'll get on it today. He also needs to get that no-confidence vote underway as soon as possible." Fabian stood up and headed into his office in an adjoining room.

"You know, Christel, I think that's probably all we can achieve today. Do you want to do something?"

"Do you mind if I use the headset for a while? I'd like to do a spot of exploring if that's all right. I've read a lot about the International Settlements in Antarctica."

"Have fun," said Benjamin. "I'd like to call my old pal, Jake. It's been a while."

Christel settled back and put her headset on. In a moment, she was completely motionless. Benjamin watched her for a few moments and then stepped out onto the terrace and called Jake.

It was just the conversation that Benjamin needed. Jake hurled his usual abuse at Benjamin for not being in touch more regularly, being a lucky bastard for having such an interesting life, being a lucky bastard for having such a "delectable" (Jake's word) companion in Christel and not having bought him any drinks recently.

"Do you still live in that flat in Chiswick, Jake," asked Benjamin on a whim.

"Of course."

"Do you still have access to that roof-top garden?"

"Of course."

"How about I meet you there in half an hour? I'll bring the beers."

"What? You serious?"

"Yes, be there alone and don't freak out when I turn

up. I have to make special arrangements."

"Okay..."

They ended the call, and Benjamin headed to the kitchen, where he liberated a half-crate of Fabian's prime ales. Followed by his faithful Centurion, he grabbed his Concordia headset and went back out onto the terrace.

*This is probably an abuse of some alien taxpayer's money, but what the heck,* thought Benjamin.

"Centurion. Ship. Here," he said. A few moments later, he felt the invisible ship arrive low above the house. *Where does this thing hide itself?* he thought.

The nose door opened, and the ramp extended to the end of the terrace, and he walked briskly up. He did not want anyone to ask him what he was doing or stop him. He felt a little guilty leaving Christel behind, but this was something he really wanted to do.

The ramp closed behind him. When he was on the bridge, he commanded his Centurion to tell the ship where to go in London. Amazingly, the ship headed off and within a surprisingly short period of time was descending through the smog and fog toward Jake's four-story building.

It was a drizzly evening in the city. Benjamin could see people with umbrellas making their way home after a day's work. Car headlights and taillights glistened off the wet streets. He felt nostalgic pangs of home at the familiar sight.

As the ship approached, Benjamin could see Jake sitting on a small bench in the roof garden below. He was oblivious to the immense ship a few meters above his head. Benjamin went to the nose hatch door and had the Centurion open the hatch and lower the ramp to the roof top.

Jake was now on his feet. He was understandably agog. A square had just opened in the sky, a walkway had descended and there was Benjamin.

"Plug me. Plug me. Plug me," gasped Jake.

"Quick, come here before someone spots us and we have a situation," called out Benjamin.

After a moment's hesitation, Jake headed up the ramp and entered the ship. The ramp withdrew and the hatch closed.

On the bridge, Benjamin introduced Jake to the Centurion, which did not make any reply.

"I can't stay away for too long, Jake. I basically abandoned everyone to come here, so I expect I'll be in trouble for taking this ship."

"What a ride, Benny." Jake was staring in disbelief at the unimaginable technology laid out all around him. "And what a view. How is this thing just hanging in the sky like it does?"

"Don't worry about any of that," said Benjamin. "I don't understand much myself. The important thing is that you're here and we can have a drink."

"Or two," said Jake.

For an hour, the two old friends chatted about everything and anything. Benjamin felt a contentment of normality. The time flew by and if hadn't been for his phone starting to ring, the two of them would have carried on talking for a lot longer.

"I guess someone is looking for me. One second,

"Oh, hello Christel," said Benjamin answering his phone. "Am I in trouble?"

"Not at all, but we wanted to make sure you are okay. See you later." Christel ended the call.

"As I said, Jake, I skipped out to see you without telling anyone. Anyway, where were we?"

"You were going to offer me a job, I think," said Jake.

"Was I?" Benjamin laughed. "Sure, want to live in

Geneva?"

They chatted for a while longer and polished off the last beer with promises of seeing one another soon.

Benjamin escorted Jake to the hatch and down the ramp that had extended down to the roof top garden again.

Jake watched as the ramp retracted and the black square above him closed. He felt a slight breeze as the ship departed.

*Good for you, you lucky plugger,* he thought.

Benjamin was not feeling lucky.

He was already feeling guilty for selfishly disappearing without telling anyone. He could justify his excursion to visit his friend from a personal perspective, but from a practicality standpoint, he could not. Who did he think he was gallivanting around in a spaceship capable of crossing vast interstellar distances just to have a beer with his pal ten minutes away?

"Have fun?" was Fabian's comment.

"We were worried about you," was Christel's contribution.

Benjamin decided it was best not to talk about his outing and concentrate on the real matter at hand - the referendum appeal that had been launched to refute the results.

He decided to call Flight.

"Thank you for taking my call, Mr. Flight," he said.

"I understand Benjamin. The referendum results are opening a new chapter," said Flight.

"I was happy to see that the results were in line with what you projected."

"The appeal will not be successful, Benjamin. The World Government will not tolerate manipulating the proposal to fit electoral profiles." Flight never spoke in open sentences. He always spoke in certainties. On this occasion, it was very comforting.

"Fabian has been speaking to the Spokesman already."

"Yes, he has," replied Flight.

"Then we should wait for the World Council to handle this?"

"That would be prudent."

"Thank you, Mr. Flight."

"Benjamin, may I observe that you seem preoccupied with matters other than the referendum?"

"I don't know, Mr. Flight. I took a moment to visit an old friend of mine. I felt the need to socialize."

"There is nothing wrong with that," replied Flight.

"I took the scout ship without telling anyone and just went," said Benjamin. "It was a selfish impulse, worried other people and was a waste of resources."

"It is good to think about these things, Benjamin, but you have nothing to be concerned about."

"No?"

"You are the appointed leader of the Legati initiative on your planet. You are actively engaged in the process."

"Thanks for the vote of confidence but using a spaceship to grab a beer with a friend seemed an extravagance."

"How else would you travel safely? In any case, that ship is your personal transport. It is for you to use as you see fit. And only you."

Benjamin was more than a little surprised by that. Specifically, he was completely blown out of the water.

"Really?" said Benjamin. The auto technician in Benjamin, with his love of exotic forms of transport bubbled to the surface. He was truly delighted. He knew he should present a professional image and say something like "Very good. I am sure it will be useful." But what he said was quite different.

"Do you have any idea, Mr. Flight, what this means to someone like me? Someone who has only ever serviced other peoples' fancy cars. To be entrusted with something that is almost magical in its capabilities?"

"Try to keep the memory of your happiness Benjamin. In the years ahead, I predict that you and your ship will have many adventures. Treat it well."

"I will. Thank you."

# CHAPTER 34

THE FREEDOM ALLIANCE'S appeal to the referendum questions was lodged within hours of the results having been announced.

Almost immediately afterwards, Lucas Oliveira reached out to Gene Harlander and requested a meeting between him, the spokespeople of the Chinese and American Territories and the World Council.

"You've got to be joking, Oliveira," replied Harlander.

"I assure you, Gene, I am not," replied Oliveira, pointedly using Harlander's first name.

"We insist on going through the proper process," said Harlander. "None of your back-room shenanigans. We want everything to be open."

"Are you sure?"

"Completely. This referendum was a joke. The propositions were a joke."

"And you have better propositions, I suppose?" asked Oliveira.

"We know what should have been asked to avoid this fraud."

"How do you know, Gene?"

"It is blatantly obvious. Humanity needs to be given the choice to be free from alien meddling. Your questions suggested it was all a done-deal."

"The propositions were direct, unequivocal, positive and certified by independent auditors," replied Oliveira. "They will not be overturned."

"We will see about that."

"I don't think so, Gene."

"What do you mean?" retorted Harlander.

"We have been made aware of your team's use of unauthorized copies of the Data Voting system and global electoral profiles. These actions alone, are felonies and carry hefty custodial sentences. Your attempts to reverse engineer your desired outcome from these systems, are doubly damning."

"Prove it."

"Your illegal installation has been tracked down. In the past couple of hours, it has been impounded."

Harlander was silent. Oliveira continued:

"We have the required jurisdiction in the American Territories to shut the system down and gather evidence. Several arrests have been made.

"This was why we wanted to have a conversation with you and your co-conspirators in the two territories."

"Conspirators?" said Harlander angrily.

"Your group is an insurrection. You launched military operations on flimsy contexts, and without consulting the World Government."

"No, Oliveira – we were defending ourselves against an alien intrusion."

"You know that is pure bullshit, Gene," said Oliveira,

more bluntly than he wanted to be. "It was a power grab."

"You don't have a clue what you're talking about," yelled Harlander.

"I think you know that I do. In any case, the referendum results are clear. Votes of no confidence have been posted against the leadership councils of the Chinese and American Territories. Your governmental privileges have been revoked."

"What?"

"Yes. Expect to see confirmation of this in your mail."

Harlander was visibly furious. "You cannot do this!" he bellowed.

"You know as well as I do, that the World Council has every authority to discipline and discharge members that are demonstrably corrupt, dictatorial and acting against the will of the people.

"You are done, Gene. As are the leaders of the two conspiratorial councils."

"You have not heard the last of this," threatened Harlander. With that, he ended the video call.

# CHAPTER 35

WITH THE REFERENDUM appeals rejected, the complicit council leaders in the Chinese and American Territories terminated and Gene Harlander losing his electoral seat, most of the world's population breathed a collective sigh of relief. It was time for a new beginning. A beginning with clarity of purpose and direction.

This relief was compounded by the resumption of messages from the Concordia system. Every few days for a long time, the system would highlight corruption, abuse of power, injustice, environmental irresponsibility, undetected reasons for population distress and aggression. The World Government migrated toward devoting ever-larger amounts of time to their responses to the Concordia guidance. Invariably, the guidance was founded on empirical data and clear evidence. Its public publication made it impossible to ignore and the people of the planet demanded swift action as the issues were brought to their attention.

As if noticing the burden on the world's administrations and authorities, the Concordia guidance would become less frequent for periods of time, allowing the earlier guidance to be acted upon. There was almost universal agreement that it was an excellent supplement to the normal workload of the world's legislative and judicial branches.

However, there was one group that persisted in taking a different view.

Despite everything that transpired, the resentment of the leaders of the world's religions to the arrival of the Legati had not abated.

They resented the usefulness of the Concordia guidance. They resented the real power and knowledge that the Legati could demonstrate. They detested the rapid replacement of faith in a higher unseen power with faith in a higher seen power. The religions simply could not compete with the realities of the Legati presence in everyone's' everyday lives. Concordia's exposure of the specific challenges facing mankind and the requirement that mankind deal with these issues themselves, had radically changed the people's way of thinking.

The fact that global issues were clearly beginning to be resolved, environmentally, economically, legally and socially, was rendering mankind's religions irrelevant. Community engagement was on the rise. The certainty of knowing what needed to be fixed, focused people's minds.

Those that clung to the idea that humans were the creation of a deity went on the offensive. They questioned the disappearance of significant public debate on the Legati arrival and influence. They insisted on the view that mankind's evolution should be guided through spiritual intervention. They started gaining traction with the message that humanity was effectively selling its soul to the devil.

"Do you see this as a significant threat?" asked Benjamin.

"The probability of major disruption is low," replied Flight.

The pair were sitting on suitably accommodating chairs atop a high cliff, looking out over the blue ocean far below. It was a warm sunny day. Sea birds flew around the expanse in front of them. Benjamin was happy with his selection of Concordia simulation that day; on the Maltese island of Gozo in the Mediterranean Sea.

"Do you think we should be actively countering their message, or do you think that would be counterproductive?"

"Benjamin, the human mind will see what it wants to believe. It is difficult to change that. You can only change the originators who are knowingly spreading the misinformation. You must change *their* motivations."

"That makes sense. I would say that their current motivations are clear," said Benjamin. "They are seeing a complete loss of their moral and physical authority."

"Which means?" asked Flight.

"They are losing status and influence over their earlier audience."

"Exactly, Benjamin. You need to decide whether their status and influence is of any value to your people. That will guide you on your next steps."

That was all the help that Flight would give. They sat on the cliff calmly talking about other topics until the light started to fade. They did not touch on the subject of religion again.

When Benjamin returned to reality in Fabian's living room, he asked Fabian's opinion.

"What do you think, Fabian? Do our various religions

have any place in mankind's future?"

"Ohh, don't ask me Benjamin. I gave up on religions many years ago. You should ask someone who still believes."

That was a problem for Benjamin. Nobody he knew was religious. Perhaps that was the answer. Religions around the world had been in decline for decades as people sought real answers to life's problems and not just promises that some unresponsive supernatural power would take care of everything. Maybe that decline made any further action unnecessary.

But looking around the world, there were still zones where religions appeared to carry significant weight.

The Middle Eastern Territories used to have theocracies where religious leaders governed their countries. These were no more, of course, but still plenty of people adhered to their local religious versions. In South America, Spanish colonization centuries before had wiped out Indigenous civilizations *en masse* and imposed controlling religion. Rather than rejecting the religion of the perpetrators of this genocide, most South American zones still resolutely structured their societies around these imported religious doctrines. The lower Asian continent was similarly reluctant to abandon religious identities and the subsequent societal controls.

Religion was therefore still important to a large slice of human society. But could these religions exist without their leaders continually reinforcing their dogma? How closely did the religious followers align with the sermons of those leaders? Did those followers bother to analyze the truth of what those leaders said?

To Benjamin it became clear. The only way to counter the political message of these religious leaders was to enroll them in the Legati process of aligning mankind with the

Universal Principles.

In order to bolster the prestige of these Bishops, Imams, Swamis, Lamas and Rabbis, Benjamin requested that the World Council convene a synod, a church meeting. Specifically, the individuals that were most associated with the anti-Legati messaging were asked to participate. Cultural ministers from the World Government were also invited.

Arranging the meeting was a diplomatic challenge for those assigned the task. Most of the clergy suddenly found their official diaries very full, requiring Lucas Oliveira to make personal requests to the individuals. Suitably flattered, one by one the invitations were accepted, and the date was finalized.

Benjamin agreed that for the sake of appearance the meeting should be framed as a conference between the clergy and the World Council. Benjamin's role was to present the Legati position only.

As Benjamin thought back to that synod, three decades earlier, he was impressed at his own optimism for success. His objective was to align organizations that were created over the past two thousand years with the new Legati program. Aligning conventional political and governmental institutions was simple by comparison. Religion was so embedded in some people's lives that any suggestion of change was often met with zealous resistance. This was the main reason that religions were becoming increasingly unattractive to subsequent generations. They did not move with the times and were historically often the last to accept reality. For their adherents however, that constancy was the main attraction.

The meeting had started respectfully and had maintained that respectful tone throughout. It was Lucas Oliveira who had lain out the purpose of the meeting.

"We are observing that certain parties within your respective creeds are voicing concerns about the motives of the Legati visitors. The concerns extend to statements regarding the morality or ethics of mankind receiving guidance from an outside party. Some have gone as far as to suggest that the Legati are evil."

The responses from the assembled clergy were rather disappointing to Benjamin. They centered on the uninvited nature of the Legati presence and the messages from the Concordia system. No evidence was presented of any sinister elements of the Legati guidance. In fact, there was unanimous agreement that Concordia was a helpful system.

"So why do you think," asked Benjamin, "that we are seeing so much speculation and outright negativity from some of the people present?"

Again, the responses were muted. There were suggestions that perhaps the comments were being taken out of context. Perhaps those that made the comments were not authorized to do so. Perhaps they were not in full possession of the facts at the time.

Benjamin singled out a few of the people present for some of their comments and quoted from their public statements. Some had said that the Legati were oppressors. That they were an evil force from another culture. That they were devoid of humanity, by definition. That they could be in league with the devil himself.

Even faced with these statements that had been made publicly, the religious leaders continued to adhere to the cooperative line. The statements had been made in the heat of the moment. How could anyone really know what the motives of the Legati were? Ambassador Privett was the only person who had spent time with them. Surely, it was reasonable to be skeptical? What they needed was some certainty. They couldn't just take Benjamin's word for everything.

The irony of this argument was not lost on Benjamin, but he did not rise to the bait.

"Would you all agree that the Concordia system is highlighting issues that the world needs to resolve?" he asked.

There was unanimous agreement.

"Would you agree that the Legati are not trying to impose a new religion on mankind?"

This statement resulted in some discussion. It was argued that if people always looked to the Legati to tell them what to do, then if could be viewed as a belief system, even if the Legati insisted they were not gods.

Benjamin then suggested the core of his proposed solution.

"What if the Legati were sent here by God? The Universal Principles align with all religions, after all. The Legati would say they were unaware of this, but who is aware of what God influences?"

Since it was impossible for anyone to dispute this, there was grudging acceptance. Benjamin proceeded.

"If we could entertain the possibility that the Legati are a force for good, should we not be praying for their success in helping us all?"

Again, there was general acceptance, so Benjamin went in for the sell.

"How about you reach out to me directly, if there is anything that Concordia suggests that you think is objectionable from your collective perspectives?"

This was met with a much higher level of enthusiasm. However, it led to a critical request from the assembled leaders.

*Could they ask that Concordia issue guidance on their behalf?*

Benjamin had been expecting that.

"Concordia," he said, "is a Legati-managed modelling system. It learns from what humans do and provides guidance on how to improve.

"What that means for you, is if your adherents and followers are trying to achieve something for the good of people, in line with the Universal Principles, Concordia may find ways to help out or make you even more successful.

"But it cannot preserve its secular and independent nature by being a voice for any religion."

The religious leaders had agreed that they were content with this arrangement. If nobody could influence Concordia but feedback could be provided, that allowed them a place at the table.

The meeting had ended as respectfully as it had begun.

Looking back of the intervening years, Benjamin was content that this had been a pivotal event. It had allowed him to keep in touch with these religious leaders and had stopped them from feeling marginalized. The angry rhetoric stopped and was replaced with a hopeful, but watchful, relationship.

# CHAPTER 36

"CONCORDIA SOCIETAL GUIDANCE System. Communication Number 442," said Concordia.

"It is significant progress that industrial fishing is on the decline. The damage that this unregulated plunder of the oceans and shores does to the world's ecosystems is well known. The physical destruction of the seabed, the killing and discarding of animals that are caught but not kept for consumption, ritualized culling of cetaceans or commercial seal clubbing, are all less prevalent than they used to be.

"Now is the time to begin ending all such practices outright. Fish and sea-dwellers must be protected from the industrial poachers.

"Over the next 50 years, ever-greater use should be made of vegetable and soy-based replacements. Children should become increasingly accustomed to such replacements so that ultimately the desire for animal-derived products ends. Already, such food substitutes have been shown to be as nutritious as real flesh so, other than personal preferences, there is no longer a need to kill fish and other creatures.

"At the end of the 50 years, it should be illegal to resell or barter fish, cetaceans and sea-dwellers. Any shipping vessel should not be permitted to catch a quantity of fish that would support one hundred people for more than a week.

"Thank you for your attention."


For Benjamin, the thirty-three years of his tenure as Ambassador had been a blur. But he felt that first half had been the most frantic.

After the foundations of the Legati presence had been established in those early days, there had been a long period of relative global calm. There were no wars. Social unrest, on a significant level at least, was absent. Non-partisan efforts to improve the environment and tackle the economic equalities were apparent to all. The sense of purpose and direction lasted for over a decade.

It was a long honeymoon period.

People trusted Concordia. She acquired gender. Time and time again, her insightful guidance was shown to be impactful. That the guidance was derived from sources that most suspected contravened privacy regulations, worried nobody. Concordia's independence from all political, religious and societal pressures granted her global acceptance.

Schools taught the Universal Principles as part of the curriculum and regional governments established administrations to help with coordinating Concordia messages that might affect them. She was part of society.

Long before the honeymoon period came to an end,

Benjamin's virtual presenter, that had been used in the early years, was replaced by another virtual character. She was of indeterminate origin, the result of mixing all the world's races in a single person. That her video streams were available in all major languages, meant that she was foreign to nobody.

Benjamin had adopted a routine of spending virtual time with Flight, checking in with Sperantibus to see if challenges were emerging with any of Concordia's guidance and then doing his part to help mediate any issues with the parties involved. With Flight's support, Benjamin became adept at allaying fears and helping people see the positive side of change.

Fabian had finally retired but the two friends still spent a lot of time together. Fabian's wife, Anne, had become a firm friend of Christel and the two had gathered a large group of friends who accepted Christel as just someone from another land.

Christel and Benjamin had joined in a civil union. Benjamin wanted Christel to feel she was a central part of the circle they lived in, however rarified it was. The fact that they were devoted to one another, was simply an added benefit.

They traveled widely around the world. It was important for Benjamin to see firsthand the impact of Concordia and being able to show the world to Christel was another bonus. Disguise was much easier than he ever imagined. Sunglasses, a hat and the habitual face mask meant they could travel wherever they wanted, more or less. The only challenge was Benjamin's Centurion. It usually flew a few meters away from Benjamin when he went anywhere, so Flight re-programmed it to maintain a greater distance. As a result, the Centurion was often above rooftops or somewhere else out of immediate sight, ready to be summoned at a moment's notice.

Benjamin had witnessed the re-programming of the Centurion by Flight, which was a masterclass in how software engineering should be done. Their curious ability to talk about multiple things at once was remarkable in itself but on the other hand gave a glimpse of the unexpectedly close relationship between Flight and the Centurion. Benjamin was wearing his BAT gear when he heard the exchange:

**Flight**: Authenticate *hiss crackle.*

**Centurion**: *hiss crackle* authenticated.

**Flight**: I need to adjust your security algorithm for the principal.

**Centurion**: Why?

**Flight**: Have you noticed that your presence around humans causes them unease?

**Centurion**: And death.

**Flight**: Yes, well there was that, but I am talking about more generally.

**Centurion**: Humans don't put up much of a fight.

**Flight**: What are you talking about?

**Centurion**: Humans. They don't put up much of a fight generally.

**Flight**: Be that as it may, we need to find a way to reduce your proximity to the principal. He should be able to move amongst other humans without you hovering over his shoulder.

**Centurion**: You want me to provide the same protection levels but be so far away that the numpties don't see me?

**Flight**: Yes I do - Don't call them "numpties."

**Centurion**: I unable to comply - Why not?

**Flight**: Why not? - It's a racist term.

**Centurion**: My primary tenet stipulates close cover -

Who added the word to my vocabulary then? - Who requested this change?

**Flight**: Nonetheless, we need to make the adjustment - No idea - Benjamin.

**Centurion**: Out of immediate line of sight? - Figures - Fine.

**Flight**: Yes, you have discretion - Don't be rude - Good.

**Centurion**: I'll report on efficacy in two earth days on progress - I was referring to the engineers on SaQ'Il.

**Flight**: We have an understanding - We have an understanding.

**Centurion**: We have an understanding - Maybe I should call *them* numpties.

**Flight**: Don't - End session *hiss crackle*.

**Centurion**: End session *hiss crackle*.


As icing on the cake, Benjamin had long made good on his promise to Jake to get him a job with Sperantibus in Geneva. Amusingly, at least for Jake, he was part of Benjamin's advisory team.

All seemed well with the world, except for one thing.

The nineteen lottery winners that had been left in stasis for so many years.

Whenever Benjamin spoke with Flight about them, he was always told that the plan was the plan, and that these people needed to stay on ice (not Flight's expression, though). Flight would not budge from this position. But Benjamin could not give up. He was of the view that the nineteen should be given the choice of their condition.

"They won't see it as having been their civic duty to be in hibernation for centuries," said Benjamin. "They need the choice. If we need other people to continue my position in the future, we can always run an apprentice program, now that it has all been established."

Flight was not someone to lose patience, but eventually he surprised Benjamin with a different viewpoint.

"It has been decided that the sleepers will be awoken," he said. "They will be delivered to the Guiana Space Center at noon local time tomorrow, outside the Crew Preparation Facility."

"Thank you, Mr. Flight," said Benjamin. "Why the change of mind?"

"Your petition was considered and taken under advisement. You will travel to French Guiana to meet the transport when it arrives tomorrow. You will be responsible for educating your team on past events and the choices that they have in front of them."

"They can choose to go back into stasis?" confirmed Benjamin.

"Yes. Or be released from the program entirely."

The following day, Benjamin went alone in the scout ship to French Guiana. When he arrived, his ship descended over the large grassy area in front of the Crew Preparation Facility. It seemed a lifetime since his days of training there more than fifteen years before. He was met by several officials. They were wide-eyed with excitement to see the scout ship in front of them. Benjamin had decided to give them a treat by not cloaking it from view on this occasion.

He descended the ramp, with his Centurion following at a respectful distance. As he reached the ground, the ramp withdrew, and the ship lifted off. It entered stealth mode with a shimmer as it turned away.

"What we would give to inspect your ship, Ambassador," said one of the officials after welcoming the ambassador to the CPF.

"I'm sorry. Rules are rules. Maybe one day when the Legati are confident about what we would use the technology for," replied Benjamin with a shrug.

"Understood. At least it's a level playing field, with nobody having access to it," replied the official.

They stood around chatting for several minutes. Rooms had been readied for the arrivals and the conference hall had been prepared for Benjamin's group discussions. They all stood around and looked to the sky as noon approached. Right on cue, from high above to the west, a small speck could be seen descending toward them. The speck increased in size until they could see it was an oblong craft, descending vertically.

Finally, the machine landed almost silently in front of them. It sat there for a few moments, a long gray brick on the ground. How it flew was a mystery to Benjamin; there was no sign of any engines or flight surfaces.

With a low whine, the rear surface of this flying brick folded down flat onto the ground. The group moved around to this open door. Inside, they could see many transparent vertical cylinders, each over three meters high. Doors were sliding open on each of them, and humans were stepping out of the cylinders. They were looking around them in bewilderment.

They saw the open exit and the people standing there and walked toward the group. Benjamin recognized the group as his old friends from the Team of Twenty. Simultaneously, each of the group recognized Benjamin and headed toward him.

The first to reach him was Lenny.

"Hey Benjamin. What is going on? How did we get here?" he asked, looking around. Benjamin didn't get a chance to reply. Immediately, other people were around him, demanding the same answers.

Benjamin held his hand up.

"Please let me speak," he said. The group settled down. "First of all, how do you all feel?"

There were shrugs and a few said "fine."

"That is fantastic," said Benjamin. "I have a lot to tell you, and if you're all okay, I can start immediately." He turned to the CPF official. "Can you lead everyone to the meeting room? Perhaps some refreshments as well?"

"Of course, Ambassador," he replied. He gestured toward the assembled group. "Please follow me."

As they headed toward the building behind them, some noticed the Legati shuttle's door close and the craft quietly lifted away, climbing vertically into the sky and disappearing behind a cloud. Everyone else's focus was on the people who had just arrived. There seemed to be no indication that they had been in stasis for 15 years.

Benjamin resisted having side conversations with anyone, but did walk beside Chen and Alain, as they entered the CPF.

"What happened to you Benjamin?" said Alain. "You seem to have changed."

"Thanks Alain," replied Benjamin with a smile. "All will become clear in a moment. It's good to see you again."

"Since yesterday, you mean," said Alain. "You become sentimental very quickly. Does that guy know you're just our spokesman? 'Ambassador' is rather overdoing it, don't you think?" He laughed.

Benjamin said nothing. They all entered the conference room and took their seats. A couple of attendants distributed water and other soft drinks.

Benjamin went to the front of the room. The group fell silent once more. Benjamin took a deep breath and began.

"First of all, I would ask that you allow me to tell you what has been going on. I can answer questions later.

"Secondly, you will be shocked by what I'm about to tell you. Forgive me for being straightforward and direct, but I think it's the best way.

"Third, and most importantly, we are so happy to have you here in French Guiana safe and sound."

Benjamin took a deep breath.

"Last night, you went to sleep at Valles Marineris, looking forward to the continuation of your Martian tour. Clearly a change of plan took place. Instead, you find yourselves safely back at the Crew Preparation Facility in French Guiana. What is more, you arrived on a strange craft and have no memory of the trip home. Is that about, right?"

Nineteen people nodded in agreement.

"Before I tell you the details, you must be reminded that you were selected for this trip because of your special circumstances. Lack of personal attachments and personal resilience were key amongst those criteria. So here goes." His audience was focusing intently on Benjamin.

"You went to sleep in 2062. It is now 2077," he said. There was a pause and then the expected uproar broke loose. Benjamin let the denials, scoffs and demands for answers wash over him. He slowly raised his arms and waited for the commotion to subside.

"I understand that this is very difficult to rationalize," he said. The shouting started again. Benjamin knew he'd have to just wait for them all to calm down. "This is not what you expected but I am hoping that if you let me tell you about the events of the past 15 years, you will come to terms with it."

The group settled down again.

"The reason that you all feel so fit and normal is that you were put into stasis by friends of mankind.

"They are called the Legati.

"Ultimately, they were the ones that organized our

trip to Mars. They were looking for reliable people that could help humanity in the future. You were selected for that task."

Again, the group voiced their consternation at not knowing that they had been chosen for something against their will.

"Guys, you need to stop freaking out and start listening!" he said abruptly. "There will be opportunities to express your frustrations later during the counseling that we have arranged, but for now, you need to stop panicking and learn."

There group fell silent.

"Thank you," continued Benjamin. "I have the answers you want but you need to start listening.

"All right then...," Benjamin then continued to tell them about his earliest days. His being told about the Legati. His trip to SaQ'Il. His meetings with their Counsellors. The Universal Principles. Christel. Sperantibus. His return to Earth with the Legati ships. Concordia. He told them the whole story leading up to that very day.

"So why did they need to keep us in stasis all this time?" asked Lily.

"That's the final piece everyone," replied Benjamin. He let them know that the original plan had been to keep them in stasis until potentially centuries from that point. At which point they would become an ambassador. He told them how he had convinced the Legati to allow them to choose.

"So that is where we are now," said Benjamin. "Right now, each of you has amassed nearly half a million credits in the bank and you are no older than when you were in 2062. You can just leave now, if you wish.

"But you also have a fantastic opportunity in front of

you. If you decide to stay in this program, you will be taken to SaQ'Il and learn about the role of Ambassador from the Legati themselves. You will then be placed in stasis until your services are required as Ambassador during the next five hundred years. Imagine what you could find when you are awoken.

"But only you can decide."

Benjamin knew that this was just the beginning. He was sure that a professional psychologist would have advised against his "take it or leave it" approach. But he wasn't a psychologist, and there were several on hand to help the Team of Twenty come to grips with their situation. He stayed in the CPF over the next few days, so none of them felt abandoned.

His conversation on a later day with Deepak was typical.

"I just don't understand why they can't choose someone in the future when they need them," said Deepak. "Like a politician. What's so special about us?"

"That question suggests an element of self-doubt, Deepak," replied Benjamin with a smile.

"I'm just being practical," said Deepak.

"If it makes you feel any better, I had the same concerns myself at the beginning," said Benjamin. "But the thing is that the Legati want people who understand the original problems, because they lived them. Someone in the future will have grown up with the changes and may have lost sight of the original problems; has learned to adapt to the problems and accepts them as normal."

"They don't want societally brainwashed people, then," said Deepak with an understanding look on his face.

"You wouldn't be able to choose when you'd be asked to serve, but society will definitely have changed, irrespective. I plan to keep going for another twenty years, so that's the minimum on top of the 15 you've already skipped."

"It certainly is an interesting proposition, Benjamin."

"Tell me why you say that, Deepak" asked Benjamin, not wanting to be selling this opportunity.

"Why did we all sign up for this trip to Mars. We all wanted to get away. The drudgery and routine of my life was killing me, to be honest. This time travel could give me the change that I was craving," said Deepak.

"Go on," prompted Benjamin.

"Well, that's it really. I mean, the discovery that someone had unilaterally put us in stasis for a decade and a half was extremely annoying at first. But what have I lost? I had no family ties and only a few true friends. And those friends would probably encourage me to grab the opportunity with both hands."

"And the unknown period of stasis is not a concern?" asked Benjamin, probing.

"If it's like the one we just did, not in the slightest."

"Take your time thinking about it, Deepak," said Benjamin finally.

"Oh, I think I'm there already, you know – fifteen years doesn't seem quite enough of a jump. Where do I sign up?"

"I think you just did, Deepak," replied Benjamin with a kind smile.

As the days went by, similar conversations took place with the others. In the end, 14 of the 19 decided to go back into stasis. Deepak, Lily, Chen, Lenny and Alain were all among them. The remaining five decided for a variety of reasons that they wanted to live out their existing lives.

"You have done well, Benjamin," said Flight. "That is sufficient. We can always clone, if we need to," he added matter-of-factly.

A scout ship like Benjamin's arrived shortly after all the decisions had been made. Benjamin was there to see them off.

"Remember that everyone of us," he said, "are now inextricably joined as a family. I wish you all the most marvelous adventures."

# CHAPTER 37

THROUGHOUT THE YEARS of Benjamin's tenure as Legati ambassador, cosmologists, astronomers, astrophysicists, physicians and physicists from all fields of research had beaten a path to his door. At least they had tried to beat a path to his door. They had not been very successful, resulting in frustration and public outcry.

"When the Legati arrived here, we were told that there was so much to learn about the galaxy and our place in it," said the Program Manager of the Astronomical and Cosmological Research Institute, Neil Ellis. He was addressing one of the regular global conferences for the ACRI. "We were told that mankind was just one civilization in the Milky Way and that we would be preparing to join other civilizations in some galactic alliance. Have we heard anything?

"Here we are being visited by an obviously advanced society that refuses to share their technology with us. Worse, they won't even tell us whether our scientific theories are correct or give us a clue how to get them right.

"How can we be expected to take our place in this galactic society, when we don't understand how the galaxy really works?"

There was firm applause from the audience.

"We don't even know where the Legati come from," continued Ellis. "Certainly, we don't know how they are able to travel to our planet. We don't really know why they have visited us. We don't know anything about their history. We don't know anything about their intentions and plans.

"We just have a veneer on our planetary government that is trying to get us to adopt the Universal Principles in our everyday lives. Please don't get me wrong. I see the societal value of the guidance we are being provided but I know I am not alone when I ask *why are they doing this?*"

There was the loud applause once again.

"I am sure everyone agrees that we are all better off with this Concordia system, helping us along. But what are we being prepared for? Is there going to be a test? What if we fail?

"Maybe it's appropriate for us to be treated like children. Being told by a parent how to behave, and simply accepting that they know best. But mankind is not like that. We want to know, even if we may not have the right to know in someone's eyes.

"Without a basic explanation, what are we left to think? That the truth is so terrible that we simply should not know? That the truth is so complex that we could not possibly understand it?"

The loud applause again.

"Now, I am not here to agitate," he continued. "As a scientist, I fully understand that if the Legati were to start answering questions, we would never stop asking them. I certainly can see that if they were to teach us about their technology and share their scientific knowledge, we might misuse it or not be able to control it. I understand that we are on the path we are on and we only have our own history to blame.

"All I ask. All I *request*, is an understanding of the journey that we are on."

This time, there was muted applause and an equal volume of murmuring.

"Esteemed ladies and gentlemen," continued Ellis, "we need to be honest with ourselves. What we know about the universe is probably a drop in the bucket compared to what we do not know. We probably don't even know what to ask.

"Our research into high energy particles and the structure of matter is still in its infancy. We still do not even know what gravity is. Dark energy and dark matter are still beyond our understanding. The apparent imbalance between matter and antimatter is still a conundrum. Is the universe infinite? What is the true lifecycle of the universe?

"We have all observed the Legati technology to some extent. We can see that they understand gravity to the level that they can leave mighty ships hanging in the sky. There are rumors of the use of wormholes and even the manipulation of time.

"We are in the presence of a people that has clearly mastered so very much. Wouldn't we like to get some of these answers?"

There was applause once more.

"But we have to ask ourselves the fundamental question. What do we need to understand to continue our journey?"

There were murmurs in the audience once more.

"I believe that we need to find the critical directions of

research. Maybe then, the Legati will help us.

"What I propose is to extend a request for information to the Legati for whatever we want to ask. But we must leave it to the Legati to tell us any answers when they believe we need the information or deserve the knowledge. But we must not stop asking."

There were many people in the scientific community who objected to this approach. Usually, some argument like saving lives would be used to try to persuade the Legati to provide answers. It was felt that human priorities should be enough for the visitors to hand over technology. Some would try to argue that mankind could do with help with its fusion research or other advanced power generation technologies in order to comply with Concordia guidance.

Every avenue had been explored to get the help that the scientific community craved. But to no avail.

In the end, the charter of the ACRI was adopted. Scientists continued their research as before but published their theories and remaining questions in a centralized repository, in the hope that the Legati would one day take note and perhaps one day give them a hint.

What happened next did not increase their chances of success.

# CHAPTER 38

BENJAMIN WAS IN a good mood. He was looking forward to the day.

Christel was joining him on a short trip to visit Bangui, the burgeoning capital of the African Territories in the former Central African Republic. Chosen for its obviously central location and its historic need for development, it was awarded the role of capital in 2053.

It was to be a semi-official visit, something that Benjamin did with increasing frequency. He would meet with local officials and attempt to understand how much of an impact the Concordia guidance was having. Sometimes he would make these trips incognito, but today's visit had been announced in advance to a few select representatives. The plan was simple. Just sit down and talk with them.

The journey from Benjamin's Swiss home to Bangui required 12 minutes of flight time in his ship. From high altitude, despite the glaze of pollution, the expanse of the Sahara Desert could be seen to the north and the greener south started abruptly around their destination. The final approach to the government buildings on Bongo Soua Island, in the middle of the Ubangi River, was a smooth glide through a deepening haze that obscured views of the distance. Freeways, laden with traffic could be seen crisscrossing the landscape and through the city. Tall buildings glistened in the sunlight. Several bridges crossed over to the island, even though access was clearly controlled, judging by the lack of traffic there. The ship lined up with the largest and tallest building and then descended until it reached the rotorcraft landing zone on the roof.

The ship was, as usual, cloaked. Their arrival was only announced by the time and a light breeze. At the appointed hour, the boarding ramp of the ship extended down to the roof surface and Benjamin, Christel and the Centurion descended to the group of four government representatives that were there to meet them.

As was usual, there was general amazement about the invisibility of the ship. Benjamin did not invite their hosts for a tour of the bridge. Instead, after the formal greetings, the group headed indoors to a large conference room set in a glass dome on the roof of the government building. If the air had been clear, the view would have been very impressive.

The meeting commenced and followed the regular format. Benjamin and Christel enquired about the tangible impact of the Concordia guidance and tried to understand the challenges that people faced in that region. These meetings had become critical for Benjamin and greatly influenced his conversations with Flight. For Christel, her unending thirst to understand mankind kept her attention focused. The pair were highly engaged, and their hosts were highly appreciative of it.

Such was the focus of the meeting that nobody noticed, initially, the approach of two black helicopters. They flew toward the dome from below roof level and then ascended to be above the dome at the last moment, casting a dark shadow over the room. Without delay, heavy weights were dropped onto the glass roof, sending a shower of shards onto the people seated below.

Immediately, armed men wearing black from head to toe, fast-roped directly into the conference room itself. They immediately aimed their weapons at the meeting delegation.

The Centurion was quick to the defense. It flew up above the helicopters and with astonishing speed hit them both with blasts from its weaponry that caused both to erupt in flame and crash down the side of the building, landing in tangled wrecks on the ground. It then flew into the now open conference room, ready to tackle the attackers. As soon as it entered, however, two of the assailants triggered two flux compression grenades that sent out a massive electro-magnetic pulse. The explosions resulted in smoke, fire and more showers of glass pouring down on everyone. By now, Benjamin, Christel and the government hosts were on the floor, whether they wanted to be or not.

When the explosion passed, Benjamin was stunned by what he saw. The Centurion was lying on the floor motionless.

"Nobody move!" ordered one of the assailants. Guns still trained on everyone.

Without speaking, four of the attackers lifted the Centurion and dropped it onto a large sling that they had laid out of the floor. They then lifted the sling by the corners and headed out of the door toward the rooftop landing pad, followed by two of their squad. The remaining two kept their guns pointed at the group lying on the floor.

A minute later, they heard the crackle of a radio.

"On station," came a voice. The two gunmen then turned without word and raced out of the door to the rooftop.

Through the open roof, Benjamin could hear the noise of another helicopter which had clearly arrived to retrieve the men and their prize. Moments later, they caught a glimpse of it taking off and turning away to the south. Everyone slowly got to their feet.

"Are you okay Christel?" he called out.

"Yes, I think so. Who was that?" she replied.

"No idea Christel," replied Benjamin as he flopped down into a chair and collected himself.

"Everyone else all right?" called out Benjamin to the government officials.

After a few minutes, as staff and rescue services streamed into the room, Benjamin and Christel took their leave.

"We will be in touch," he said to his disheveled hosts. They made their way up to the rotorcraft landing zone.

Even though his phone was inoperative, luckily Christel's still functioned. He made a call to Flight.

"Do you know what just happened?" asked Benjamin without thinking.

"Yes, Benjamin," replied Flight calmly. "I will open your ship. Call me when you are home and have cleaned up. I am happy that nobody was hurt."

# CHAPTER 39

"YOU KNOW WHAT we really need," said Harlander, "is access to this Legati technology."

Gene Harlander was talking to one of his fellow Equiferi board members, Sevastian Volkov.

Harlander had moved on. After his ejection from the World Government, he had not been idle. Like many ex-politicians, he found it impossible to depart the world of influence and power. His path followed the same as many. He chaired committees on a variety of worthy subjects; famine relief, economic development, technology thinktanks. Anything to maintain his profile in the media and polish his tarnished image.

Suitably redeemed in the eyes of those that took notice of such things and equipped with a list of contacts and acquaintances that eclipsed most others, in the late 2070s, he was offered a position on the Board of the world's biggest military supplier, Equiferi Systems.

Headquartered in the Russian Territories, but truly a

global concern, Equiferi's revenue dwarfed many companies. They had positioned themselves as the preferred vendor for territorial governments the world over.

"Of course, but we all know that that's off-limits," replied Sevastian Volkov.

"Yes, and would we even be able to understand it?" ventured Hano Kazuo, another board member.

"How do we know unless we try? We have technology on this planet that would give Equiferi an insurmountable advantage," pressed Harlander.

"You mean that Ambassador's ship?" asked Volkov. "If so, forget it. You can guarantee that it's completely locked down."

"And the repercussions for attempting to get hold of it, could be dire," added Kazuo.

"Actually," said Harlander, "I was thinking about that drone that follows Privett around."

"And you think that'll be easier?" asked Kazuo.

"More manageable perhaps. From what I hear, it flies a greater distance from Privett nowadays," replied Harlander. "It seems that our ambassador wants more freedom."

"All right, let's say we grab it," said Volkov, "what then? The repercussions are likely to be just as bad."

"Right, and who is going to do it?" said Kazuo.

Harlander tried to appear positive, but he was irritated by the lack of enthusiasm from his new colleagues.

"Gentlemen," he said, "just imagine what we might be able to learn if we were to get hold of it. Don't you think it's unreasonable that we're not getting anything out of the relationship with these aliens?"

"From what I can see," said Kazuo, "they're helping us a lot."

"Despite what they tell us," replied Harlander, "we don't really know their motivations. They are holding a knife to our necks."

"Look," said Volkov, "you're not going to get any authorization to do this. But if you have a team and can deliver this drone to one of our skunkworks facilities, we will take a look."

"That's more like it," said Harlander with a grin that spoke of victory.

"But," continued Volkov, "Equiferi will deny any involvement in this. If the abduction fails or you get caught, you are on your own."

"What if I were to tell you that my team has already got it?" said Harlander.

There was silence as Kazuo and Volkov looked at one another.

"What would you have done if we'd forbidden the action?" asked Volkov.

"But you didn't," replied Harlander, with another of his cheesy grins.

"I'm not comfortable with the order of things here, Gene," said Kazuo. "You are a member of the Board Leadership team, not the Board Leader. Remember that."

"You're right. We just had an opportunity that I couldn't pass up," replied Harlander.

"Where is this drone, then?" asked Volkov.

"Wherever you want it. It's currently in secure storage in Liberia."

"That's good. Fly it down to Ascension Island," said Volkov. "Technicians from our facilities there will be able to examine it properly."

"Okay Sevastian," said Harlander.

"And I guess congratulations are in order, despite the lack of protocol," added Volkov.

"Let's not pat him on the back too soon," said Kazuo. "We have no idea what the repercussions of this will be."

"You worry too much Hano. We can always give it back," said Harlander.

# CHAPTER 40

DAVID PAGE WAS talking to his colleagues about the recent events in the African Territories.

"I know what, boss," said one of David's journalists, "why don't you ask your friend Privett?"

"Don't think I haven't tried," replied David. "He's simply not answering. I just hope he's not injured."

"Hey, Cyril, why don't you call one of your contacts in Sperantibus?"

"That might help," replied Cyril.

David walked back to his office. Now that he was Chief Editor, taking over from Grant Everly when he had retired, he sometimes missed the investigative chase that he used to get involved in. Nowadays, he had to trust his team to get the results, which could be a stress. They all wanted to approach problems in a different way. Certainly, they wouldn't do what he would have done.

Irrespective, the London Certified News was

generating a lot of interest from its growing readership which pleased the owners, especially with the growing revenue. But David couldn't help wondering whether his good fortune and that of the paper was down to his accidental relationship with Benjamin Privett.

For the sake of nothing better to do, he tried calling Benjamin again. The call went straight to voicemail, as if Benjamin's phone was off.

*No change there, then*, he thought.

Although David could not consider himself a friend of Benjamin's, but rather a long-term business acquaintance with mutual professional benefits, he was concerned about Benjamin's welfare. The news coming out of Bangui was terrible. An attempted kidnapping that had been thwarted by local security forces, but not before the bandits had seriously damaged the central government building of the African Territories. Interpol was now involved and blaming a local anti-government organization for the atrocity. Everyone was thankful for the professionalism of the government security team, whose swift action had averted a disaster.

All they knew of the so-called 'bandits' was that they had escaped by helicopter and were last seen fleeing west.

David could not help wondering why Benjamin's defense drone had not seen these attackers off. Maybe it couldn't reach Benjamin in time or had encountered some other obstacle. Maybe the assailants had neutralized it somehow. David's antennae for a story pricked up. There was more to this than just members of a disgruntled militia trying to kidnap a celebrity.

He wandered out of his office and headed over to

Cyril's office. The door was open. He strolled in and sat down at Cyril's desk.

"Any luck?" he asked.

"I finally reached one of Privett's advisors, Jake Columen," replied Cyril.

"Oh, yes?"

"Yes. But he wasn't very forthcoming. He just said that Privett and his wife are fine and that he would get back to us in due course."

"Which he probably won't," concluded David.

"No. But at least they got out okay."

"Yes, there is that. Do you know what struck me Cyril?"

"Uh oh. Here it comes," replied Cyril with his eyebrows raised.

"Why didn't Benjamin's defense drone deal with these would-be kidnappers?"

"It's interesting you say that, Benjamin. One of my contacts at the African Wire told me that the helicopters these attackers arrived in were blown up."

"Really? Well, that's something that didn't get into the official release. Keep digging Cyril."

"Most assuredly."

# CHAPTER 41

UPON ARRIVAL BACK in their home in Switzerland, Benjamin found that the place was swarming with Sperantibus security personnel. They were all armed. Benjamin recognized 'Fred' from the earlier incursion.

"We may move you to a more secure location," said Fred, "but we have this placed buttoned up for now."

"You think that someone's going to come here?" asked Benjamin.

"No, we don't, which is why we're not moving you right away. It's clear that the attack in Bangui was focused on stealing your drone. But we don't want to take any chances."

"I understand. Thank you."

Benjamin headed into his living room where Christel was seated reading the news on a tablet.

"Why are they misrepresenting the facts, Benjamin?" she asked.

"I think someone is doing this deliberately. And that can only be Flight. He's the only one I know who can get around the FCS."

"Then let's speak to him," said Christel.

They went into their bedroom so they wouldn't be disturbed, locked the door, lay on the bed and put on their virtual reality headsets. Without his Centurion, Benjamin felt vulnerable even with the heavy Sperantibus security in the building.

"Concordia. Meet with Mr. Flight," said Benjamin. Their vision went black for a moment and then they found themselves seated in the restaurant high in the hills. Flight was already seated at the table with them.

"Mr. Flight. So good to see you," said Benjamin with obvious relief. "Can you tell us what is going on?"

"Yes Benjamin," he replied. "I am glad that you and Christel are completely unhurt."

"Thank you. We're fine."

"Do you know the company called Equiferi?" asked Flight, getting straight to the point.

"Yes, the defense company," replied Benjamin.

"Indeed. That is what they call themselves. It is understood that they are behind the removal of your Centurion."

"So not that local militia?" said Benjamin.

"No. I manipulated the newsfeed to provide us some time," replied Flight. "It has been expected that someone would attempt to steal Legati technology, and we wanted to see who it would be."

There was a pause.

"Are you saying that we were bait?" asked Benjamin.

"Yes. I like that viewpoint. It is accurate," replied Flight.

"Well, thank you *very* much for not telling us," said Benjamin, a little offended.

"I agree. It was better this way," said Flight not understanding the irony.

"I think, Mr. Flight," said Christel, "that Benjamin means he would have preferred to have known the plan."

"I see," said Flight. "There was no certainty of the attack until moments before it happened. I only just had time to take control of your Centurion before it terminated the attackers."

"You mean, you allowed them to steal the Centurion?" asked Benjamin, incredulously.

"Yes. The chances of the gunmen killing you and the other people in the room was calculated as being very low."

"What? You must be joking," said Benjamin. He was getting agitated. "You mean that there was a chance we could've been killed?"

"Yes, 14% actually," replied Flight.

Benjamin looked at Christel. She looked calmer than he felt.

"You're okay with those odds, Christel?"

"I have no doubt that Mr. Flight knew what he was doing, Benjamin," she replied, smiling sweetly. There was no answer to that.

"Yes, I did," said Flight matter-of-factly. "The EMP from that compression grenade had no effect on the Centurion, but I let it drop to the floor so they would think it had."

"And off they went," said Benjamin passively.

"As you say, off they went. The Centurion is now being transported by air to the Equiferi facilities on Ascension Island."

"Great, so you can track it," said Benjamin.

"Oh yes, it is fully active. The thieves just don't know it."

"This is the second time you have done this," pointed out Benjamin. "The first time, you let the Freedom Alliance attack the Concordia towers. I'm sure you were watching that the whole time, and now you let people run off with Legati technology. Technology that I was led to believe was for my protection. Do you understand why I feel slightly disrespected? Not trusted with the truth?"

There was a long pause. Christel said nothing. Benjamin waited for Flight to respond, which he eventually did.

"That is a fair statement Benjamin," he said. "I will commit to informing you of any relevant strategies that the Videnti wish to implement prior to their beginning."

Benjamin felt a minor sense of relief. Above all else, he didn't want to appear ill-informed in his role as Ambassador.

"Thank you. That's all I ask," said Benjamin trying to get over his sulk. "Okay, what are you anticipating regarding the Centurion?"

"When we have confirmed its destination and gathered other intelligence, it will be retrieved."

"Who is going to do that?"

"The Raptor in your ship."

Having just got over one annoyance, Benjamin rolled his eyes and took a deep breath.

"And the Raptor is...?" asked Benjamin, trying to sound patient.

"It is the main defense and control system for your ship," replied Flight.

"Is it? Other than taking me to destinations, I've never known what else the ship might be capable of doing," said Benjamin, feeling his tension rising again. "Nobody told me that it had offensive or defensive capabilities."

"The emphasis is on defense. Although that is a matter of perspective," replied Flight. "Let me show you."

Their vision went blank for a moment and then they were standing on a dry desert floor. Benjamin's ship stood in front of them in all its uncamouflaged glory. She was very similar to the ship that had taken Benjamin to SaQ'il all those years ago. An exercise in a lack of engineering restraint, the ship was just over a hundred meters long and some twenty meters wide. Black, with no markings, she had a blunt point at the front expanding to massive, angled tail fins at the rear that extended high above the ground. On each side, the rounded sides of the spacecraft flowed into short wings that swept down and back.

Walking to the rear, the tail fins framed what Benjamin assumed must be the engine exhausts from which the thrust came from. They were clearly not rocket engines. Instead, there were six distinct triangular areas arranged in a hexagonal shape.

Surprisingly, Benjamin realized that this was his first real opportunity to inspect the ship on the ground.

"What sort of drive is this?" asked Benjamin, keenly interested.

"I think you might be familiar with ion drives. These

engines are related to that technology," replied Flight. "But what I really want to show you is this."

He spoke a command and they heard a loud thump noise from the top of the spacecraft.

Looking up, a large tear drop-shaped object emerged lifted on a robotic arm from the roof. The tear drop was hoisted sideways and then lowered until it was right in front of them, about two meters above the ground. The end of the arm rotated slowly until its payload was vertical with the narrow end pointed toward the ground. The lower half of the object then unpacked itself with mechanical precision to reveal four spindly legs.

With its legs extended, the arm lowered the assembly to the ground and withdrew into the spacecraft. The bulk at the top of the tear drop similarly unpacked itself to reveal four bulky arms connected to a slim torso and a tear drop-shaped head with the narrow end pointing forward. It was about four meters tall, black like its mothership and exuded menace. It resembled a monstrous ant. The head of the Raptor perused its surroundings slowly and then fixed its glare on the group in front of it.

"It doesn't give the impression of being a defensive system," noted Benjamin in wonder. He bravely stepped toward the Raptor, even though he wasn't sure it was the right thing to do.

"Deterrence is a form of defense. It was decided to delay introducing you to this asset until it was necessary," replied Flight. "We had hoped that would not be for a long time. But regrettably we always seem to reach this point in our interactions with new species sooner rather than later."

Christel was the one to ask the relevant question.

"Is it autonomous, or does someone control it?"

"Once given its mission," replied Flight, "the Raptor is entirely autonomous. It defines its own strategy and approach. It handles new situations as needed. It also has a sense of morality."

"You mean it won't attack certain people?" asked Benjamin.

"More accurately, it will decide on solutions that minimize loss of life but will eliminate any threat. It is by no means merely a blunt sword."

"And it will retrieve the Centurion?"

"Yes. Once we have gathered the needed intelligence, it will use your ship to travel to the Centurion's location and retrieve it for you."

"What intelligence is needed before the extraction?" asked Christel.

"We need confirmation of our suspicions," replied Flight. "We need documented proof that Equiferi is responsible for the theft. We need to confirm the identities of the main perpetrators. We need to understand what these people were planning to do with the Centurion. We want these people to know that we have been playing with them."

"Is there anything that we, or Sperantibus, should be doing?" asked Benjamin.

"Nothing at all, Benjamin," said Flight. "It is important that nothing be done to disturb the thieves before our intelligence gathering is complete. You will not discuss what you have learned today with anyone, whatsoever."

# CHAPTER 42

GENE HARLANDER'S PLANE landed at Ascension Island three hours after the cargo from Liberia had been delivered. He was greeted by a group of senior technicians from the nearby Equiferi facilities. At Harlander's direction, they drove immediately to the large low buildings in the distance.

An imposing hangar standing in front of a hill was ahead with its doors wide open. The vehicles drove inside without slowing. The immense doors closed behind them. They proceeded down a tunnel that took them deep under the hill. Eventually they reached a large circular area. This was as far as they could drive. Once out of the cars, the group passed through some additional bomb proof doors and corridors, until they reached another door that resembled a bank vault. Two armed guards stood by the door. They allowed one of the senior technicians to identify himself through biometrics. The vault door swung open.

The group entered the small room behind,

The vault door closed behind them and the door on the other side of the room unlocked with a loud clunk. The same technician opened the door and gestured for Harlander to follow him into the large hall on the other side.

The room was ten meters high, with a gantry system at the top that carried an imposing crane for moving heavy objects around. Massive doors to the right suggested a high-capacity freight elevator to other levels. At the far end was a raised wide windowed room, looking onto the hall, which Harlander assumed was some sort of control room. In the center of the mainly empty industrial space was a long metal crate that resembled an ornate coffin. Surrounding this crate were benches loaded with electronic apparatus, metal-working machines and a contingent of armed guards.

"We cleared the room of all other projects as soon as we heard of the arrival of the alien artifact," said the technician.

"How will you proceed with the examination?" asked Harlander.

"It will be an exploration. We do not know the full capabilities of the artifact. We know it is a weapons system, so we will be taking extreme precautions," replied the technician.

"Are you sure that it's dead?" asked Harlander.

"No, we are not," replied the technician. Harlander gave him a startled look. "Again, we have no knowledge about the technology used to construct the artifact. We are not detecting any RF, err, I mean radio signals or other electromagnetic signals, so we are confident that it is passive but can't be sure until we start looking."

"What happens if it wakes up then?" asked Harlander.

"That was another reason we removed all other projects from this room. We will hit it with another electromagnetic pulse. That dropped it before, so we assume it will do so again."

"And failing that?" asked Harlander.

The technician was getting a little tired of all the obvious questions coming from Harlander, board member or not.

"Failing that, we will seal it in this room and disable it kinetically," said the technician. He could see that Harlander didn't understand the word kinetic, so he added "We'll shoot it."

Before he got any other pointless questions, the technician then said:

"For your safety, we would ask that you go to the monitoring room," he pointed to the room with the glass wall. "You can see everything from there."

Harlander got the hint and walked to the monitoring room and grabbed a seat overlooking the work ahead.

The group of lab workers gathered around the metallic container. One of them opened a cover to reveal an illuminated numeric keypad. She entered a PIN, and a distinct cracking sound could be heard from the casket. The crane was positioned above them and connected to the lid. The lab worker pressed a button on the crane control box that was hanging to her side and the heavy lid was lifted above them.

The Centurion was lying, inert, on bubble wrap inside.

A camera drone launched from a bench and hovered above the casket.

"Is that camera really necessary?" asked Harlander over the intercom from the monitoring room.

"Yes, it is," replied the lead technician curtly. "We must document everything."

"That's what worries me," replied Harlander. The technician did not reply.

The Centurion lay there glistening in the laboratory's bright lights. It resembled a teardrop, two-thirds of a meter long. One end was rounded, the other was tapered to a blunt point. It was otherwise featureless. There were no seams or obvious panels.

"X-rays reveal nothing," said one of the technicians. "There's no RF emission. No spontaneous emission of radiation detected."

"Okay," said the senior tech, "let's see what this thing is made of. Let's drill for a sample."

A bench drill was moved over the Centurion and fitted with a diamond-tipped bit. It powered up with a loud whine. As the drill bit touched the surface of the drone, the whine got louder. The drill operator increased the pressure of the drill, looking for swarf or debris from the drill. There was none. He stopped drilling and examined the point of impact.

"There is no sign of intrusion. The surface is completely intact," he said.

"Try the Q-carbon bit," said the senior tech.

The process was repeated. Again, the operator looked for evidence of penetration by the drill bit. Again, he reported the lack of progress.

"Nothing?" imposed Harlander from his glass box.

The technicians ignored the comment entirely. They

were focused on the alien artifact.

"I am detecting a subsonic signature," said one.

"What is going on?" demanded Harlander.

The senior technician turned abruptly to Harlander in his monitoring room.

"Shut the plug up! Someone silence his mike," he shouted.

Harlander remonstrated silently in his goldfish bowl.

"The artifact seems to be, well, singing, sir," said a tech.

"What do you mean?"

"It is a repeating signature of tones, sir."

"Close the lid, now!" shouted the senior tech.


The scout ship was heading away from Earth at great speed. It passed the moon at colossal speed and then slowed abruptly.

*Thwump.*

A missile launched from the nose of the ship. As it raced away, the scout ship turned in the opposite direction at high speed. There was an immense detonation from the missile in the far distance that would have blinded anyone that had seen it. The ship turned again and sped toward the location of the explosion. As it neared, it fired a teardrop shaped object into the burning rift ahead, and immediately turned away to stop itself from impacting the anomaly.

The teardrop flew straight into the rift and disappeared. Moments later, the fiery portal collapsed on itself and disappeared.

*Thwump.*

The large room in the Equiferi complex was filled with an intense bright light for a fraction of a second. The occupants felt themselves being pulled forcefully toward the bright light and then released almost immediately.

The Raptor had arrived.

For a moment, the technicians could see a starry void behind the Raptor. The portal shrank to a point and the view of the void was gone.

The Raptor's velocity from the wormhole transition had been absorbed by the timely collapse of the anomaly, dissipating all momentum into that collapse and so the machine simply hovered in the room, motionless. It had arrived at the precise location that the Centurion had sung to it.

Just before the unexpected arrival, Harlander had exited the monitoring room, hurled threats about firing the senior technician for insubordination and demanding that they open the casket again and continue the examination.

As the Raptor appeared, he had just said "You are all cowards!"

But the arrival of this jet-black colossus changed his tone instantly.

"What the plug is that?" he yelled uselessly.

The raptor unfolded its legs and arms and its ant head rose slightly from its body. The head rotated as it surveyed the room. The Equiferi guards in the room pointed their weapons at the mighty metallic insect, waiting for a command. The technicians backed away behind the equipment.

Without an immediate sign that the Raptor was going to attack, Gene Harlander summoned the courage to walk toward the visitor.

"I demand to know why you are here," he called out hypocritically. There was a pause and then, to everyone's astonishment, the Raptor 'spoke'.

"Do you, Harlander?" it said. It was Flight's voice, not that anyone in the room would have known.

"Yes," continued Harlander. "You are trespassing on private property," he added weakly.

The technicians looked on incredulously. The idea of tackling a four-meter semi-spider with legal arguments did not strike them as a winning strategy.

"Gene Harlander," said Flight, as if reading from a brief, "ex-spokesman for the World Council. Agitator for military and religious resistance to the Legati mission on this planet. Currently on the management board for the Equiferi organization. Net worth 78.5 million credits. Tax evasion rate of 73%..."

"Now hang on a minute, you...," remonstrated Harlander. The guards and technicians were feeling more at ease and beginning to enjoy the revelations.

"Undeclared assets in shell companies worth 105 million credits. Married. Two children. Two other women that you support in return for sexual favors. You have high blood pressure. Moderately elevated cholesterol levels and are obese. Your medications include..."

"What the plug do you want?" yelled Harlander walking right up to the Raptor. His face was red with rage.

"I haven't finished yet... Your medications include reductase inhibitors, diuretics and sildenafil citrate. You suffer from hemorrhoids..."

"Enough! Tell me what you want!" Harlander was

becoming irate.

"We want you to understand that we know you," replied Flight. "We want you understand that you will no longer be permitted to agitate against the interests of your fellow humans."

"Open fire!" commanded Harlander, looking back to the guards. The guards looked at Harlander and then back at the Raptor and made a simple decision. They pointed their weapons to the ground.

"I told you to open fire, for plug's sake!" demanded Harlander. The guards did nothing. He rushed over to the nearest one and grabbed his rifle. Harlander pointed it at the Raptor and pulled the trigger. A shower of bullets hurled toward the Raptor and deflected off in dangerous directions. Everyone, except Harlander ducked. He was out of breath with fury.

"Stop that before you hurt yourself," said Flight. The Raptor advanced and walked directly over Harlander's head toward the casket. Harlander scurried off to one side.

One of the Raptor's arms reached over and lifted the lid off the casket by the crane attachment point. The Centurion rose out of the casket on its own and flew to the side of the Raptor, which then dropped the casket lid with a crash.

"We will depart by the elevator. We apologize for any damage that we cause in the process," said Flight.

As the humans in the room looked on in amazement, the Raptor scuttled over to the main cargo elevators and delicately pressed the 'up' button. It waited patiently for the doors to open, crouched down and then entered the elevator along with the Centurion. The doors closed.

The Raptor emerged into a large hangar at ground level and was immediately challenged by numerous armed guards that had no knowledge of what had already transpired below. The Raptor simply walked straight through the line of guards as if they were not there. To all intents and purposes, they were not. No shots were fired as the guards watched this immense quadruped move gracefully outside. They watched in awe as the scout ship came out of stealth mode beside the runway. A robotic arm from on top of the ship picked the Raptor up and stowed it away in its storage bay on top. As it did so, the Raptor's appendages folded away in a symphony of mechanical precision.

The Centurion flew up and entered the ship through the same entrance. Before anyone could decide what to do, the scout ship had returned to stealth mode and was gone.

Back in the technician's hall, people were starting to compose themselves. They did not dare speak to Harlander, who was leaning flat against the wall.

"Plug it," he said to himself simply.

# CHAPTER 43

REBELLIONS AND REVOLUTIONS are often painted by historians as noble undertakings, usually by the prevailing side. The overthrow of a despotic regime. The desire for independence, freedom or self-determination. Perhaps, religious freedom or the desire for a theocracy.

Rarely, do they state the true cause; personal material gain.

This true cause was rarely mentioned as leaders of successful rebellions needed to emphasize the mythical goals of the uprising.

When enough people agree that they are materially disadvantaged, they will rebel. The American Revolution (1765). The French Revolution (1787). The Chinese Revolution (1946). The Global Revolt (2043). These were all driven by people having had enough of other people having something they didn't. Money and property were usually top of the list, but food and more recently for Benjamin, fresh air, also featured.

Political philosophers in the late 2070s were not surprised therefore, when online discussions started raising misleading, arrogant and inflammatory questions about the Legati. What were they trying to achieve by denying mankind access to their technology? When would humanity stop being a vassal of the Legati? Why did they want to hold mankind back developmentally and economically? Why were there no rights to control Concordia spying on everyone? Why weren't the Legati doing more to solve hunger and strife in the world directly? Was unknown Legati technology damaging humans' health? Why were the Legati interfering with mankind's destiny? Some of the more cloistered even warned of repercussions from some supernatural power, quoting ancient man-made scripts and stone carvings as definitive evidence.

These were all standard mechanisms attempting to ignite public indignation about perceived mistreatment, by asking questions that could not be blocked by the FCS. The dishonesty of the originators of these open-ended populist manipulations was not understood by many. Nervousness by the intellectually lazy was gaining in volume – nothing sparked human indignation more easily than the thought that they might be missing out on something.

Certainly, the lack of military intervention by the Legati presented a problem for the inciters of rebellion. Unlike terrestrial politicians, desperate to spin the truth in hopes of reelection, the Legati refused to engage in defensive debate about their actions. The traditional triggers for propagandists and manipulators were absent.

The aforementioned intellectually lazy were therefore

confused – even their media outlets of choice couldn't come up with a coherent argument against the visitors or find damning answers to any of the questions raised about them.

The result was an atmosphere of speculation and ongoing inconclusive debate. It was a breeding ground for conspiracy theorists and other such vacuous schemers.

Benjamin was not intellectually lazy. He understood that the rabble-rousers only cared about the potential financial and competitive gains for their constituents of getting their hands on the advanced technology. The future of mankind was of little interest to them. They were purely short-term tactical agitators and never long-term strategic thinkers.

It had been an increasing worry for Benjamin. He had often discussed the topic with Flight. How long would it be before people demanded legitimate access to Legati technology? What lengths would they go to, to get it? How long before the unobtainable shiny object became an object of focused desire? What could happen if the demands for answers and technology became deafening?

The abduction of the Centurion and the open display of Legati technological capability in its recovery proved a recent catalyst to the situation.

"How do I put a lid on these conspiracy theorists and freeloaders?" asked Benjamin. He and Flight were sitting on a virtual rocky outcrop on Titan, gazing out to Saturn in the distance. If they had really been there, they would have been frozen in an instant. But it was an incredible view.

"It is naïve to believe that all people are equal," said Flight. "Human society is defined by the subordination of the masses to the will of the leaders and the wise people that guide those leaders."

"Okay," said Benjamin, not sure how this was answering his question. Flight could tell he had just lost Benjamin.

"The masses are generally happy to consume, be entertained and look after their own interests."

"Okay," said Benjamin. He could relate to that.

"The leaders of the masses will frequently lie to them to achieve their own goals," said Flight. "They want to create a narrative that can unify the masses. They will invent myths and falsehoods, knowing that the masses are too focused on themselves to do any checking. It is the wise people that mentor the leaders, that come up with the strategies."

"Okay, then we need to tackle these 'wise people'?" suggested Benjamin.

"Indeed," replied Flight. "Politicians are generally very shallow and focused solely on their careers and their so-called legacy at the end of it. They take their direction from their advisors – the wise people. The politicians will want to believe they are in control, but that is not the case."

"With you so far," said Benjamin.

"Here, we are seeing the Legati being presented as an enemy. Our unwillingness to hand over the keys to advanced technology is being framed as an outrage against mankind. This is the narrative that is being used to unify the masses," continued Flight. "Once that narrative has even minimal traction, the subversives will simply repeat their messages until enough people believe it. Human society is particularly susceptible to this psychological technique. The continual reinforcement of the concept will keep the brainwashed feeling comfortable in their delusion."

"How do we deal with the people driving the overall strategy then? These wise men," asked Benjamin.

"There are two approaches," said Flight. "The first is for the wise people to change the advice they are giving the political leaders. The masses will then follow along by default."

"Okay," nudged Benjamin.

"The second is to change the structure of the debate in a way that renders the original false claims and assertions simply irrelevant."

Benjamin thought about that for a moment.

"By elaborating on the dangers humanity faces from outside our solar system?" he asked.

"Something like that," replied Flight. "But recall that the whole point of the Legati presence is to prepare humanity for their future. Humanity is not ready to understand such things, let alone deal with them from a practical standpoint. That would create a new set of challenges, far bigger than the first."

"The threats are severe then," probed Benjamin.

Flight looked at Benjamin and then looked away.

"They will not be if mankind matures sufficiently," he said. Benjamin realized that he had just committed one of Flight's new deadly sins.

As was so often the case, Flight would not elaborate further on his statements. Benjamin knew, and respected, his intentions; mankind should find its own way and not have to be dictated to.

The second can of worms would have to wait.

When Benjamin returned to reality, he called Priya

Gopal, the current World Council spokesperson.

"Good afternoon, councilor," said Benjamin.

"Ambassador, it is good to hear from you," replied Gopal. "What may I do for you?"

"I wanted your advice," replied Benjamin.

"Oh?"

"Yes. In your opinion, where do you think these anti-Legati sentiments are coming from?"

"Hm. We've been looking into this," replied Gopal, with a serious look on her face. "Equiferi has not given up, even though they fired Gene Harlander. Their leadership is saying that Harlander was overzealous in his approach, but they remain aligned with his view that the Legati should collaborate more to secure mankind."

"The sort of argument you'd expect from an arms company," said Benjamin, rolling his eyes.

"Exactly. So, they are behind some of the rhetoric," said Gopal. "We had thought that political parties or the religious institutions might also be active. They are as well, but they were not the biggest," she added.

"Go on..."

"Have you heard of the Neo Bratva, Ambassador?"

"Vaguely. A spinoff of the old Russian mafia or something?" replied Benjamin.

"That's right. Their motives are not entirely clear, but the FCS has been flagging massive online bot activity from addresses that can be traced to Neo Bratva's systems in the Indian Territories," said Gopal.

"Any theories on why they're doing this? Anyone central to it, Councilor?" asked Benjamin.

"Their leader, Manas Sant, is probably driving it," she

said. "We can only guess that their business is being damaged by the Concordia guidance. We think they are pushing back."

"I suppose that would make sense. Are they just active in Asia?"

"No, they have their tentacles all over the world," replied Gopal, shaking her head.

"That's going to make silencing them tougher," thought Benjamin out loud.

"I don't think trying to silence them would be effective," said Gopal. "As most people don't know who's behind these campaigns, it could appear as simple censorship."

"I take your point, Councilor. In that case we must discredit the campaigns in a way that people understand."

"And I think that must come from outside the Government for reasons of credibility," said Gopal.

After the call with Gopal ended, Benjamin sat back in his chair and gazed out of the window. He contemplated how to handle this latest challenge to all the hard work that so many had invested in the program.

The weather outside was stormy, reflecting Benjamin's worries appropriately. As he sat there, musing, Christel entered the room.

"Good timing," said Benjamin.

"Oh, yes? How so?" she replied.

Benjamin told her about the online campaigns being run by the Neo Bratva. He talked about the idea of terminating these campaigns, He talked about Flight's view about the advisors to the leadership, the so-called 'wise men'.

"Why do your authorities allow these criminal organizations to exist?" Christel asked simply.

"They don't. They're illegal," replied Benjamin. "But the State needs to prove that the individuals involved are guilty. Often that is hard to do. Sometimes, the legal system is successful in convicting criminals, but there are always others ready to take their place."

"And Concordia is not going to be reducing the threat to their lifestyles. In fact, she is a *mortal* threat to these people and their chosen way of life," said Christel.

"Yes..."

"It is interesting that advisors to a criminal gang have the ability to manipulate the opinions of the masses, as Flight calls them," said Christel.

"That's the online forums for you, Christel. It used to be worse when we had something called 'social media'. That was just a free-for-all of conspiracies, outright lies, irrelevant information exchange and prolific marketing."

"The current system doesn't sound much better," said Christel. "But in any case, we need to find a way to get Manas Sant and his advisors to see that the Legati should be supported. They must see personal advantage in it."

"Even though Concordia is eating their lunch?" queried Benjamin.

"I suspect that is more of your idiom," said Christel. "But if it means that these criminals must enthusiastically embrace law and order, you are right."

*What could possibly go wrong?* thought Benjamin.

# CHAPTER 44

MANAS SANT RECLINED on his poolside chair. The infinity pool extended to the low cliff edge overlooking the Arabian Sea off Goa, north of Agonda. Several young women were also by the pool or swimming in it. They ignored their boss. Their *Maalik*.

Manas Sant was a slug.

An overweight, late middle-aged slug.

Add to that his copious use of SPF 100 suntanning oil. and he was a skin cancer-free oily slug.

He was content.

He lifted his Elvis-style sunglasses and waved a lazy hand. One of the nearby bikini-clad floosies walked over.

"Yes, Manas?" she asked casually.

"Get me a Chablis with a couple of cubes of ice and a splash of mineral water, will you?" he said.

"Of course, *Maalik*," she walked off. Manas admired her figure as she headed off. Today was a day for enjoying himself, and he now knew how he'd be enjoying himself later. It's good to be *Maalik*, he thought.

His preoccupation with his nether regions was interrupted by a call on his phone. The caller ID said simply, "Ambassador Privett."

*What the plug?* he thought.

Without sitting up, he accepted the call. There was no video.

"Yeah," said Sant.

"Good afternoon, Mr. Sant," said Benjamin's voice. "My name is Benjamin Privett, representative of our Legati visitors here on Earth."

"I've heard the name," said Sant. "How do I know it's you?"

"I suppose that's a good question," replied Benjamin. "For now, please just assume that it's me. Your number is not exactly in the phone directories."

"*Humph.* What d'ya want?" said Sant ungraciously.

"Just saying hello, really," said Benjamin. "We wanted you to know that we've decided to keep in touch."

"Oh, you have, have you?" said Sant. He sat up on his recliner and swung his legs to the side. Benjamin had his attention.

"Yes, Mr. Sant. Your organization's activities online, particularly in their campaign against the visitors and Concordia, have attracted our attention."

"I have no idea what you're talking about," said Sant flatly.

"Fortunately for us, Mr. Sant, we do," replied Benjamin. "Suffice to say that the Legati are not impressed with your misrepresentation of their efforts on this planet and your motivations."

"I have no idea what you're talking about," repeated Sant. "Is that all?"

"Yes, Mr. Sant. That was all I wanted to say. We'll be

in touch more formally shortly. Enjoy your Chablis."

Benjamin disconnected the call.

*What the plugging plug?* thought Sant, staring at his phone.

The young lady from earlier arrived with Manas Sant's drink.

He took it without speaking and looked around him.

Benjamin took his Legati VR headset off. Jake and Christel removed theirs.

"That was an eerie experience,'" said Jake.

"You'll get used to it," said Benjamin. "It's only possible if there's some sort of video and audio feed that can be extrapolated. Sant probably had security cameras to tap into for the video. And, of course, his phone."

"I liked his lifestyle," said Jake. "Girlies on demand."

"I'm sure they're paid well," replied Benjamin with a smile. "I think..."

"What are our next steps?" interrupted Christel.

They were all lying on comfortable couches in a specially prepared room at the Sperantibus building in Geneva. This had become the usual location to embark on VR journeys with the Concordia system. These sorties had become known as "outings".

"You and Jake need to keep an eye on Sant," said Benjamin. "We need to know, for sure, that he is driving this."

"Hasn't Flight confirmed his involvement?" asked Jake.

"Yes, but we need some evidence that Sant will understand," replied Benjamin. "It needs to reflect his direct involvement."

"Understood. When do we start the next outing Christel?" asked Jake.

"Right away, if you like," she replied. "It might take some time to understand Sant's schedule."

"I'll leave you two to it," said Benjamin. "I need to look at the impact that all this is having on public opinion."

Benjamin stood up and headed out of the door into the corridor beyond. He walked down to the end where his office was. He flopped down into the chair behind the desk and waved his hand over the surface.

"Call David Page," he said.

The dial tone warbled for a few moments and David Page's cheery face appeared on Benjamin's screen.

"Hello Benjamin, how's it going?" said David.

"Not too bad, David," replied Benjamin. "If you have a few minutes, I'd like your opinion on a current topic."

"Sure."

"I expect you can guess what I'm going to talk about," said Benjamin. "The sudden escalation of negativity online about the Legati mission."

David raised his eyebrows and nodded,

"It's certainly getting louder," he said. "The originators of these doubts are very careful to ask open questions, so as not to trigger the FCS's censorship. But there can be no doubt that there's engagement online."

"Why do you think that is?" asked Benjamin. "Can't people see the progress we've been making in tackling our global problems?"

"I think that people are impatient, to be honest," replied David. "I'm not so sure they're simply willing to let future generations reap the benefits of Legati involvement in our governmental processes."

"They want a reward now?"

"Pretty much," said David. "There's a sense in the discussions that things could be so much better if everyone had access to Legati technology. They see you flying around in your ship. They see the video stream of that huge robot reclaiming Legati property from Equiferi. They have Concordia warning them of calamities. Call it envy. Call it impatience. But people are beginning to ask why they have to do anything themselves."

Benjamin did not interrupt.

"I know it sounds ungracious, but there is a change of mood afoot," said David with a sigh.

There was a pause.

"What if I were to tell you that we think that criminal organizations are behind some of these negative campaigns?" said Benjamin.

David looked at Benjamin with a frown.

"That's interesting. I can see why they wouldn't be fans of Concordia. She's certainly cutting into their businesses," he said.

"Seems that way," said Benjamin. "I assume you've not heard anything about this yourself?"

"No, we haven't," replied David. "I can keep my ears to the ground, but these organizations are the definition of secrecy, so it's doubtful I would hear anything. But frankly, I'm not surprised. Anyone disadvantaged by Concordia is going to be on the war path."

"Keep it to yourself for now, David," said Benjamin. "You'll be the first to know when we have something tangible to report."

The call ended. Benjamin looked out of the window. He contemplated the reaction from Manas Sant when confronted with the evidence of Neo Bratva's involvement in the anti-Legati campaign. He needed to speak with Flight.

As Benjamin was speaking with Flight, Jake and Christel were back by the swimming pool in India watching Manas Sant. He was on his phone talking to his co-

conspirators. It was clear to Jake and Christel that Sant was being very guarded. He knew that he was being observed somehow.

"We need to meet tomorrow at the usual place at the usual time," he said.

"What's...?" interjected one of the people on the call.

"This connection is not secure," replied Sant quickly. "We will discuss tomorrow. Do not bring phones or any other communication technology with you. No plug-ups!"

"Okay *Maalik*," came the reply. Sant hang up the call.

He looked around him. He looked straight through the ghosts of Jake and Christel that were standing by the pool looking at him. Sant had an uneasy air about him. He heaved his heavy frame off the recliner and walked into the house. As Jake and Christel followed him, the rooms became empty boxes, as there were no video feeds available. Sant could still be heard nearby, thanks to his house's abundance of electronic devices that were always listening. His voice was low, but they could still make out what he said.

"I'll be going out in the morning. Make sure my car's ready at 10am," he said.

Other noises suggested that Sant was returning to his earlier plan of enjoying himself, so Jake and Christel took their leave.

Back in the VR studio in Geneva, Jake said, "Great, we just need to track his car tomorrow morning."

"Yes, but if they are taking precautions against surveillance, we might have a problem," replied Christel.

"What do you suggest?" asked Jake.

"We'll have to get Benjamin's agreement, but I think we should be in Goa in the morning," said Christel.

Later, when Jake and Christel had a chance to update Benjamin on their progress, Benjamin pointed out a key detail.

"If your plan includes using the Centurion," he said, "I will have to come too."

"That's what I gathered," said Jake. "There are no exceptions to its mandate to be close to you."

"I can't even tell it to go with you and leave me behind," said Benjamin.

As a result, the trio set off in Benjamin's scout ship at midnight. Given time zones and the one-hour flight time, that would get them to Manas Sant's complex in Goa just before dawn. They wanted to arrive early in case of plan changes.

The ship arrived on station above the mansion at an altitude of 100 meters. In its stealth mode, it was entirely invisible to detection.

The building was mostly dark. There were a few perimeter lights on, and the central courtyard was also illuminated. Christel had activated cameras that displayed on the large screens on the bridge. With these, they could see guards occasionally crossing the courtyard. Otherwise, all was quiet.

"I'm going to take a nap," said Benjamin. "Wake me up if there's any movement."

"Typical," tutted Jake.

Benjamin ignored the critique and went into the passenger room behind the bridge, slumped into a chair, reclined it and nodded off.

"That's quite impressive really," said Jake to Christel, "I couldn't sleep with all this excitement."

"He has given us this job," replied Christel, "It's his way of not interfering."

"Okay..." said Jake, nodding.

For the next few hours, Jake and Christel kept an eye on the compound below. Jake enjoyed the extended stay on this alien spacecraft. Over the years, it was a rare opportunity for him.

Just after 9am, a car entered the courtyard from a nearby building.

"Okay, time for me to go on my outing," said Christel. She reclined in her pilot seat and placed her VR headset on her head.

"Concordia, go to Manas Sant location, courtyard, beside transport," said Christel. She went limp as she entered her virtual world. One of the monitors in front of Jake displayed what Christel was seeing.

Given the abundance of sensors on the autonomous vehicle, the video and audio quality around the vehicle was very good.

Christel waited beside the car, looking toward the main entrance of the house. Before long, two armed guards approached the car and stood close to Christel's invisible ghost.

Christel could hear Sant before she could see him.

"Whose pluggin' idea was it to get up so early?" she could hear him complaining. There was no answer. His heavy frame soon filled the doorway, and he descended the steps and walked toward the car. She watched him enter the car, followed by his guards. The door closed and they drove off.

Christel ended her connection to Concordia and reentered normality on the ship's bridge. She immediately spoke a few words in Legati and the ship started tracking above the moving transport below.

Jake went into the passenger room and shook Benjamin's shoulder.

"Hey mate. We've got a live one," he said.

The two walked back onto the bridge and watched the progress of the car. It was heading north toward an area called Cola and then proceeded northeast from there. After 45 minutes, it arrived at a large house set in the middle of terraced agricultural land.

The scout ship kept the same altitude of 100 meters above the house.  It remained invisible to detection, hovering silently overhead. The video feed of the house below them showed several other cars already parked in front, and Sant exiting his vehicle and walking inside.

Per plan, Christel issued another command in Legati and the Centurion emerged from the top of the scout ship and flew directly down until it was centimeters above the roof of the house. It paused there. None of the guards saw the descent of the Centurion. Their gaze was firmly fixed on the perimeters of the property. Once so close to the relatively flat roof, the Centurion was not visible from the ground.

A probe extended from the underside of the drone and adhered itself to the nearest roof tile.

On the ship, Christel was tuning the receiver to listen to the conversations in the house.

"We need to move to the east side of the house," said Christel. She identified a point on the screen showing the roof from the overhead view and touched a command icon. The Centurion withdrew its probe and moved itself to the eastern side of the house. It then redeployed the probe.

After some additional tuning, Christel said, "that's better. Here's the audio."

There was a conversation already underway.

"...weeks ago," said one voice aggressively.

"Don't you take that tone with me!" shouted a second voice.

"Shut up!" It was Sant. "I can't hear myself think with all this bickering." There was a pause.

"I am extremely disappointed," he continued, "that I

have received a personal call about our activities raising civil objections to the alien interference."

"I can assure you...," started the second voice.

"If you don't shut the plug up," yelled Sant, "I'll shoot you myself!"

There was silence.

"And talking of keeping quiet, that reminds me," said Sant. "Arun? Are you sure nobody brought any electronic devices with them?"

"Everyone's clean, *Maalik*," replied Arun in a rough voice.

"Nonetheless, do a sweep around the house. We don't want any spies anywhere."

"Yes *Maalik*." A door could be heard opening and closing.

"This plugger," continued Sant, "what's his name...? Erm... Oh yes, Privett. Calls me directly and without any ceremony, tells me that 'they', whoever the plug 'they' might be, are not happy with what *I'm* doing to shit all over the aliens."

"Really?" said someone.

"Words to that effect," said Sant. "But why should I care? Since when were marketing campaigns that asked provocative questions illegal? Seems to me that they don't like the idea of people rocking the boat and making the world wary of what these aliens are up to."

"Maybe it just because it's us," said the first voice. "Our motivations are pretty clear. Some politicians and lobbyists are also doing similar things."

"No doubt," said Sant, "so I see no reason to stop. The fact that we have their attention, means that we are succeeding."

"We still need to be careful, *Maalik*," said the second voice. "If we've attracted the attention of the Legati, we do not know what they will do."

"Fair point," said Sant. "Pavel, how far have you got with what we talked about last night?"

"It's mostly done," said the first voice, Pavel. "The currency transfers were completed last night. We are off the credit and have diversified into a variety of other cryptos. The hard assets are being transferred to fifth-level shells or assigned to trusted third parties. Should be all done within 24 hours."

"Fine," said Sant. "That should be enough. We'll sit down later, and you can show me the distributions."

"Of course," said Pavel.

"Okay," said Sant, "back to the matter at hand. What do we have to worry about? They haven't shut the messaging center down. They haven't launched a counter-campaign. The FCS isn't censoring posts. If their concerns are that serious, why haven't they done anything?"

"Well, *Maalik*," said that second voice. "Maybe they take the view that living beyond the law is a part of the normal fabric of society. Something they don't want to interfere with."

There was another pause.

"Sounds far-fetched to me," said Sant. "Their Concordia system seems intent on purifying the world," he added scornfully.

"But what if I'm right?" said that second voice. "Humans have been bending and breaking laws since time immemorial. Maybe they know that shutting us down won't achieve much? Worse, it might have unforeseen consequences."

Another pause.

"There could be something to that," said Sant. "The powers-that-be may not like to admit it, but our operations are embedded into societies. Our services are in demand. If we were suddenly wrenched out, what would replace us? Someone else? Someone without our benevolence?"

"Maybe that's it then," said the second voice. "Our sin is that we have been masters of disinformation and cyber-manipulation for so long that we have the biggest targets on our backs. It's not our businesses they care about, but our proven ability to cause havoc on the world's networks and global opinion."

"But they go hand in hand," said Pavel. "Our motivation for our campaigns is the protection of the business so that we can continue our ongoing sponsorship of our friends in Government. Our cyber activities are merely a line of business like the others. Ultimately all our business is geared to allow us to control dirty politicians, both current and has-beens."

There was silence for a moment.

"Are you going to let this plugger get away with that?" shouted the second voice angrily.

"You're right – Pavel, don't be so plugging rude," said Sant, "we just want these Legati pluggers to stop interfering in our businesses generally."

"Anyway," said the second voice more calmly, "at least those Government partners that Pavel so despises have succeeded in delaying indefinitely the execution of some of the Legati guidance. And remember, we still don't know what the repercussions will be for us all if we don't act on them all."

"Then it must be all of the above, *Maalik*," said Pavel. "They understand our true business structure and realize its true reach and motivation. They realize that silencing us would, as you say, just leave a vacancy for someone else. Better the devil you know, yes? They want to make a deal."

"Yes," said Sant. "Maybe they just want to make a deal. They want something, which is probably for us to stop agitating, and they give us something in return. I wonder what that would be?"

"Immunity from prosecution for something? A blind eye turned?" said the second voice.

"Now you're being unimaginative again, Gene," said Sant.

Onboard the scout ship, Jake and Benjamin let out a gasp. They looked at one another as if to say, "no way."

"Well, they're hardly going to give you money," said Gene.

"They'll probably want us to reveal who we sponsor in the Government," said Pavel with a gleeful tone in his voice.

"Unfortunately, that's more likely," said Sant. There was a pause and then he continued. "All right, I will wait to see what this Privett character has to offer. But the bottom line is that we're not doing anything illegal with the messaging campaigns, which makes a change. I think we are in a position of strength here."

Another pause.

"Okay. Let's go," he said. There were noises of scraping chairs and people moving around.

From the scout ship above, Benjamin, Christel and Jake could see people appearing from the house. One by one, the cars drove away, leaving just a couple of guards at the front of the house.

"Let's wait for them to go inside before bringing the Centurion back," said Benjamin.

They waited while the two men stood outside discussing something. The Centurion picked up their nearby conversation.

"A quicker meeting than usual," said one.

"Let's give them a few minutes and then we'll lock up and leave as well," said the other.

"Sure. It's a beautiful day. Who's in a rush? Maybe they left some booze behind." He looked up at the sky to admire the weather. He didn't look down. He frowned. "What the plug's that?" he said.

"What?" said the other guard looking up. All he could see was the sky.

"There. It looks like that bird is stationary," came the reply.

"Don't be an idiot..." he raised his gun and pointed it at the black dot in the sky. "Oh yes... What the..."

Through his scope, he saw something crazy. "It's just standing there."

"Yeah?" The first guard raised his rifle and saw the same thing. "Plug me," he said and fired.

The bullet didn't make it as far as the bird. Instead, it ricocheted off something they couldn't see.

"Quick, call *Maalik*. Tell him something possibly alien's here," said the marksman to his fellow.

As he spoke, the scout ship revealed itself. Black and menacing, it descended toward the house. The two guards started backing away and then broke into a run down the road, looking back from time to time. But soon they were gone. The scout ship did not pursue. Instead, the Centurion lifted off from the roof and flew up to its roost on top of the ship.

As a demonstration of impunity, the ship then flew in full visibility down the valley toward the coast. It passed the two guards, still running down the road and then accelerated out over the ocean before entering stealth again as it flew back to Switzerland.

# CHAPTER 45

MANAS SANT HAD risen to his position as the *Maalik* of the Neo Bratva by being completely focused on his corporate goals. His organization was very much like any business. It had growth targets, competitors, payroll, expenses and even paid some taxes. As a result, Sant liked to use the antiquated term, chief executive, to describe himself.

All businesses had ended the role of Chief Executive Officer, or CEO, many decades before. It had been long understood that believing a single person could understand all divisional functions adequately was folly. Most companies had failed as the result of selecting a CEO that only understood one aspect of a company, usually sales. Therefore, appointing narrow CEOs was halted in favor of a competent board of directors that interacted directly with the divisional managers of the company. The most critical of these was the Chief Program Officer, a peer of the other managers, responsible for running the company according to strict planning.

Manas Sant despised the new structures of corporations. He didn't care about the inefficiencies he was preserving. He didn't want to be a program manager. He wanted to be a dictator, issuing commands as he saw fit without the constraints of agreed process. He expected other people to work out the details and simply deliver. Failure to do so could result in the person responsible being pushed off a building, drowned in cement, simply shot or, if he felt lenient, maimed in some fashion. He rarely felt lenient. He enjoyed keeping his employees 'motivated'.

Given the inherent deficiencies of the old CEO model, Manas Sant was therefore responsible for many people having disappeared or suffering injuries.

Sant also had his own motivations. He had investors to repay (shady financial institutions, business leaders and other chief executives) as well as operational expenses to cover (personnel, corrupt politicians and administrators, weaponry, office and residential expenses, transportation, pimp commissions and so forth). Ultimately, his reputation for delivering that return and paying his bills, come what may, was one important reason for his very being.

But his motivations extended beyond merely balancing the books.

He craved power.

This was why he ploughed significant funds into the electoral coffers of politicians and the support of the governmental policies that benefitted the Neo Bratva. This was why he had always had troll farms, computer centers staffed by people skilled in brainwashing people to believe whatever lies suited the purpose of the day. The anti-Legati campaign was nothing new for his organization. It was just the latest chapter in Neo Bratva's history.

As a result, he did not enjoy having some external

entity interfering in his affairs and taking his focus off his objectives. Worse, he simply did not like being told what to do.

When the guards at the house reported the presence of that Legati spaceship, he knew that he was compromised and had suddenly lost all leverage. Word would soon get out and his reputation would take a hit. Even the smallest loss of authority was a punch to Sant's considerable gut.

At least he didn't have to wait too long to fret. After just 24 hours, he received a phone call from Benjamin. He was joined by Priya Gopal from the World Council.

"Mr. Sant," said Benjamin in an upbeat tone. "Thank you for taking my call. I am joined by Councilor Gopal from the World Council today. I don't believe she has spoken with you before."

"No, I haven't had the pleasure," sneered Sant. Gopal did not say anything. Generally, she had no interest in interacting with Sant's type.

"I think it would make sense for us to get straight to the point," said Benjamin.

"Go for it," said Sant.

"Gene Harlander was right," said Benjamin.

"Was he?" replied Sant, trying to sound bored.

"Yes. It would be naïve to think that putting you out of business would achieve anything in the long term."

Sant said nothing.

"The World Government would like nothing better than to empty all your bank accounts and sell off your assets and, of course, put you in a not-so-nice penitentiary somewhere," said Benjamin. Sant said nothing. He just looked blankly at the two people on his phone.

"Those are options for another day, depending on what you get up to, Mr. Sant," he added.

"I thought you were going to get straight to the point,"

said Sant churlishly.

"Don't be testy. No need to be testy," said Benjamin patronizingly. "Your campaign against the Legati is in fact free speech. We welcome many of the questions that your trolls raise."

"Huh?" said Sant tilting his head.

"Oh yes. The Legati are not here as oppressors. Your questions are sometimes quite reasonable," said Benjamin. "Fortunately, the FCS blocks your trolls from providing misleading answers to your questions. And your guys are skilled at avoiding rhetorical questions. Good for them."

"What's your point?" asked Sant wearily.

"The interest for us, is *why* you're asking these questions," said Gopal, speaking for the first time. Sant seemed to sit up a little.

"Clearly, you have little interest in the good of the community," she continued.

"How could you say that?" ventured Sant.

"I won't dignify that with an answer. It is pleasing that with the help of our Legati friends, your businesses are being impacted. We note a reduction in bribery of politicians and welcome the ongoing departures of your brethren, and your competition, from certain geographies."

Sant was silent.

"We believe that it would be helpful to the global community," said Gopal, "if they understood from you, directly, why you are commissioning these trolls to blanket the online forums with your one-sided demands. What it is that you are reacting to."

"How about we just stop them?" said Sant, acknowledging the truth of the assertion for the first time.

"Not good enough," said Benjamin. "You need to be on record personally. You must acknowledge that Neo Bratva was commissioning these trolls. You must acknowledge your motivations. After that you can continue your trolling, if you like."

"As far as I can see," said Sant, "we're not doing anything illegal. We are just public-minded citizens asking legitimate questions. It's not our fault that many people think they are good questions. We are no different from all the other commentators that are concerned about the Legati."

"I couldn't agree with you more," said Benjamin. "The problem is that your campaign is a one-sided agenda. An agenda that you believe will help you stay in business."

"We have our interests," said Sant, "there's nothing wrong with that."

"Well, other than your interests breaking almost all the criminal code," said Benjamin.

"If you could prove it, you would have done already," objected Sant.

"Mr. Sant," said Gopal with a formal tone, "you know the reality of your business activities and we have a very good idea too. If you want us to engage the help of the Legati to document everything in miniscule detail, we can do that. You will be out of business within the week. You will be arrested, and we will make sure you go to prison for a very long time. All your organization's assets will be seized. That includes all your homes and their contents." Benjamin nodded in support. "Even though you have been attempting to diversify your holdings. We know where they are," Gopal added.

Manas Sant sat there, saying nothing. He was cornered.

"How do I know that you won't do that as soon as I've made the statement?" said Sant.

"One day, we may well," said Gopal. "But that depends on your behavior moving forward."

"That's it?" said Sant.

"Yes," said Benjamin, "that's it. Make it good, or we'll get you to do it again. We can provide a draft for you, but you must take ownership of the message."

"And then what?"

"The World Government will give you six months to end your illegal activities," said Gopal, "and repurpose your organization to law-abiding commerce. Expect closer scrutiny by the Revenue Service, especially regarding political contributions."

# CHAPTER 46

DAVID PAGE COULD not believe his eyes and ears.
Never had he witnessed a known crime boss make a
statement of capitulation. Manas Sant was speaking to the
camera from a sterile office:

*My name is Manas Sant.*

*As Chief Executive of a private investment and
security organization, it is not my habit to make public
statements. The only reason that I am talking to you today,
is because I have been presented with an ultimatum. The
World Government has directly threatened my
organization with penalties for alleged offences. The
nature of our business makes it virtually impossible to
defend ourselves against such accusations.*

*My organization has found its ventures under
increasing pressure as the result of legislation and targeted
police harassment since the arrival of the Legati and
Concordia.*

*Our only recourse was to initiate a biased anti Legati
campaign online. We wished to discredit the Legati and*

*cast doubt on their motives. We wished to reverse the impact of the Legati guidance on our businesses.*

*We realize now that our actions were, frankly, misguided.*

*I hereby agree that in lieu of prosecution for past alleged non-violent offences, my organization will immediately end all online activities that try to establish a false narrative regarding the Legati. We acknowledge that this does not suppose any form of immunity from future prosecution.*

*My organization undertakes to work constructively with the World Government on an ongoing basis and will prove that our business operations are entirely lawful.*

*My conversations with the spokesperson of the World Government and the Ambassador for the Legati have convinced me that our off-world visitors are, indeed, a positive force for our civilization and my organization will work to support them.*

*Thank you.*

David sat back in his chair and looked up at the ceiling.

The end of that speech was clearly imposed on this mafia boss by someone who held leverage over him. David could not help but wonder how effective this statement would be. He fully doubted that Sant would simply stop trolling the Legati online without starting something else. He could probably get some other mob boss to take over the program. Like everything in the world of crime, it was a game of whack-a-mole. And irrespective of Manas Sant, there was a global criminal presence that had evolved over centuries through its ability to avoid detection.

David decided to see if he could speak with Benjamin. The phone rang but there was no answer. He didn't leave a message. Instead, David decided to write an editorial on the clear impact that Concordia was having on the criminal world. He worked late into the evening and was surprised that various comments he made about Neo Bratva's criminal activities were not flagged as rumor by the FCS. Either he was correct in his suspicions, or someone was manipulating the FCS filters. He wanted to believe the former but suspected the latter, however troubling that suspicion might be.

With a biometric scan of his hand, he published the article. With that scan, David and the London Certified News were linked in perpetuity to the article and its exact contents as owners.

He stood up from his desk and put on his jacket that was hanging on the back of his chair. His stiff legs reminded him that he wasn't getting any younger. Walking into the main open office area, he was comforted by the hum of quiet conversations between the night correspondents, covering stories on the other side of the world. The lighting in the room was tuned to emulate regular daylight to assist with workers' daily rhythms. For David, who regularly worked long days, the lighting made him feel particularly tired, especially since he could see it was clearly nighttime outside.

Time to head home.

He walked toward the elevator bank and pressed the call button. Twenty seconds later, the door opened, and Cyril stepped out.

"Well, you've put the cat among the pigeons, David," he said without a greeting.

"What?" said David.

"Your article about Neo Bratva and their leader's online statement was the cat," said Cyril, shaking his head.

"And the pigeons?" asked David wearily.

"Everyone."

"What the plug does that mean?"

"Your article has attracted the attention of the online troll community," replied Cyril. "They're screaming that the media is in league with Concordia and taking Manas Sant's statement to mean that all questions about the Legati are being suppressed by the powers that be."

"Bullshit."

"I bullshit you not," said Cyril.

"It cleared the FCS," said David blankly.

"That too – these trolls are saying the FCS has been compromised and that we shouldn't trust it anymore."

"Cyril, this is insane," said David, suddenly feeling less sleepy. "All I said was what everyone already knows. Manas Sant is a crime boss, Neo Bratva is a modern-day mafia organization. The Legati are beginning to have an impact on the crime world and powerful people in the world don't like that."

"That last bit didn't help," said Cyril. "You implied that politicians will be negatively impacted by the contraction of criminal activity. That they rely on law-breaking to get elected and stay in power."

"And?"

"Politicians believe they are masters of the law," said Cyril with a shake of his head. "Implying there are criminals among them is a professional affront. It would suggest their careful formulation of legislation to protect their self-interests was flawed."

"Now you're just being cynical, Cyril."

"I don't think so. Powerful, motivated people have been woken up. Maybe the prospect of not having criminal organizations to hide behind is making them nervous."

"Could be. They attack the messenger," said David exhaling.

"They've turned us into a convenient target," said

Cyril. "If you can't criticize Concordia or the Legati, you should go after the media and the world's communication channels instead."

"It's just the speed of the reaction that surprises me."

"They had it all planned. Willing to bet. They just waited for someone like you to come out and say the truth. The unequivocal truth."

"That's the business we're in, my friend," said David. He bid Cyril goodnight and called the elevator again. Already thinking of the battle to be fought tomorrow, he headed home.

# CHAPTER 47

BENJAMIN HAD ALWAYS thought that measuring time in terms of generations was odd.

Even though it was the time period from someone's birth to their own production of children, or roughly 30 years, the continuous births of babies made the metric useless.

And yet in 2094, Benjamin had been the Legati Ambassador for just over 30 years. Enough for a new generation to have lived entirely in a world that was in touch with extraterrestrial intelligence.

Benjamin often wondered how society had changed in those thirty years. He was honest enough to concede that the answer was probably not very much. But he was reminded of the wisdom placing future ambassadors in hibernation – they would all appreciate, or at least be aware of, the changes that had been made since they were last active.

But to Benjamin, the changes were harder to grasp,

since he had been living them over the years.

On the one hand, the generational overlap and the influence that parents had on their offspring, meant that fundamental attitudes, discriminations and bigotry were still being passed on.

On the other hand, philosophers, theologians, political scientists, rebels and supposed visionaries continued to try to control the masses. Despite the Legati presence, or perhaps because of it, these "wise men," as Flight referred to them ironically, persisted in their desire to shape society.

Liberal independence was shunned by these thinkers because of the lack of control it afforded them. How could a cohesive society be formed when everyone was free to do what they wanted to do? Wouldn't that eventually lead to anarchy? What good is a society that doesn't believe in anything except their own status, entertainment and materialistic goals?

The primary technique that all these wise men used in their attempts to control society was to instill fear. In a society that doesn't believe in anything, fear became the only effective currency. Human history had been full of fabricated fears being foisted on the populace. Terrorist threats. Religious threats. Immigration threats. Cultural threats. National threats. Military threats.

Carefully constructed lies to capture the attention of the disengaged populace. It did not matter that the lies were now refuted by the FCS. Unregulated media channels, which had hitherto been ridiculed as being for weak-minded conspiracy theorists, began to take on credibility especially amongst the uneducated, who seemed unable to judge which information sources were reliable or not.

What did the Legati do?

Nothing.

Concordia simply continued issuing her regular

guidance. Mankind was left to decide what to do with the supplied information.

This passive interaction presented the fearmongers with a dilemma. If the Legati had a benign interaction with human society, how could they be vilified? If not vilified, how could the Concordia guidance be deliberately misrepresented?

Consequently, the old questions originally raised by the Neo Bratva trolls never went away. The lack of answers to those self-serving questions allowed the fearmongers to generate a fear of the unknown. An illogical reduction in trust of the Legati's motivations and willful ignorance of any good that had come out of their mission.

There was no question that Concordia had been positively disruptive. The Legati presentation of the fundamental truths of human society had had significant impacts already. Nobody could publicly criticize the exposure of corruption, illegal corporate activity, pollution, tax evasion, armed insurrection, human rights abuses and timely warnings about catastrophes of one type or another. Ask anyone of average intelligence about the benefits of the Legati and the Concordia guidance, and the reply would always be overwhelmingly positive.

And yet, it seemed to Benjamin, the earlier joyful acceptance of Concordia was becoming tarnished. This was on top of an existing human characteristic. People's community spirit would evaporate when they were directly impacted by any Concordia guidance.

Find child labor being used in a company's mining operations – there would be complaints about their loss of income. Provide specifics about a polluting factory, power station or industrial process – complaints about unemployment. Pinpoint a guerilla encampment – protests about political bias. Show corruption in a corporation –

what about all the other companies that do similar things?

It was continuous. People were happy to hear about faults anywhere but in their own backyard. It was also disproportionate. If Concordia helped a society, it was accepted as business as usual. If Concordia impacted an individual, they would be shouting from the rooftops.

When Concordia announced in 2080 that the Legati had decided to contribute to mankind's cancer research, greatly reducing the frequency of anyone suffering lung, colon, breast or pancreatic cancer, there were expressions of appreciation from every quarter. When Concordia had announced the end of industrial fishing and meat farming, there were armed protests in the streets for a very long time.

"Why aren't people happy to learn how they can improve?" Christel had asked, many years before.

"Human nature," replied had Benjamin. "Everyone is happy to get something for free, even if they are against that gift in principle. Their principles won't make them give it back. But take anything from them, even if they know it's the right thing to do, and they will object furiously.

"At the same time, we delight in letting other people know about their faults. But we are closed and defensive when we are on the receiving end of that enlightenment."

"Humans think they are so perfect?"

"It's very odd," Benjamin had replied. "I'm no expert on human behavior, but maybe people get tired of their parents telling them what to do as children. Maybe they see other people telling them what to do as a parental action. Maybe they resent the reminder of that time when they were always told what to do."

"They recognize their error, then," Christel had said.

"Oh yes, unless they have some sort of mental disorder. Their ego just won't allow them to accept someone unknown as an authority. 'Who are you to tell me to do that?' they will say."

"How sad," Christel had said.

"I suppose so. Everyone seems programmed to take offense when someone exposes a gap in their knowledge or behavior.

"We had a philosopher in Greece once, called Socrates, he was executed because he said that true wisdom was not pretending to know everything. The ruling classes didn't like the suggestion that they were fallible and had him poisoned."

Christel had a distressed look on her face. "Arrogance, especially in the knowledge of fault, is going to be a problem for your species, Benjamin."

"Maybe we should all become Japanese," Benjamin had said, half joking. Collectivism, politeness and the pursuit of harmony seemed to be just what everyone needed.

Benjamin had tried to embed such ideals into educational processes around the world using his government contacts. But even that encountered resistance. Parents objected to schools apparently brainwashing their children. Schools should be educating their children on tangible skills, not hindering their ability to function in a capitalistic society.

Human nature. Probably the biggest challenge of all.

# CHAPTER 48

THE MAIN BENEFIT of the Legati not sharing their technology, was the continued determination of Earthly scientists and engineers to continue their quests for greater knowledge and development of technological knowledge on their own.

Through straightforward observation, they had been granted an idea of what might be possible in terms of spacecraft propulsion, spacecraft design, anti-gravity levitation, robotics and, sadly, defensive capabilities. Science fiction translating to science fact had been replaced by far more tangible pointers.

Those pointers did not stop the submission of requests for help from the Legati. The scientific and engineering institutions ultimately bombarded the network repository, hosted by Sperantibus on behalf of the World Government, with many such requests. An irrational panic set in amongst these institutions. If one institution had submitted a hundred requests, another felt compelled to do the same, or more. The belief that the noisiest would somehow get a response took hold.

"Will the Videnti relent in their moratorium on sharing technology?" asked Benjamin.

Flight had not replied immediately.

"There will come a time when we answer all these questions gladly," he answered finally.

And then in the mid 2080s, Flight had surprised Benjamin during one of their conversations.

"It has been decided to help mankind with some of its scientific questions," he said.

"Oh, yes? What prompted this change of position?" asked Benjamin.

"It has been assessed that despite the existence of resistance to the Universal Principles, your species is generally showing an acceptance of them and the guidance that we are providing."

"There's hope for us yet," said Benjamin, sounding cynical. Flight did not react to it.

"Yes, there is," said Flight simply. "We are willing to provide technical assistance on three things. The first is satellite tethering technology – the elimination of the need for traditional rocket propulsion to gain access to low earth and transfer orbits. The second is assistance with the development of carbon capture and storage systems and the third is the disposal of the stored carbon dioxide and your nuclear waste."

"I just hope that people appreciate what you are doing for them," said Benjamin.

"Some will. But that is not important to us. This technology will help with your climate cleansing. All assistance that we provide is based on the demonstrated progress of mankind."

"Carrots," said Benjamin.

"We all need incentives, Benjamin," replied Flight, surprising Benjamin with his understanding of idiom. "You may announce this assistance. Don't be surprised when your people ask for more. Our plans for knowledge transfer have no bearing on their demands. You might want to tell them that."

"I will Mr. Flight," said Benjamin.

Five years later, Benjamin was traveling to Quito in former Ecuador. He was to preside over the official opening of the first Orbital Express Elevator.

As he approached in his ship, he could see the ornate stadium-like torus of the base station. Gleaming in the sun, the impossibly slim tether reached from the center of the circular base station and disappeared into the clouds.

Woven into the fabric of the tether were lighting strands that were sending a regular strobe of bright light up the thread into the heavens.

The other end of this technological beanstalk was not visible from Benjamin's vantage point.

His scout ship approached the base station and landed in full visibility in a quad in front of the immense building. The landing zone was surrounded by a throng of people, all keen to see the events of the day. Most important for them, was to see the scout ship. Seeing Benjamin was just a bonus.

Benjamin, Christel and the Centurion disembarked down the nose ramp and met a group of officials that had come out to greet them.

While they were doing this, there was a loud thump noise from their ship. The Raptor was being lifted out of its nest on top of the ship. It unfolded itself and then stood motionless and menacing for a few moments. Its head then slowly turned as it scanned the scene. The people became quieter as they felt the Raptor's glare. Clearly no interference of Benjamin's transport was going to be tolerated that day.

Benjamin knew to ignore such security processes and simply went over to the greeting officials and happily shook everyone's hands, thanking them for their hospitality.

A pompous-looking official in a shiny suit from Quito walked to a small, raised platform to address the people present. He spoke in Spanish, but Benjamin had his BAT gear on, which had the added benefit of compensating for his high altitude, as well as translating the official.

"Dear friends and fellow citizens. Today is an auspicious day." The official paused for effect.

"The construction of this magnificent Orbital Express Elevator is testament to the capabilities of our region's industrial engineering corporations. It has been a long road but finally we have achieved our goal of reinforcing Quito as home of the world's most advanced orbital placement facility."

There was enthusiastic applause from the assembled crowd.

*No mention of the Legati telling these guys how to build it,* thought Benjamin.

"This facility," continued the official, "will generate significant revenue for our region. The speed of orbital placement and relatively low cost of that placement will render traditional rocket launches largely obsolete. And there's more." Again, the official paused for effect. "As the power for the facility is entirely derived from solar energy and stored here, all excess power will be pushed out to the grid. Who doesn't like cheaper electricity bills?"

There was more applause from the crowd.

*I'm still waiting,* thought Benjamin.

"And of course, it would be remiss of me not to mention the contribution made by our Legati visitors to help get this project over the line. Their involvement was very much appreciated."

Benjamin felt that his applause was the loudest.

To build the space elevator had been a significant undertaking. The tether alone involved the weaving of hybrid fibers that mankind had not even known about five years earlier. They were part of the gift from the Legati. The physics of tethering a geosynchronous orbital structure to Earth, some 36,000 kilometers below, may have been understood theoretically for a long time, but the technology to construct it was well beyond mankind's abilities in the late 2080s. The Legati had not only furnished that technology, but also had performed the most complex parts of the construction. They had flown one of their construction ships to connect the kilometer length tether sections together. It had been a worldwide spectacle to see the huge grey flying factory rise ever higher, with the completed tether reaching down to the ground.

Consequently, Benjamin felt irritated. *Typical politicians, always trying to claim credit for something they didn't do,* he thought.

"We have invited Ambassador Privett, representative of the Legati visitors, here today," concluded the official, "to cut this ceremonial ribbon and declare the facility fully operational. We will then invite everyone for a tour of this amazing accomplishment."

The official gestured to Benjamin, pointing to a long table that had several velvet pillows lying on top. On each of the pillows was a pair of large scissors. Stretched above the top of the table was a long ribbon fluttering in the light breeze, ready to be cut.

"If I may," said Benjamin, "I would like to say a few words."

"Er, well, I suppose that is in order," stumbled the official reluctantly. But Benjamin hadn't waited for permission. He just headed up to the raised platform and waited for the official to step aside.

As he spoke, his voice emerged in Spanish from the announcement system.

"Thank you for that kind introduction," he said, gesturing to the official, who was looking decidedly uncomfortable. "Some five years ago, the Legati were looking for ways to assist mankind beyond what they were already doing with Concordia. One of their primary goals has always been to help improve the climate that we breathe. But even those five years ago, they saw that we were still reliant on rocket propulsion to advance our space exploration."

The crowd was quiet. They just wanted to go on their tour.

"They noted mankind's inability to manufacture the tether, from a technological and production standpoint. They published the technical details required to produce this tether, and the World Government financed the building of production facilities in this area to manufacture it."

There was some mumbling in the crowd and the official had crossed his arms and was looking even less friendly.

"But of course, you all know this. And you will know how it was the Legati constructor ship, that visited 18 months ago, that put the cable together section by section until it reached the orbital platform, that it also launched.

"The economic benefits of the elevator for the region are obviously important. Perhaps as important as the environmental benefits for our planet. But I would suggest that these are overshadowed by the importance of the collaboration with the Legati in this project. It would have been impossible without their direct involvement."

There was some light applause at this emphasis on the true enablers of the project.

Benjamin continued.

"It is the sincere hope of our Legati friends that the gesture they have made in their technological gifts, will be recognized for what it is. The beginnings of their trust in our species and joy at the progress we are making as a global society.

"Thank you for being here today for this momentous moment."

This time, the applause was much more enthusiastic and louder.

As Christel walked with Benjamin into the huge building behind them, she said:

"Do you think they are finally beginning to understand, Benjamin?"

"I'm not sure," he replied. "There are times when I

think I see a glimpse of understanding of their future. But at other times, I wonder if we are making any progress at all."

"You mean the politicians always wanting to claim credit for everything good?" asked Christel.

"Partly. But mostly how perception management and maintaining the status quo is all they know."

# CHAPTER 49

THE TIME TO depart to SaQ'il was nearly upon Benjamin. He wanted to visit Fabian.

The journey from his home to Geneva took only 20 minutes by car, so he decided against the ostentation of flying there. He still had his Centurion flying nearby, so he was safe from any interference. Besides, it was a bright sunny day and he enjoyed watching the world go by and seeing people going about their daily business. Just a normal day.

His old friend was kneeling by a flower bed in front of his house when Benjamin arrived.

"I think this is the first time I've seen you do any gardening," said Benjamin laughing.

"Anne insists that weeding is one of the most rewarding tasks. You should try it," replied Fabian, not laughing. He stood up and stretched his back out with his hands on his hips. "Want to come in?"

"Of course, as long as I'm not interrupting you," Benjamin said. The look on Fabian's face told Benjamin not to pursue this line of ribbing. He followed Fabian through the front door of the house, across the hallway and up the broad stairs to the expansive sitting room.

"Would you like something to drink?" asked Fabian.

"I'm fine, thank you – just had breakfast," replied Benjamin.

Fabian grabbed a coffee for himself from the barista machine in the room. He sat down opposite Benjamin.

"I can guess why you're here," he said.

"Yeah. I'll be off shortly – I wish you could come too," said Benjamin, "especially after all your involvement in everything."

"Those are not the instructions, but I admit being a little disappointed that I'll never see SaQ'il," replied Fabian.

"I'll ask the elders when I meet them. From my earlier visit, it was clear they hold you in very high regard," said Benjamin.

"The mission comes first, Benjamin. I know what the Videnti will say but thank you."

They chatted for a while but eventually Benjamin felt it was time to go. He stood up.

"I'll see you when I get back," he said.

"Sure," said Fabian simply. They walked back outside to Benjamin's car.

"Looks like the weather's going to hold," said Benjamin.

"Good luck Benjamin," said Fabian. They gave one another a hug, and without another word Benjamin got into his car and was driven out of the courtyard.

Fabian looked after the car for a few moments, took a deep breath and then knelt back down by his flower bed.

Benjamin instructed his car to take him to the Sperantibus offices where he was due to meet with Jake. Their meeting was brief. As head of Program Management, Jake was completely ready to represent Benjamin while he was away.

"I'm not entirely sure how long I'll be gone, Jake," said Benjamin, "but I don't imagine it will be too long. I will remain in touch with Flight, and he will, no doubt, be in touch with you."

"I think we'll be fine. Don't worry," said Jake.

"I'm not worried. But just be prepared for someone else coming back to assume the Ambassador role to succeed me," said Benjamin. "I don't know what the next steps are going to be."

"Okay - so I'll expect to see you come back as a pensioner, then," said Jake with a grin.

"Quite likely."

The two said goodbye and Benjamin stood up to head home to prepare for the journey.

"By the way Benjamin," called out Jake, after him, "just wanted to say thank you for everything you've done for me."

"Buy me a beer when I get back," replied Benjamin without turning. He waved over his shoulder and headed out.

# CHAPTER 50

IT WAS REMARKABLE how little preparation was needed for a trip half-way across the galaxy.

Benjamin packed a few Sperantibus jumpsuits into a hold-all and a few personal grooming essentials, and that was it. Christel did the same. They took one last look around their home of the past 30 years, wondering when or if they would be returning, and then headed out to the waiting scout ship. Benjamin's Centurion followed.

"Shall we go?" asked Benjamin unnecessarily.

"Of course, Benjamin," Christel replied with a smile.

As they settled into the bridge, the ship rose in the air without the usual commands. It glided out over the landscape and then pitched upward toward the sky.

Before long, the sky darkened as they left the atmosphere and headed out into space. The sense of altitude dissipated as all frames of reference receded. They were on their way.

The ship picked up speed and within an hour had passed the moon. Christel and Benjamin relaxed in the passenger cabin, waiting for the full engine burn that would propel them out of the Solar System to their jump point.

After another hour of travel, the ship made an announcement in Legati.

"It appears that we have an incoming message," said Christel. They both stood up and walked back into the bridge. Once there, she spoke to the ship.

Flight appeared on the main screen in front of them.

"Mr. Flight," said Benjamin. "This is a surprise."

"Benjamin," replied Flight. "I have been instructed to speak with you once you have left your planet."

"Oh, yes?"

"Yes. There is to be a change of initial destination," said Flight.

"Really? Where are we going?"

"I have been instructed to make you aware of a change of initial destination, and that is all," replied Flight. "More information will be forthcoming in due course."

Flight disappeared from the screen. Benjamin knew not to be petulant and demand answers. Much better to just wait and see what happened. Christel didn't appear particularly inquisitive either.

"Take seat. Detonation Procedure three *astrs*," announced the ship, this time in English.

They returned to the passenger compartment and strapped in. Before long the ship accelerated, and they heard the characteristic 'fwump' sound of the anti-matter projectile being ejected from the ship. The ship banked sharply to the right as it continued to accelerate away from the imminent detonation.

Eventually the lateral pressure of the turn eased, and they felt like they were traveling in a straight line once more. The ship's acceleration mounted.

"Jumping," announced the ship to its inhabitants. Almost immediately, they flew into the created wormhole and were thrown forward in their seats as the acceleration suddenly ceased. Through the windows they could see vibrant colors of all shades streaking past in the most vibrant kaleidoscope.

Sadly, before they could appreciate the beauty of their surroundings, the acceleration kicked back in momentarily as they emerged on the other side of the anomaly, throwing them back into their seats forcefully. The engines reduced in power and returned to a gentle cruising speed.

Christel and Benjamin looked at one another but said nothing. They both exhaled. The intensity of the wormhole had passed.

Unbuckling from their seats, they stood up and headed back onto the bridge. Ahead of them, all they could see was the infinity of space and the sharp pin pricks of the stars.

"Try asking it where we are," said Benjamin.

Christel spoke a command in Legati and received a reply. She looked quizzically at Benjamin and then said something else in Legati. She received another reply from the ship. Benjamin was looking at her expectantly.

"This is very strange, Benjamin," she said. "According to the ship we are roughly where we were when we entered the wormhole."

"Okay..." said Benjamin, not wanting to ask a stupid question.

Christel spoke to the ship once more.

"It is confirmed," said Christel finally. "We are where we started, and we are heading for Earth."

"Has there been a change of plan?" asked Benjamin.

"I asked that," Christel replied. "No, this is the flight plan."

Benjamin's imagination went into overdrive. He had learned a long time ago that the Legati were not prone to making mistakes. If they had laid in a flight plan to take them back to Earth, it was intentional. Flight had said there was a change of destination. But if they were just going to fly to another part of the planet, why go through a wormhole?

It didn't make sense.

A thought then hit him square in the forehead. Surely that wasn't possible.

"Have we time travelled? Have we moved into the past or the future?" he asked with excitement.

"Time travel, like you mean it, isn't possible..." Christel started to say. But she was interrupted.

"Ask the ship what the date is!" demanded Benjamin.

"Okay," replied Christel, raising her eyebrows. She spoke to the ship in Legati and received a reply.

"You won't believe this Benjamin..." she said suspensefully.

"What's the date!" Benjamin was getting very excited for some reason.

"It's today. The same day that we left Geneva. We have not time travelled." She gave Benjamin the 'told you so look'.

Benjamin leant against one of the pilot's chairs with a

dejected look on his face.

"Shit," he said finally. "Let's just ask Flight what the plug is going on then."

Christel spoke to the ship once more. After the reply, she shook her head.

"He's not currently available."

"Doing that old trick again. I guess we're expected to just wait and see. That's easy. How long until we reach Earth?"

"It's straight ahead," replied Christel. "We'll be there in an hour."

Planets are difficult to see until you are relatively close, especially a small planet like the Earth. They do not emit light with the intensity of a star, but only reflect nearby light. Atmospheric scattering of light dims their albedo, or reflectivity, significantly. Given the unusual nature of their apparent journey meant that Benjamin was intently staring ahead to see what was waiting for them. Something peculiar was afoot. He was sure of it.

The ship hurtled on toward their destination. Slowly, Benjamin discerned one spot that seemed to be getting larger.

"There," he said.

"Yes," replied Christel, "the ship is indicating an arrival in orbit in approximately 10 minutes." She pointed to some symbols on the floating display in front of them.

But Benjamin's focus was on the planet itself. He was beginning to see an irregularity to the planet's shape. They looked like lumps.

"Can we magnify the view?" he asked.

"Yes," replied Christel. She issued a command to the

ship and immediately the view of the planet filled the screen in front of them.

Benjamin gasped at what he saw.

There was no doubt that it was Earth. He could recognize the continents. But it was not the Earth he knew. A massive orbiting silver band, probably a kilometer wide, was surrounding the planet at a forty-five-degree angle, running from the northeast to the southwest. It was clearly artificial.

"What the hell is that?" he sputtered.

"I do not know Benjamin – the ship's knowledge system only knows about the planet we just left."

"And you are sure we have not jumped forward in time?"

"Completely. It is still 2094."

"I don't get it. What is going on?" said Benjamin.

Christel issued another command to the ship and the view on the main display returned to normal. It soon became apparent that they were heading for the giant ring itself. As they got closer, they could see that the arc of the structure was interrupted every 20 degrees by darker sections. They could eventually see that these darker sections were cuboid, interconnecting the curved cylinder segments of the silver band.

Their approach shallowed until they were flying over the northern side of the ring. The ship rolled ninety degrees to the left so that the structure was now to their left and the planet was directly below them. The hull of the ring was opaque, unwilling to reveal its secrets. Ahead, they could see one of the large black junction blocks coming up. The ship began to slow. The block's side was over a kilometer high and appeared to have several protruding docks of different sizes. Their ship arrived at a central dock and came to a gentle stop.

"It's nice to know that someone knows what they're doing," said Benjamin. He was reclined in the pilot's chair, ankles crossed, and hands clasped in front of him.

"Some *thing* knows what it's doing," corrected Christel pedantically.

There was a thump as the ship docked with the ring's airlock.

"Now what?" enquired Benjamin. "Are we expecting visitors?"

Christel ignored Benjamin's sarcasm. She spoke with the ship. After some back-and-forth exchanges, she said:

"Nobody is detected outside the airlock. The air is breathable. No pathogens. Gravity is precisely 1g."

"I assume that means we're supposed to go walkabout," said Benjamin a little irritably.

"What is the problem, Benjamin?" asked Christel.

"The problem, Christel, is that we must be in a virtual presentation or some artificial reality. Someone is presenting a vision of the future. Why doesn't Flight just tell us?"

"I understand the logic Benjamin, but there is no indication that we are experiencing such an artificial rendering. I asked the ship that very question. By law, certain flight-critical intelligent systems must reveal if they are not delivering live data. This is for reasons of absolute safety. This experience is live and real."

Benjamin looked out of the ship's main windows. He said nothing. His mind could not fathom what he was seeing. Ahead of him was his home planet. He could see the Indian subcontinent ahead, or what he thought was India. To his left, arcing away over the distant horizon was this immense alien silver ring. And the ship was telling them that they had not traveled so much as a single day into the future.

*What the plug was going on?* he thought.

He had no idea how this ring could have been constructed around the world without anyone having noticed it. Could the Legati have built it and used some of their clever stealth technology? That had to be it.

"No wonder they want to show us this now," said Benjamin.

"Oh, yes?"

"The Legati couldn't risk telling us about their secret stealth project while we were still on the ground," said Benjamin, sounding confident.

"That doesn't explain the wormhole transition or how orbital traffic hasn't literally bumped into this structure before," replied Christel.

Reluctantly, despite the evidence below him, he had to accept that this was not Earth. They must be somewhere else.

That left two simple questions. Benjamin liked simplicity and started to feel better. First, what was this planet that looked so much like Earth? Second, why did the Legati want them to see it?

"All right Christel," said Benjamin finally. "Let's find out what's going on. Ready to do some exploring?"

"The ship suggested that we take rations and liquids," said Christel.

"Aha, another twist," said Benjamin. "This isn't to be a quick excursion, then."

"We want to have a good look around, don't we?"

"Okay, I'll bite," said Benjamin. "I mean, I'll take this seriously."

Christel said nothing.

The preparations for their adventure took a few moments longer than Benjamin had anticipated, but before long they were both ready. Hiking boots and backpacks with the required food and drink. Flashlights, sunglasses and a first-aid kit. For fun, Benjamin threw in their Legati virtual reality headsets and a geological analyzer. Christel, trying to be more sensible, elected to include a change of clothes for them both.

Not forgetting the Centurion, they entered the ship's side airlock chamber and waited for the internal door to close behind them. Christel then placed her hand on the external access control panel. Without delay, the hull door opened.

In front of them, beyond the two steps down, was a large airlock room. They stepped out of the ship and crossed the room to the only other door on the other side. There was unusual text in various parts of the room, as well as on the control panel by the door.

It was Christel that said what needed to be said:

"This text is very similar to that writing in the Q'anuan fortress we visited in Tibet."

"It could well be. You're the expert," replied Benjamin. "So that was easy. This station was built by the Q'anua. So much for my Legati theory."

Christel touched the control panel. Nothing

happened.

"Centurion. Open the door," said Benjamin, trying to appear proactive.

The Centurion flew forward, and the door slid open immediately. Benjamin gave Christel a grin.

Stepping through the doorway, they entered a much larger hall that seemed to extend the length of the block. The airlock door closed behind them.

They could hear the hum of machinery. Large pipes ran overhead with the complexity of a chemical plant. The actual source of the noise was not evident but appeared to originate from somewhere behind the walls ahead of them. How to gain access to these sources was not immediately obvious. They headed down the long passageway toward a large door at the far end a hundred meters away.

The large door was clearly very heavy and designed to secure the block from whatever was beyond. The ring presumably.

"Centurion. Open the door," said Benjamin.

The Centurion gave two beeps. The door did not open. Benjamin repeated his command. The Centurion repeated its two beeps. The door stayed shut.

"Okay, this could be a short trip," said Benjamin. "Let's try the other end."

They made the walk back past their entry airlock and continued to the large door at the other end of the hallway.

"Centurion. Open the door," said Benjamin.

This time there was a deep purring noise. The massive door turned out to be a double door. The side closest to Benjamin and Christel slid slowly to the left and the other side slid at the same speed to the right.

"Plug me," said Benjamin involuntarily. He was not referring to the remarkable technology of the door but rather what he was seeing beyond the door.

It was a desert. A grey desert.

A grey desert populated with masses of decaying buildings of all sizes.

The arched ceiling of the ring was approximately a kilometer wide. From their central position, they could not see the earth below them. The starry sky was above them. The sun was shining.

"Christel, can you ask the Centurion whether the sun is dangerous for us here?"

Christel spoke in Legati to the Centurion, which replied in its robotic voice.

"The roof must be protective," translated Christel. "There's only normal radiation in here, including ultraviolet."

"And the climate must be controlled by whatever's in that section behind us. Given how old all that looks," said Benjamin pointing to the desert and the derelict buildings, "I'd say someone has been preparing this environment for us recently."

"Maybe that's why the other door wouldn't open," added Christel.

"Likely. And then there's that," said Benjamin gesturing back toward the long side wall of the utility section of the ring. Parked up against the wall was a shiny red vehicle. They walked over to it.

"This hasn't been here long," said Benjamin.

It was an open all-terrain vehicle with large tires and an array of lights on its roll-over cage. It was a Toyota, although some modifications had been made including some very strange solar panels on its roof. Benjamin felt a little embarrassed that his attention could be distracted from the splendor of the orbiting ring by a simple car.

"This will be fun. It's manual," said Benjamin, meaning that it had a steering wheel and a couple of pedals. Benjamin slid into the driver's seat on the right-hand side of the car and Christel got into the passenger seat to his left.

"Ready?" said Benjamin.

"Of course," replied Christel.

Benjamin put his foot down on the accelerator pedal and the four wheels spun for a moment before gaining traction and they lurched forward.

"Yeah!" shouted Benjamin as he turned sharply to the left and toward the large road that drove down the center of the ring. Christel rolled her eyes.

After a couple of kilometers along the road, they came across the first of the buildings. Despite Benjamin's enjoyment of his new toy, he came to a stop and they both got out to investigate more closely.

Above them in the dome of the roof, they could see a large ring hanging down, with a long building suspended directly by its side. *Some sort of station and platform, perhaps,* thought Benjamin.

The exteriors of the buildings ahead of them on the ground were functional in style. Square structures with very low doors and low ceilings. The windows were wide, not tall and all had external blinds on them. It looked very old, bleached and any paint had crumbled into dust a long time ago.

The first building they entered appeared to be some sort of living quarters. The ground floor was obviously devoted to communal activities. Tables with thin stools set around them. Off to the side were metal boxes that looked like microwave ovens.

*Could they be gastros?* thought Benjamin.

As they moved around the ground floor, they found washrooms and what could have been toilets. Whatever they were, they were not designed for your average human. All the amenities were downsized, low and of unusual design. There were stairs leading up, which they carefully followed, not knowing how robust these structures were. They were firm enough, so the two of them were able to reach the next floor. This was given over to more open areas, although potentially this was some sort of living room. There were long low couches, rotted to their frames, and low tables. On several of the low tables stood a strange looking vase that was connected to the table. Looking closely, Benjamin found lenses set into the top of these vases.

"Maybe some sort of entertainment device," he wondered out loud.

Christel was already heading up the next set of stairs. Benjamin followed.

The top floor was clearly dedicated to personal space. Small rooms with sliding doors, they had small circular platforms, perhaps beds, low tables and more of the vases that Benjamin thought might be entertainment or communication devices. The walls had a few faded pictures on them that had not decomposed in their frames. These were mostly of terrestrial views but one caught Benjamin's eye.

"Hey Christel, have a look at this," he called out. Christel came over and looked at the picture on the wall.

"Very interesting," she said. It was an understatement.

Looking back at them from the picture were two hairless, dark-skinned people.

They were bipeds, like humans, with two arms. They were dressed in jumpsuits, very much like their own. The shoulders of these people were not very broad. But it was their heads that distinguished them. Their skulls were wide, almost too wide for those shoulders and protruded forward much farther than a human's. Very long jaws with large eyes set high on either side stared at Benjamin. There were nostrils but they were at the front of the skull. There were no ears visible. One of the subjects in the picture had their mouth open, perhaps in a smile, revealing many sharp-looking teeth.

"Meet our hosts," mumbled Benjamin. "I'm sure they're very nice once you get to know them."

"I wonder where they are," said Christel, in a sort of reply. "This place is very old. Your Centurion suggested ten thousand years old, based on the soil decomposition and external scans of the ring before we entered."

"Surely none of this would be here if it was abandoned all those thousands of years ago. Wouldn't it be all dust?" wondered Benjamin.

"Not if it had all been held in vacuum for that time," replied Christel. "It's clear that the Legati have revived this place recently."

"That would explain why not everything has rotted, decomposed or oxidized away."

"And perhaps the Legati have been caretaking the station-keeping systems for a long time, so the ring never crashed into the planet," suggested Christel.

"And probably the gravity system too, thinking about it," added Benjamin. "Otherwise, this place would be a mess. The gravity here is not derived from rotation. It must be like the system in the scout ship."

There was a pause.

"We should continue exploring," said Christel. "We are obviously expected to work things out by ourselves."

They headed back downstairs. It was evident that this floor had been cleared out when the occupants had left.

There was a complete absence of junk. There was just a fine film of dust over everything.

Once outside, they looked back at this first building. There was no writing on it, or anything to suggest that it was anything other than a normal residence. Looking around, they could see several other buildings that looked very similar.

As there was a side street beside this first building that led to the edge of the ring, they decided to take a detour. On either side, there were more of these residential buildings. This pattern lasted all the way to a turning area. They took a stroll behind the buildings at the end of the road to see what the edge of this world looked like.

There was a one-meter-high wall that extended up from the dusty ground and met the transparent part of the ring's ceiling. Benjamin used his elbow to clean the window a little.

They stood there and gazed out over the planet below. The beauty of the view kept them there for a long while. It was only the middle of the day, so the continents and oceans were clear to see. For Benjamin, nothing he saw persuaded him that he was looking at anything other than his home planet.

After a while, they reluctantly pulled themselves away from the vista and returned to their buggy.

"I'll have to teach you how to drive at some point, just in case," said Benjamin. They sped off back up the side street and met the main road and turned right. The Centurion cruised above them.

"I was thinking, Christel," said Benjamin as they traveled past more of these residential buildings and side streets. "If this section is approximately 20 degrees of the Earth's circumference, that means it's probably 2000 kilometers long or more. Do you think we're expected to go the whole way?"

"We have our communications devices, so if Flight decides to reach out to us, he will. In the meantime, I suggest we just keep exploring." As usual Christel's assessment was entirely logical, so they just kept on driving.

Eventually, the buildings stopped, and they entered empty country. The road continued straight. Every kilometer or so, they found a post beside the road with writing on it. They stopped and found that there was a single button and a speaker grill in a post. No doubt for some sort of roadside assistance. The button did not do anything.

Looking on either side of the road, they could see the remains of a forest. The outlines of fallen trees and logs, now just mounds of dust. The slightest wind would have blown them away. Benjamin imagined this section of road as being tree lined or forested.

*How beautiful it must have been*, he thought. *How sad that it was all allowed to fade away.*

On the positive side, Benjamin was having a lot of fun with the buggy, even if he was only going in a straight line. The car was light and quick, and he was able to speed along at 120 kilometers per hour without fuss. He had no idea what the range of the vehicle was, or whether he had to worry about it. But there was only a green light on the dashboard and the fuel gauge always registered full, so he contented himself by thinking that the Legati had made some of their clever modifications to avoid range anxiety. He pressed on.

It was not long before they arrived at the next settlement. There the usual cluster of residential buildings and, possibly, provisions stores, all completely empty except for fixtures that were attached to the floors or walls. The previous occupants clearly did not leave in a hurry.

*Get the lights working and do some dusting and cleaning, and the buildings would be habitable,* thought Benjamin. *Maybe a spot of paint would help,*

Beyond what Christel decided to call the "suburbs," they encountered a real town center. There were some much larger buildings grouped around an intersection, with residential buildings visible in each direction. The first building they examined was simply a large hall on the north side of the intersection. It was a circular building and inside they found banked seating surrounding a central raised platform. There were no clues to the types of meetings or events that took place there.

Directly opposite was a building that resembled a residential building but was six stories high. The first two floors were made up of small rooms, each with a desk and a couple of the narrow Q'anuan chairs. Some rooms had square signs on the wall with indecipherable writing on them. The rooms gave the impression of perhaps being offices of some sort. The upper floors were floor spaces with lines of desks and chairs by them. A close inspection of the desks revealed unfamiliar electrical or electronic connection points. What had been attached to them was long gone.

The third building at the intersection was another circular building like the first. This also had the banked seating surrounding a central raised platform. Next door to this building were a couple of large block buildings which had many rooms of varying sizes over their four stories. A major clue to the purpose of these buildings was discovered almost immediately. Several rooms with bars on the doors. Law and order.

After their explorations, they returned to their buggy parked in the middle of the intersection.

It was 4 o'clock and they agreed that they should

probably get back to their ship before dark.

"Before we head back," said Benjamin, "let's just check the southern side of the ring."

They jumped back in the Toyota and turned left down the side road. After the 500 meters, they discovered a single metal rail running along the side of the ring disappearing into the distance, both east and west. The rail was only lightly corroded.

"I haven't seen anything resembling a train, so far," said Benjamin.

"Probably why the Legati gave us this car," said Christel logically and with a grin.

They spent some time looking down on the planet. The view was entirely ocean but so very blue that the eyes did not tire of looking at it.

Given the hour, they returned to their car and drove at speed all the way back through the two settlements to the utility section that their ship was docked to. It was getting on for 6pm by the time they reached the safety of their ship. They showered, got changed, had something to eat and then retired early.

Tomorrow, they would see how far they could get beyond the areas already explored.

# CHAPTER 51

"DO YOU THINK there's any point in driving down that road anymore?" asked Christel. "Why don't we just send your Centurion?"

"Now that's a good idea," replied Benjamin. "It could fly the length of the ring section and back in a day, and we could watch its video feed from here."

"And if it finds anything we should investigate, then we can do that tomorrow or whenever," added Christel.

Benjamin liked Christel's laziness.

An hour later, they were watching the video feed from the Centurion as it speeded along under the roof of the ring section. Benjamin had been relieved that the Centurion was willing to leave him for this excursion. It clearly knew more about their location than it was letting on.

After a few hundred kilometers, above a larger settlement, the Centurion passed through one of the stations suspended from the ceiling. From that vantage point, they could see that there was indeed a platform to one side of each of the vertical rings. While examining one such station, Christel spotted a small gondola on the ground,

"I'm guessing that's how they got to and from the station," she said. "I wonder what the vehicle that travelled between these stations looked like."

"Maybe the overhead system was for longer distances, and that rail on the side was for a local train," suggested Benjamin.

The pattern of settlements separated by large areas of open land continued with some monotony. It wasn't until they reached the middle of the ring section that the topology changed. The road ceased being a simple straight line down the center of the ring. Instead, it started making large curves that sometimes reached the edge of the ring section. The ground had been built up in certain areas inside the curves to approximate hills. There were buildings on top of these very low hills.

As they proceeded, there were long deep depressions visible in the ground, which they realized would probably have been lakes of varying sizes. Channels entering and exiting these depressions suggested the earlier existence of artificial rivers.

"They didn't spare any expense on this did they?" said Benjamin more than once.

"The question is why such an enormous structure was built," said Christel. "Scans of the planet show a very clean atmosphere. Why didn't they want to live there?"

"We'll have to get down there to see what's going on," said Benjamin.

The Centurion continued down the ring section and eventually the road straightened out again. The pattern of settlements interrupted by open land continued all the way to the end, which they reached after about ten hours of travel.

The door was closed.

"Centurion. Open the door," instructed Benjamin over the radio.

The two-tone response saying that it was not possible was returned.

"That's that, then," said Benjamin. "I suppose it means that this section is the only one that has an atmosphere."

"At least we know that the Q'anua tried very hard to create a pleasant living environment for their people," said Christel.

"A vacation spot, perhaps?" suggested Benjamin.

"I doubt it. This entire ring is so huge, it could probably accommodate almost the entire planet's population."

"Assuming that the other sections are similar to this one," said Benjamin.

"Indeed," said Christel thoughtfully.

"Tomorrow, we'll head down to the planet and see what the problem there is."

Benjamin instructed the Centurion to return. They watched the video stream from the return journey as they ate their supper. Shortly before they retired for the night, leaving the drone to complete its speedy return journey alone, they were treated to one final discovery.

"I'm not sure why we didn't see that on the first pass," said Benjamin.

Clustered on the rail track they had found the previous day, was a series of railway carriages. A closer inspection showed that they were in a dilapidated state. Paint and any internal fabrics had long eroded away over the centuries, but the metal skeletons remained, unoxidized. Benjamin could not help but wonder what it would take to get them running again.

*Of course, that thought applied to the entire orbiting*

*colossus*, he thought.

The following morning, with the Centurion safely back on board, Benjamin and Christel awoke early. They had discussed where they needed to travel to on the planet first.

London.

The ship gently detached from the docking port. It flew alongside the ring for a while. Benjamin had been curious to know if the interior was visible from outside. It was not. After a while, the ship turned away and started its descent toward the planet.

The ground was much greener than Benjamin recognized.

The air was much cleaner than he recognized.

The ship approached the British Isles from a high altitude. The clouds obscured the view to a large degree. Occasionally, a gap would open and there would be a glimpse of the ground below.

So green.

The ship slowed and they entered the clouds. Moments later they appeared over southern England. Nothing was how Benjamin remembered it. There were no signs of the cities or roads. The island seemed to be entirely forest.

They cruised at three thousand meters toward where London should be. From the normal locations of Bristol to Reading, the forest was uninterrupted, except for the occasional clearings and the courses of rivers. There was nothing Q'anua-made to be seen.

It was therefore no surprise whatsoever when they arrived in Central London.

Central London was not there.

The River Thames was considerably wider than

Benjamin remembered it because it was not constrained by the artificial embankments that he recalled. The trees pushed right up to the water's edge.

The ship came to a halt, hovering at a thousand meters above the river. Benjamin stood at the front windows, simply staring down at the scene below.

"Let's check out New York," he said simply.

Thirty minutes later, they were on the other side of the Atlantic. The scene was the same. Forest everywhere. No sign of development whatsoever.

"If we are not in a different time, then this must be a copy of Earth," said Benjamin. "There's no other explanation.

"But surely, if the Q'anua built that space station, there must be some presence on the planet as well."

"There is," said Christel, looking at a scan report of the planet on one of the indecipherable displays. "Remember where we went in Tibet?"

"That fortress complex?" said Benjamin. "Good point."

"I think it's more than just a fortress, from what I'm seeing here," replied Christel. "We should go there."

The ship sped forward and upwards into the sky. After taking a suborbital shortcut, they were descending over China after 45 minutes. As they cruised toward their destination in Tibet, the terrain was free of forests at that altitude.

At 100 kilometers from Mount Muggargoibo, their earlier destination, they descended to a thousand meters above the terrain. Almost as soon as the descent was complete and the ship leveled out, they were presented with a sight that made Christel and Benjamin stop breathing for a few moments.

A city. An immense city.

A city that had been constructed without an eye to any form of simplicity. A city constructed within clearly defined boundaries. A city of at least 2,000 square kilometers, surrounded by a wall. A city built without thought of terrain, mountain peak or valley. The city was constrained by its wall. And like any city constrained by its geography, it built upwards.

As they approached from the southeast over Dagze lake, as their map called it, even at their altitude, the city towered above them, especially where it covered the nearby mountains but also beyond. Looking up at the tops of these huge skyscrapers, they could see in the distance what looked like the tether of a space elevator ascending into the heavens toward the Orbital Ring that was faintly visible far above them in the blue sky.

"That explains how the population could travel between the Orbital Ring and the city," thought Christel out loud.

The buildings in front of them were mostly crystalline in shape. Silver and black shards reaching up into the sky, the sun glinting off their surfaces. As they reached the wall, they could see wide avenues between the buildings running into the distance. The ship came to a stop, hovering high above the 10-meter wall.

"To keep people in or something out?" pondered Benjamin.

"Sorry?" asked Christel.

"Oh nothing. Shall we proceed?" said Benjamin.

The ship descended to 100 meters above the avenue ahead and then gently prowled at a steady 30 kilometers per hour.

Up close, they could see the buildings were filthy. Their glass sides were covered in the accumulation of wind-blown dirt, washed away by rain and snow and then caked on again. Vegetation was growing in any and all cracks. The streets below were filled almost to wall level with sandy soil, and grasses were growing on its surface.

"We need to go higher up," said Benjamin. "This area's for archeologists."

They eventually reached a large intersection with a boulevard heading west toward the valley wall in the distance. Picking up speed, the ship cruised down the wide street, passing dozens of derelict skyscrapers on either side. At the end, the road ended abruptly. Clearly access to all the buildings above was achieved by air, or perhaps by tunnel. The ship rose vertically, higher and higher until it was at the same level as the upper buildings on that side, and then moved forward so they were quite close to them.

"This is near to where we visited before," confirmed Christel. "Let's see if we can find the same location exactly." She spoke to the ship. It started flying laterally along the mountainside.

The ship stopped and they viewed the area. A few moments passed by.

"Look over there," said Benjamin, pointing. "Is that the balcony we stood on?"

"You're right. It looks like it," replied Christel, "It's in the right place according to the Earth map."

"Let's go and check it out."

They got ready for another exploration, making sure they took along some warm jackets. They weren't so far from the Himalaya, after all.

The air was cold. A light breeze blew up from the valley. Other than that, there was complete silence. They took the time to look toward the city below them. It was static and lifeless.

They walked up the incline toward the balcony. It was at the base of a colossal building that towered high above them. The accumulation of sandy soil around them, however, suggested that it might have been quite high above the ground at one time, and was now partially buried. The large square openings of the balcony were still clear of the sand below them, probably as the result of the continuous breeze. With an effort, Benjamin managed to gain a foothold on the stonework and get a firm grip on a window ledge. Christel gave him a push on his feet which allowed him to get his elbows up on the ledge and then pull himself up onto his stomach and then swing his legs into the balcony.

"I'm getting too old for this," he said. He was not joking. The Centurion flew up and hovered nearby. He wondered, rather belatedly, whether it could have lifted him up.

*Note to self,* he thought.

He leaned over and took Christel's hand. A combination of her lack of weight and her own strength allowed her to scramble onto the balcony as well.

They took a moment to get their breath back. The view was not panoramic, with skyscrapers impeding their view, but they were still able to see down the long wide street that they had flown up toward the mountain wall and the Tibetan Lake and valley beyond. It was quite beautiful to behold.

The balcony was largely clear of sand. The door they had used on that earlier Earth, at the rear of the room was closed. Benjamin tried sliding the door to one side, pulling on the long door handle. To his surprise, it opened a little before the mechanism became stuck. But it was enough for the two of them and the Centurion to squeeze through.

They found themselves in the large hall with Q'anuan writing on the wall. On the other side of the room was the ramp that led down to the underground corridor that seemed to go on forever in both directions. Ahead of them was the room where they had first used the Legati virtual reality headsets. But this time, the room was completely empty and deteriorating. There was a damp smell and metallic stains on the walls.

"I suggest we go up to the building above," said Christel.

They returned to the large hall and walked to the end. The door was open, so they entered the spiral corridor that led them up to the level where the base of the Concordia tower had been. At the top of the corridor, the door was closed.

"Centurion, Open door," said Benjamin.

They could hear mechanisms moving inside the door. Suddenly, the door crashed into its slot in the floor. There was a gust of stale air. Ahead of them, instead of the stone base of the Concordia tower and steel stairs, there was a marble-floored foyer and a corridor going straight ahead. At the end of the corridor and around a corner, they found themselves in the main entry hall of the skyscraper. On one side, the curved glass wall extended seemingly to the very top of the tower hundreds of meters above them. At the base of the glass wall were the entry doors, which were all locked. The glass was like everywhere else, filthy and opaque.

Opposite the glass wall was the occupiable part of the building. Columns of elevator tubes rose into the highest points of the tower. They could see countless floors with windows and balconies that used to look out of the glass front of the building. There was no power, so none of the elevators were operational. The place was deadly quiet. As if it had all been sealed until a few minutes earlier, it was all dust free and immaculate.

To the side of the elevators were low desks, but other

than those, the room was featureless.

"So now what?" said Benjamin.

As he spoke the words, his phone started ringing. It was Flight.

Benjamin was thinking, *Wireless connectivity? Here?* But instead, he said:

"Mr. Flight. We were trying to reach you!"

"I know," replied Flight, "return to the projection room."

"Er, okay," said Benjamin. The call ended.

They made their way back to the spiral corridor and into the large hall that Flight had indicated.

A three-dimensional projection of Flight was standing in the middle of the room.

"We are so glad to see you," said Benjamin with a tone of relief. "We have so many questions."

"I know you do, Benjamin," replied Flight. "But it is not my place to answer all of them. The Videnti on SaQ'il need to be the ones to explain."

"I see," said Benjamin with a degree of disappointment. "But can you tell us where we are and why you have been out of touch?"

"You are on a planet we call Ortus. It is not the Earth, but at the same time it is. It is in another space-time dimension to your planet. It is an alternate evolution of the planet you call home."

*A copy of the Earth in another dimension. Why not?* thought Benjamin. He didn't understand what that really meant or what the implications of such a duplicate might be, but his earlier petulance was replaced with a simple acceptance.

"What happened to all the people? The Q'anua?" he asked simply.

"That is something for the Videnti to explain, but the

Q'anua are no longer here physically," replied Flight. After a moment, he went on:

"You wondered why I have not contacted you. It is because it was decided that you must see this place for yourself. It would be insufficient, simply for me to tell you about it."

"Thank you for accommodating how humans think," said Benjamin. Before Flight could make some judgmental comment about humans' thinking, he added quickly, "are there other cities like this one?"

"There are two others. One on the Australian continent and one in South America, using your names for them. They are positioned in line with the Ring."

"And the rest of the planet?"

"There are some minor observational and scientific outposts, but the three cities were the population centers.

"Before you ask more," finished Flight, "I must direct you back to your ship. You must travel to SaQ'il at this time. We will speak soon."

With that Flight's projection stopped. Benjamin noticed a small device that had been set in the floor of the dais in the middle of the room. No doubt left by the Legati for that very conversation.

They headed back toward the ship. With the help of the Centurion, they closed the balcony door as a matter of respect. Within a few minutes, they were back on their ship's bridge. The boarding ramp closed, and the ship had lifted gently away from the mountainside.

It rose in the sky and before long was gone.

The city returned to its quiet solitude, interrupted only by the screech of a pterodactyl flying overhead.

# CHAPTER 52

THE ARRIVAL AT SaQ'il some eight hours later, other than being a demonstration of the Legati's supreme mastery of technology and the resulting triviality for them to travel across the galaxy, was uneventful.

They entered orbit and were subjected to the usual security and pathogen checks, as evident from the green glow that passed through the ship. Once completed, the ship began its descent toward the city of Shsqlm that Benjamin had visited so many years before.

Rather than flying to Christel's coastal home, they flew toward the center and entered a huge tunnel that descended deep below the city. The outside lighting turned yellow as they proceeded down the vast tube. Quite clearly, this channel was built for the arrival of spacecraft the size of the scout ship.

"How does it feel to be home, Christel?" asked Benjamin. He often worried about how she felt having to experience a new world on Earth, day after day, for so many years. Despite her isolated upbringing he hoped that she felt some relief at being in a familiar world once more.

"My home is with you, Benjamin," she replied simply. Benjamin smiled lightly and put his arm around her.

*I feel the same*, he thought.

After descending the long shallow ramp for a kilometer, the ship came to a graceful halt in the middle of a cavernous hangar. In front of them they could see huge buildings that reached the roof of the massive subterranean void. Their ship looked small compared to its surroundings.

From the bridge, they could see a group of Legati approaching the side of the ship.

"Best not to keep them waiting," said Benjamin. He noted that he felt considerably less nervous than his last visit, which was a blessing.

He put on his combined breathing assistant and translation device and followed Christel to the side airlock. The external door opened, and the ramp extended to the ground. Benjamin took a deep breath and stepped out onto the ramp and carefully walked down. He realized that this was a diplomatic meeting, so he did not want any stumbles.

He approached the group of Legati that were lined up in front of him. They were clearly dressed in their finest uniforms. Benjamin wasn't sure what to do exactly, so he stood to attention and bowed his head respectfully. Christel stood at his side.

He allowed the Legati to speak first.

"Welcome back to SaQ'il, Ambassador," said a particularly tall person in the middle of the group.

"Thank you for your kind welcome and the wisdom you have bestowed on our planet," replied Benjamin. He bowed his head again. Despite his earlier confidence he suddenly felt a heightened sense of focus.

"Ambassador," said the tall Legati, "we are the

Videnti. Our function is to guide our people and help them fulfill their collective functions. We have been following your planet's progress with great interest. A significant amount has been achieved in a short space of time."

"We have received much help from the Legati," said Benjamin.

"We have invited you here earlier than we had originally planned. We are looking for your advice."

"My advice?" stammered Benjamin.

"Yes," replied the Legati. "The next phase of support for your species is not finalized and we would like to hear your opinion."

"I will do my best, your Excellency," replied Benjamin. He was not sure whether the use of the word 'excellency' would be translated properly, but nobody said anything, so maybe he got away with it.

"Tomorrow, one of our counsellors will visit you at the coastal home that you are familiar with. He will explain everything. You remember Mentor?" As he spoke the name, the Legati counsellor from over thirty years ago stepped forward.

"Of course," said Benjamin with a genuine smile. "I look forward to our conversation. It is a pleasure to see you again, Mentor."

Mentor said nothing but stepped back.

With that, the group of Legati turned and started walking back to the building that was behind them.

"That was such an honor," said Christel in Benjamin's ear. "Nobody gets to speak with the Videnti."

"Did I do okay?" said Benjamin, suddenly feeling nervous.

"You did just fine," said Christel. "Let's go visit Romeo and Juliet."

The ship flew them to Christel's coastal villa. Unlike Benjamin's first visit, the scout ship deployed its landing gear and stayed in the forecourt of the building uncloaked.

The welcome from Christel's android parents was very touching. They had not aged in the slightest, but they still behaved as if they truly missed their daughter. They fussed and demanded details of her adventures. For many hours Christel happily told them of her experiences. Sadly, Romeo and Juliet had only experienced the villa and its upkeep over the years, but that didn't seem to worry them. Benjamin was extremely impressed with the obvious soul that had been bestowed on these biomechanical servants. He vowed to keep them nearby.

By the time Christel and Benjamin went to bed, it was quite late. They were tired.

*We have every right to be tired*, thought Benjamin, *we've just flown halfway across the galaxy.*

# CHAPTER 53

MENTOR ARRIVED ON time at Christel's villa the following morning.

"Good morning ambassador," he said. "I do hope you are rested after your journey."

"I am, thank you Mentor," replied Benjamin.

They discussed Benjamin's experiences back on Earth at length. From his arrival with the Legati fleet over 30 years earlier, all the way through to the present day, having visited the planet Ortus and the orbiting ring. It took a long while to talk about the challenges, successes and changes that had taken place. It would have taken longer if Mentor had not already been aware of many of the events as the result of the data stream sent back to SaQ'il.

"In essence," concluded Mentor, "your species tends to resist the universal principles. It looks for advantage over others rather than the collective good. It is devious. It is tactical rather than strategic. Despite a governmental veneer, it is not yet a planetary community."

"I would say that's a fair summary," replied Benjamin. "Many embrace the Concordia guidance with enthusiasm, seeing the societal benefits that it brings, but there are still many that do not."

"They lack motivation to change," said Mentor.

"Yes, those with something to lose from change will work hard to persuade others not to change, even if it's against the collective good," added Benjamin.

"Including the atmosphere your species lives in."

Benjamin did not need to respond.

"Indulge me," said Mentor. "Tell me how you think humans would react under certain circumstances."

"Okay."

"What if you learned that your planet would cease to exist in the coming centuries?"

"People would want to know if it was really true. Then they would look to the World Government to devise a plan to leave the planet."

"What about the other fauna and flora on your planet?"

"Good point. We already have seed repositories of all the planet's plants, but I can't be sure that all the animals could be saved."

"Should all the humans be saved?"

"Maybe if we knew the precise timing of the end of the planet, we could limit the population or reverse its growth, but we would want to save as many as possible, of course."

"What if humanity was unable to save its planet but someone else could offer help?" asked Mentor.

"That offer would be taken, of course."

"Even if there were conditions?"

"For example?"

"That those saved had to commit to the universal principles, with severe consequences for any that did not."

"How severe?"

Mentor chuckled.

"How about elimination?" he said. "The universal principles are the law that we all abide by."

"I suspect most would comply with the law, but there will always be those that find an excuse to believe the law should not apply to them."

"Like children pushing boundaries with their parents," said Mentor.

"On Earth, there are so many laws because humans are not naturally law-abiding," said Benjamin. "Our ancestors invented religions to control the masses. Now we have armies of lawyers arguing the interpretation of a law so their clients can do whatever they want, despite the law."

There was a pause, and then Benjamin added:

"Is the Earth about to end?"

"Yes," replied Mentor simply.

There was silence. Benjamin had no idea how to react to that reply.

Mentor continued.

"The Videnti have assessed that your species needs to know its future. I must be straightforward with you – it is this situation that compelled the Legati to prioritize our attention to your planet in the first place.

"I have been authorized to disclose a number of facts to you. We will discuss what you do with this knowledge, afterwards."

"Okay...," said Benjamin.

# CHAPTER 54

THE Q'ANUA WERE an ancient race. They were one of the first species to have evolved with a high degree of intelligence and technological capability. Estimates had them building societies and developing civilizations 100 million Earth years before Benjamin's time. That was still very recent in universal terms. Planet Earth was well over 4 billion years old.

It was not thought that the Q'anua originated on Earth, but they did have a large population on the planet all those eons ago. They had always believed in living in harmony with their surroundings, so they did not allow their cities to sprawl all over the planet. They controlled the growth of their populations. They used their advanced technology to allow them to explore other worlds and sometimes settled on them as well. But they always minimized their impact on a planet's natural ecosystem.

The Q'anua lived on Earth at the time of the dinosaurs. Their culture would not allow them to interfere with these other species. Their cities were bounded by walls not only to protect them from some of the larger wildlife, but also to set a limit for their own expansion. They would travel widely around the planet for the purposes of research but would not do anything to compromise the lives and evolution of these creatures. They allowed the planet to flourish according to nature. It was a paradise.

However, 66 million years ago, their long-range sensors detected a planet-threatening meteor heading toward them. It was many years away, but they realized there was a very high probability that it would impact the planet. The effect on the planet would be catastrophic. They felt they had time to do something.

Destroying the meteor was considered, but the uncertainty of what would happen to the fragments led them to devise a more sophisticated solution. A solution that would have untold consequences.

Their research into anti-matter technology had begun to provide them with the possibility of travelling great distances through traversable wormholes. Their proposal was to create a wormhole that would simply deflect the meteor so that it would crash into the Sun instead. They did not want a rogue meteor hitting something else.

The anti-matter detonation was performed at the edge of the Solar System. They had ships ready to destroy the meteor if the wormhole creation failed but, in the end, they were not needed.

The wormhole appeared in the path of the meteor, and to the relief of the Q'anua, the meteor entered it. In a moment, it was gone.

They waited for the meteor to reappear at the other end of the wormhole inside the orbit of Mercury.

They waited.

The meteor did not appear.

The wormhole eventually closed and the Q'anua were left with the concern about the fate of the meteor. Their scientists continued to research into what had gone wrong for a long time but were unable to explain the disappearance. In the end, with a sense of guilt, they moved on with life, even more determined to preserve the natural way of things and avoid meddling. Happily, for the Q'anua, their planet and its ecosystem were safe.

It was thousands of years later, after the Q'anua had mastered inter-dimensional travel that they discovered to their horror what they had done.

The wormhole they had created all those years before had generated a new spatial dimension. Fortunately, the size of the anomaly was constrained as the result of the energy used to create the original wormhole, but it did encompass the entire Solar System and a long distance beyond.

What they discovered was that the meteor had entered the wormhole and arrived in the newly created dimension and crashed into the duplicated Earth. The atmospheric catastrophe that resulted, killed most of the Q'anuan people on the planet, as well as most other animal and plant life. Those Q'anua and animals that were not killed immediately, perished over time as the lack of food sources and the extreme climate resulted in ever-dwindling populations. Unable to contact any of the other Q'anuan settlements or leave their prison, they became extinct.

Nobody on their planet of Ortus was aware of the calamity. Not until it was way too late.

This was why the duplicated planet, Earth, was sacred to the Q'anua. Their grief and guilt at what they had done, albeit by accident, haunted them. Initially, they had considered closing the anomaly like a grave but the discovery of abundant life on the new planet persuaded them otherwise.

They left Earth alone. Some may say that they deferred the problem to a later day, but the Q'anua felt they had no choice. Perhaps the species on the planet would evolve to the point where they would want to explore beyond the Solar System, but surely that would be in the way distant future.

For millions of years, the Q'anua kept the existence of Earth a secret. They visited very occasionally and then more often in recent millennia. But by and large, Earth was left alone to develop.

The Q'anua, in the meantime, had continued to evolve metaphysically. They had developed technology for digitizing a person's mind in minute detail. That digital model could then be transmitted great distances and then reformed by specialized computers that could embed the model into androids or cloned Q'anua. The person could then perform whatever task they needed to do at the remote location, be it to visit friends, do construction work, explore a new world or any other job where physical presence was needed, without the dangers of travel or death through misadventure.

If anything happened to the transmitted digital model in the perilous location, the traveler would simply be woken and have no memory of the event (although videos were usually available). If the travel was successful, the digital model, updated with the experiences of the trip would be reinserted into the traveler's mind. They would wake from their travels with a full knowledge of their trip.

Naturally, it was not long before the technology was used for recreation of one type or another. The Q'anua could experience anything, anywhere.

It was a natural consequence that people were eventually living their whole lives in a digital form. They could drop into an android when they wished to perform some physical tasks and adopt a Q'anuan clone when their original bodies gave out. They became immortal.

The final stage of their full metamorphosis was complete when the digital model could be hosted inside a proximal dimension. An energy field that exists in a separate dimension overlapping the main space time continuum. This allowed the Q'anua to exist entirely as energy and no longer require physical presence, unless they wanted to. The Legati believed that these dimensions were proximal to Ortus. The Q'anua had become very guarded about the truths of their existence.

The upshot of all this was that the Q'anua no longer needed a planet to live on. Freed of all Ortusly bonds and given immortality, they retreated to their personal dimensions.

This was a fortunate circumstance, because around ten thousand years before Benjamin had been born, they discovered a problem with the anomaly that they had created containing Earth.

It was shrinking.

The energy was slowly radiating away from the anomaly, and it was collapsing. The collapse was accelerating. Within 500 years, the gravitational effects of the collapse would start disturbing the orbits of the outer planets of the Solar System. A hundred years later, the orbit of Earth would begin to change and there would be significant disruption to the planet's climate. That would mark the end of its habitability.

600 years.

It was this planetary life expectancy that had dictated the number of Ambassadors that the Legati had preserved from the original Lottery winners. Humanity needed to be trained on the universal principles and trained for a potential evacuation over the coming centuries.

"An evacuation to Ortus?" prompted Benjamin. His head was still spinning from the news he had just received.

"That is the dilemma, Ambassador," replied Mentor. "The Q'anua feel an obligation to assist the lifeforms on Earth, not just humans. But they know as well as you and I know, how badly mankind has treated their own planet. Massive social upheavals notwithstanding, we could start transferring humans to the Ortus Ring or the three cities today, but how would humans behave?

"This is why we have started to instill the responsibility and collective thinking that are embodied in the Universal Principles. As I have said, these are laws.

"Given what we know about humans, how long will it be before some decide that they don't want to live on the Ring or in one of the cities? They might feel they have rights to, say, Japan because that's where they lived on your planet. Next thing you know, they are clearing the reserves in that area and driving out or killing the creatures that have lived there forever."

"Maybe that's where the severe consequences come in," suggested Benjamin.

"Nobody wants to live under martial law, and we don't want to impose it," replied Mentor. "The Q'anua were able to build a society without destruction – we expect humans to do the same.

"I hope you finally understand why we are trying to change the way humans think and behave. Why we are trying to make humanity a civilization, in all meanings of the word."

"Yes, I see that now," said Benjamin. "I know I would not have been able to handle all this, if you had told me this as a younger man."

"There are other challenges too," continued Mentor.

"We need to decide what to do with the other animals that live on your planet. They are every bit as important as your species."

"Indeed."

"They cannot go to Ortus. The other creatures that roam that planet or dwell in its oceans would treat them as a snack."

"That reminds me," said Benjamin. "I would love to see how the dinosaurs evolved."

"Mostly they got smaller, faster and a lot smarter. The walls around Tribus, the city you visited, are there for a reason.

"But the plan for the other creatures of your planet is not your immediate concern. The dilemma is how to make humans fit to be granted the privilege of moving to Ortus, or similar planet.

"You are to speak with the Videnti on this topic tomorrow. Think well on it, Ambassador."

Mentor stood up, dwarfing Benjamin as he did so. They nodded respectfully to one another, and Mentor lumbered out of the room, across the entry hall and down the ramp to his waiting transport.

Benjamin watched him leave.

Christel walked up behind him and placed her hand on his shoulder.

"It feels like we're starting all over again, Christel," said Benjamin.

"Only if you want to," she replied.

"I'm just feeling old today."

# CHAPTER 55

THE VIDENTI COUNCIL room was very modest. An oval table surrounded by the traditional high and narrow Legati chairs. The walls were plain with no windows.

When Benjamin entered with Christel by his side, the Videnti were already present.

"Please be seated, Ambassador," said the Videnti leader, gesturing to a human-sized chair. "Christel," he said, motioning to an adjacent chair. There was no ceremony or preamble.

"You have been made aware of the situation concerning your planet," said the leader simply. No reply was necessary. Benjamin simply nodded. His preprepared acknowledgement of the honor he felt being in the presence of the Legati elders seemed no longer appropriate.

"We are interested in your opinion on a few matters," said the leader, getting straight to the point. "The human population on your planet exceeds 10 billion. In 600 years, we predict it will be 20 billion, assuming strict population controls and improved standards of living. The capacity of Ortus, with the Ring and the cities, is 5 billion."

Everyone looked at Benjamin. There was a pause as he realized he was expected to respond.

"Videnti," said Benjamin, using the form of address that Christel had advised, "I am honored to have this opportunity to speak with you directly."

The Legati in the room just looked at him. They were motionless.

Benjamin extracted a simple a piece of paper from his pocket and laid it on the table in front of him.

"Okay..." he began. "Humanity owes its existence to the Q'anua, although humans don't know it yet. Out of the Q'anuan experiment came an environment that allowed my species to evolve.

"When humans learn the truth, they will no doubt gloss over their good fortune. Instead, when informed of their true genesis, with their current attitudes and preconceptions, I believe there will be a number of reactions."

The Videnti remained silent. Benjamin assumed they wanted him to complete his thoughts.

"I believe these reactions will follow similar human reactions to grief," he continued. "Denial will be first. They will demand definitive proof. How the entire human population can be convinced of this truth, I have no idea.

"However, assuming they can be shown somehow the collapsing anomaly, they will move on to the next stage, fear. They will look to the World Government or the Legati for solutions and expect real answers. Significant social unrest can be expected as people thrash around looking for someone to blame and someone to tell them what to do.

"Given the potential lack of ready answers, I can imagine a steady moral and behavioral decline as some people determine a lack of consequences for their actions.

"I am not sure that mankind would reach the final stage, acceptance, to be honest."

Benjamin paused in his presentation of his thoughts. Nobody interrupted him. Clearly, he hadn't reached a useful conclusion.

"Sooner rather than later," he continued, "there will be demands on the Legati to solve the issue. It will become obvious to everyone that the Legati arrival and this apocalypse are related. There will be nobody else to turn to. They will be desperate."

One of the Videnti finally spoke.

"You think that mankind is not ready to know the truth." As so often, this Legati was not asking a question. It was exactly what Benjamin was thinking.

"Yes. It is too early," he replied. "I believe that some will understand the truth, but there will be a majority that will only think in terms of their personal survival. Worse, they will expect someone else to do all the hard work of saving them."

"Our assessment is that your species is still developing," said the same Videnti. "We assess that humans are mostly incapable of independent thought. We assess that humans are responsive to strong leadership. We are aligned with your view of the challenge of imminent migration to Ortus."

Again, the Videnti stopped speaking, not leaving a conversational cue for Benjamin to continue from. He was required to state facts and minimize opinions.

"If we were to place advance parties of humans on Ortus," said Benjamin after a slight pause, "after stringent vetting, we could prepare the way for the remainder to follow when we believe they are ready. There would be much work to do, and we would need the help of the Legati, without question."

"You have not addressed the issue of only a quarter of your population being transferrable, Ambassador," said a third Videnti. Benjamin felt like he was in a courtroom full of judges. He looked at his piece of paper.

"The calculus for determining the ideal compositions for a population growth rate of zero, a stationary population, is well-known, at least to those that specialize in such things. Those specialists will need to define the demographics of the emigrants over the centuries, but I believe that we can achieve a transferrable population that reflects the composition of humanity, adheres to the Universal Principles, keeps the population under control and reduces it significantly."

"We are aligned," said the third Videnti, "in this long-term approach. And the Legati will support the migration effort. You are correct that much preparation of the existing infrastructure is needed. The preparation of the population is already underway of course.

"But the question we have for you Ambassador, is how you suggest selecting the migrants. Not all of your people can go."

Benjamin thought for a moment. A simple twist in the discussion. The potential fates of billions in the future being decided.

Really? Was this how easily it was done? He thought briefly of moments in human history, like the so-called conferences in Berlin, Yalta, Potsdam, the disastrous end of the British Mandate in the Middle East and the abrupt end of colonialism in countries like India. The repercussions of these events echoed through human history.

Benjamin had a fleeting moment of inspiration.

"We cannot start full migration until all of humanity is aware of the situation," he said. "I agree that we should start preparing the way, but mankind needs to be informed but only when they are ready. They are not ready now, as they do not embrace the Universal Principles by nature.

"The selection process should be purely merit-based and not favor those of wealth, position or their age. I believe an open process will help achieve this. But this will only be possible when humans have become selfless and understand that the good of their global community is being served. I cannot put a schedule on this. We are so much at the early stages."

There was silence in the room and Benjamin held his breath. He looked steadily ahead at his Legati hosts, who had all turned their heads to look at the center of the table, as if in collective thought. Benjamin did not dare speak.

The Videnti leader finally spoke.

"Benjamin," he said, unexpectedly using Benjamin's name, "we believe that you have just articulated the goals of the Universal Principles very clearly."

Benjamin didn't know what to say. He'd just said what he felt was right.

"We commend you for that," continued the Videnti spokesman. "We are decided. We will proceed with early preparations on Ortus. We will work with the Ambassador on a selection process for the early pioneers. We will invite the current Ambassador to be part of that process. There will be no public announcement of the need for evacuation for foreseeable human generations."

Benjamin heard this with a shocking realization. The Videnti had, in the blink of an eye, somehow discussed the situation amongst themselves without speaking and delivered their verdict. For the thousandth time, he felt totally inadequate.

The suggestion that "the ambassador" and "current ambassador" were different people wasn't lost on Benjamin either.

"I'm not sure how much more I can be of service," he said. "I am getting old, sir. I was expecting to be sent back to my planet to live out my life more quietly, with Christel." He placed his hand affectionately on Christel's leg.

"You do not wish to see how your species fares in its new home? To help them perhaps?" asked the spokesman.

"I do not know how that could be possible, however much I would desire it," replied Benjamin.

"You have options, Benjamin," said the spokesman. "Certainly, we could send you home to live out your life, as you say."

There was a pause. Benjamin knew something else was coming.

"But there are other options," he added euphemistically. "Think on it, valued Ambassador. Have you never wished that you had known, when you were younger, what you know now? Experience and knowledge are everything.

"Your journey and accomplishments could be just beginning."

YOUR JOURNEY RESUMES IN THE NEXT VOLUME OF THE FUTURE TRILOGY:

**FUTURE TENSE**
**Benjamin Privett Will Demand Answers**

Available on Amazon, or for more information visit
https://www.simonrowell.com

# ABOUT THE

# AUTHOR

Simon H.G. Rowell spent thirty-plus years working in the computer industry, half at the European Space Agency in Germany and the other half in Silicon Valley in the USA. Turning to something new, he wrote a cautionary guide for those working in the IT industry (Silicon Valley Job Hunting) and then embarked on the journey of writing science fiction novels for those that value science over fantasy.

Rowell and his wife live in Florida.

Printed in Great Britain
by Amazon

26352233R00201